SCREAM FOR ME

SCREAM FOR ME

ELIZABETH WASHBURN

Library of Congress Control Number:		2013913932
ISBN:	Hardcover	978-1-4836-7836-8
	Softcover	978-1-4836-7835-1
	Ebook	978-1-4836-7837-5

Rev. date: 09/04/2013

To order additional copies of this book, contact:
Xlibris LLC
1-888-795-4274
www.Xlibris.com
Orders@Xlibris.com
138792

DEDICATION

To my kids

Acknowledgement

There are so many who helped me reach my dream of making this book a reality :

-Marisa Marks—without you this never would have happened.

-All my friends—reading early drafts and giving me feedback and support.

-My team at Xlibris—helping me through the publishing process creating what you'll read.

-Kate Kelly—for your amazing cover art to create atmosphere and set the tone for the reader.

-My Thursday Night Crew—Ken Herr, Steve Mortenson, Kyle Dobiszewski, and Kyle Mahoney who all dutifully read my book in the early stages.

-And last but not least my family—My husband, David, for all his support and encouragement and my fantastic kids, Davey, Mikey, Robbie, and Tory, you are my world!

Chapter 1

Susan Starks slowly opened her pale grey eyes. She looked around the dark, cramped room and tried to figure out what had happened. How did she get here? Her mouth was dry, her lips so brittle that the edges cracked as she began to open her mouth, so dry she tasted blood. No sound came from her lips as she tried to speak. The pain was so severe it felt like her head would split open any second. As she tried to lift her hand to her face, she couldn't and realized she was bound, both her hands and feet. Panic set in as she looked frantically around the closet-sized room and saw a small door but no windows and no other furniture besides the cot she was on. As she became more aware, she realized that she really had to go to the bathroom. That intense feeling distracted her and actually worked to calm her down, if just a little bit. She really didn't want to piss all over herself.

"Hey," she croaked out. "I really have to go to the bathroom . . . Please . . . I can't wait . . . I need to go . . . Can you hear me? Can anybody hear me?"

Silence. Minutes, maybe even an hour passed and still no sound. The pressure on her bladder finally overwhelmed her, and she felt the warm stream of urine. Trying to stop the flow only seemed to make it come out faster. She started crying. She had never felt so helpless and terrified. *Stop crying! You have to get yourself out of here!* After a while, she finally calmed herself enough to stop crying. Susan looked around the room, searching her mind for some answers.

While she tried to piece together what she could remember, fuzzy images entered her mind. She visualized a man coming out from behind a tree, that sickly sweet smelling cloth covering her nose, dizziness overwhelming her, and then nothing. Now, she remembered the terror of her last few seconds of consciousness.

She was working herself into a frenzy even though her mind kept screaming, "Remain calm!" Was she now the third one to vanish into thin air? It was the big news at the diner where she had a temp job as a waitress. Several stories circulated as people discussed what they thought had happened. For the most part, everyone assumed that the creep who kidnapped the two young women already killed them and buried the bodies somewhere in the woods. But no bodies had been found, and there were certainly an over-abundance of trees in South Carolina, so those girls may never be found. She should never have gotten up to go running alone, but that was her daily routine. With two missing girls, Arcadia Lakes just wasn't safe, and now, as her wrists ached, she knew she was another victim.

Was anyone missing her? She wasn't supposed to work until tomorrow night's dinner crowd, or was it today? She had lost her concept of time. Was it still daylight, or was it midnight? How long did she sleep? Was the creep coming to wake her up soon? She was driving herself crazy thinking about all the different scenarios, her mind constantly asking questions. The only certainty was that she didn't want to die. She just started getting her life together. She planned to be her own boss. Waitressing was just a way to make money until she got enough credits to become a certified interior decorator. She had good friends, and she had just started thinking that now was the time to be finding someone steady to date.

Looking around the room, a black cloud of defeat was beginning to manifest itself, and tears began to flow again, uncontrollably.

He sat at the computer, editing the last of the footage he shot last night. It was going to be a masterpiece. Everything was coming together nicely. Filming it in color brought the moments back to life. It was so vivid he felt the rush of adrenaline flow through his body and the blood rushing to his groin. Sally Anne will be a big hit on the web. He couldn't wait to see the number of hits his film would get, and his skin was tight with the anticipation of seeing himself in a starring role. He planned out the rape and torture scenes carefully to make sure he caught all the angles. He set up eight different cameras to capture Sally Anne's last breath and his climax into her body. He shuddered at the thought, anticipation racing through his blood. A shame he had to wear a condom, but with the sophisticated crime labs, police can find even the smallest trace of evidence. He'd never get caught anyway. He's smarter than the cops, especially in the south where they can't find their way out of a paper bag and collectively have an IQ equal to a bunch of grapes.

He knows what precautions to take. That's why he waxes all the hair from his body. Plus, he loves the biting sting of the cloth as he pulls the wax off. The pain gets him off. He's always been meticulous about removing any possibility of lingering evidence that could be used against him. As he sat naked, his skin sticking to his leather chair, he smiled to himself knowing that the police would never find a clue, never find him. He couldn't wait to see the final project, his heart pounding faster with excitement. The computer finished saving the .wav file. Time for the show to begin.

He did the final editing on his Mac and added his own titles, uploading his film. He was going to go to Columbia and find a Starbucks; he would use the free wireless there so that the police couldn't trace the IP address back to him. He didn't think that Starbucks had cameras anywhere except near the cash register, but he would wear a disguise and hoodie to hide his face anyway. *Always be prepared!* He had learned that lesson the hard way. He'll just sit at one of the tables and have his double macchiato, and just like that, his film will be on the web for all to see. It suddenly occurred to him. *How would people find it?* He knew the police were a bunch of dummies, and it would take them forever to locate his footage. He needed a way to get the news out fast. He needed to make it sensational.

After contemplating his situation for a while, discarding several possibilities that most likely wouldn't work, he finally came up with the idea to alert someone in the media. It had to be someone respectable, but not too famous, or they might not see it as their big break. Enter Seth Roberts of *The State*; he would be the perfect patsy. Roberts wanted to go to one of the big city papers. He even wrote about it in his "Dreams" series that appeared in *The State* every week. He wrote about local people and their wishes for what they wanted to do with their lives. Things were coming together nicely: he would be famous, and he gave most of the credit to Sally Anne Myers. He'd have to think of a good e-mail name that he could use. He mulled over a few like Slash—no, that's an eighties rock dude. How about Cutter? No, that's a ship. Ah, Carver. That would be perfect, and he didn't think it had been used before. He would become Carver. *Classy, nice, and so applicable.*

He went back to thinking about Sally Anne. She was his first muse, and he congratulated himself on the inspiration to use the Mike Myers mask. How cool was it that Myers was killed by a Myers! A stroke of genius! His new Goregasmic! film will definitely be a hit! He surpassed all his other efforts by a mile. He had killed before, but he never thought about the artistic creativity that careful planning and videotaping would bring him. He never thought it would give a whole new dimension to his enjoyment of flaying his girls. He could relive the torture in living color, over and over again. What a turn-on, listening to them begging him to stop, screaming for him to stop. Damn, that felt good. Beads of sweat broke out over his upper lip. He got an erection just thinking about the screams, the ragged moans as their voices hoarsely cried out in desperation and pain. Starting tomorrow, everyone would be checking out the film. His inspired work of art he created with Sally Anne's tortured body would make him famous, even a legend.

P387
Assist other agencies — SES
1hr
No Power No FSE
No Phones

SCOTT STANLEY 0409 736 030
TOBEX 000 1483

TREGEAR

WILKS, DEBORAH.

GAS TORCHES IN USE.

LOUISE GREWCOCK 0429 632 497

~~JOHN~~ 2, SIR JOSEPH BANKS

KURNELL

SYD DESALINATE

WELDING, CUTTING, GRINDING,

PERMIT TOBEX 000 1590

11/424
0080002

Chapter 2

It was a colder-than-usual April morning when Detective Elizabeth Bowlyn awoke to the sound of her cell phone. Lizzie slowly came out of her deep slumber and rubbed the sleep from her eyes, trying to focus on the digital readout of the time on her iHome. She saw five o'clock, but it was too early for her to think. In her twelve years of being a cop, early morning phone calls were always bad news. She wondered what problem awaited her this time. She finally jumped out of bed, barely avoiding the sharp corner of her nightstand, and grabbed her cell before it went to voice mail. It was one of her staff sergeants calling, telling her that her presence was required at the Forest Lake Country Club in Arcadia Lakes. There was a report of a dead body, and she would need to oversee the scene. *No!* she screamed in her head. *This is not supposed to happen in Arcadia Lakes. Was this some twisted April Fools' joke a day late?* Missing girls were one thing; a dead body made it feel like she was back in Memphis.

With the annual town picnic only two weeks from Sunday, the last thing Lizzie needed was the news of a homicide. She was trying to think what could have happened. Against all reality, she prayed that the two young women were just missing and soon to be found alive. That's the worse that should happen in Arcadia Lakes. Not a murder. She processed the news about a female body found dead, mutilated, and still fairly warm. It was most likely freshly dumped. She had to face reality. The missing girls didn't skip town voluntarily; they were most likely abducted and killed. Lizzie's cop instincts were always right. She just didn't want to believe them this time. Arcadia Lakes was her sanctuary. Now, that had changed. This was beautiful, perfect, sheltered Arcadia Lakes. It was not the kind of place where gruesome murders were supposed to happen. *What could possibly draw a killer here?*

Lizzie's white little fluffy Maltipoo was stretching across one of the pillows and then started crawling over to her master like a graveling commando, crawling stomach to the ground under a fence. Mandy joyously started licking Lizzie's face, her way of saying good morning. It was a bit of sweetness in Lizzie's tough line of work.

"Ready to go outside, Mander?" Her dog's name was Mandy, but she created the nicknames Mander and Pup 'n' Chow for her cuddly puppy. Not really knowing where those names came from, she still liked the made-up cutesy-pie sounding names for her dog. Mandy was only nine months old, still a puppy, and squirmed like crazy. She would wag her tail, and the whole lower half of her body wiggled. It was the most adorable thing Lizzie had ever seen, and that's why she got the puppy in the first place; she couldn't resist that wiggly butt.

Lizzie always wanted a dog, but her parents, being older, didn't want the mess associated with an animal. When she married Matt Bowlyn right after she graduated from college, Lizzie found out Matt was really a cat person. Right then and there, she should have known that they wouldn't work out. Since cats and dogs don't get along, the same was true with humans. Dog people really don't get along with cat people.

Lizzie opened the back door in the kitchen and watched Mandy dash outside to do her morning routine. Lizzie filled the food and water bowls and headed back upstairs. She always gave Mandy a solid fifteen minutes to roam the fenced-in yard. That gave her enough time to drag herself into the bathroom and start the shower. As the steam began billowing out over the top of the glass door, she was thinking about what the murder would do to Arcadia Lakes. This wasn't Memphis, Detroit, or even Columbia. Murders happen in those places all the time. This girl was found dead and mutilated in the sweet boundaries of Arcadia Lakes, South Carolina. All two hundred and fifty families know each other, and heck, there are only eight hundred and eighty people in the whole town. She had searched high and low for this little perfect slice of America. Even though it is only five miles north east of Columbia, it was a different world entirely. Major crime didn't really touch Arcadia Lakes. It was one of the richer towns in South Carolina with fairly homogeneous white neighborhoods; a large, stable middle class; and no significant poor section. A lot of the people worked virtually, and there were many well-off single people, perfect for her in every way.

Lizzie remembered getting phone calls all hours of the night for murders or other 911 horrors happening in Memphis. That's one of the reasons she left. That and the disaster that was her husband. Every time she thought about her ex, her stomach would roil. No time to think about that now. She needs to focus on getting ready and over to the country club.

She dressed herself in her usual outfit, a kind of uniform of her own making. She started with a silk blouse, always done up to the next to top button to play down her large breasts, dark J.Crew trousers that hugged her slim hips, flat black leather Tory Burch shoes, and a navy blue Ralph Lauren blazer. She may have been a civil servant, but she knew how to find a great sale, so she always looked sharp. She tried to play up the plain Jane look, but her clothing was all designer. She checked her standard-issue handgun, a .40-caliber 16-shot Glock 22. After clipping her badge to her belt, she was ready to head out. She opened the door to her reliable three-year-old Nissan Altima, with Mandy jumping in to ride shotgun. Mandy was small and so well-trained that most of the day she just stayed tucked under the desk at Lizzie's feet. A crate was kept neatly under Lizzie's desk so that if she had to leave for any reason, the crate door would be shut, and Mandy would sleep soundly for a few hours. Most of the time, however, this little Maltipoo was Lizzie's shadow, trotting around the squad room, dutifully following her master and trying not to get stepped on in the process.

Lizzie found her way to the murder site by six o'clock that morning. The area was ablaze with flashing lights, and police activity was everywhere. She got out of the car, giving Mandy a quick pat and a firm "stay." As she trudged over to the crime scene, her instincts started to take over. Everywhere she looked, she filed away what she saw to think about later. Lizzie was known for catching even the tiniest detail. She saw something out of the ordinary, something that didn't belong, and invariably, it would be a clue to finding the killer. She showed her badge from the South Carolina Law Enforcement Division to the local Arcadia police officers patrolling the scene. A rather large potbellied officer let her go beyond the taped-off area and commented, "It ain't pretty, Lizzie." Great, already there was a crowd gathering. Lizzie felt some relief when she finally spotted her partner.

"Mornin', Lizzie." Her partner of almost two years greeted her with a cup of piping hot coffee, three sugars and lots of milk, just the way she liked it. His rather short stature made for all sorts of Mutt and Jeff jokes. Dave Dubowski looked about fifteen years older than his fifty years. His hair was white, beginning to bald in the center of the back of his head. His "third eye," he would joke. His face always seemed to be on the verge of a smirk, always the first with some inappropriate wisecrack. Even though he was twelve years older than Lizzie, she was still senior detective, and he reported to her.

"Mornin', Dave. What do we have?"

"Pretty sure it's Sally Anne Myers, the first missing girl, although it's tough to tell with what that SOB did to her face. Her body's also real bad. That poor girl. No one should be put through that. Hopefully, she was dead when he mutilated the body. The medical examiner and photographer are with her now. She fits size-wise: really tall, thin frame. I think the hair is blond, it's hard to tell with all the blood. But I think the tattoo on her leg fits the description of the one noted in her missing person's file. The ME will be able to tell us if it's her or not."

"I was really hoping that she went on one of her friendly camping trips and just didn't tell anyone she was going," Lizzie muttered under her breath.

It was very strange. A month ago, when they started the investigation, Sally Anne Myers just seemed to have disappeared off the face of the earth. The local police had checked her home. She lived in a charming wood-framed cottage, just one of several similar houses that were close together, lining both sides of the street. She had a shabby-chic theme throughout the house. Everything inside was neat, clean, and sparsely but thoughtfully decorated. In addition to having her own web design business, she was an amateur photographer and had an entire wall devoted to artsy black-and-white photos. It looked like she had just run out for a minute and would be right back. But she wasn't right back. It had been four weeks since she was reported missing. She didn't have a steady boyfriend, just a couple of girlfriends who never really worried if she didn't call. Her family didn't miss her immediately because she frequently took off to go camping with the newest boyfriend or a hike to take some pictures.

Sally Anne Myers was a typical example of the type of person who lived in Arcadia Lakes. She was single and worked from home, doing Internet website design, and had just finished two big projects. She had time until her next few projects were due. The initial theory was that she just took some time off to go camping since her gear and camera were missing. Her friends and family agreed, but then too much time had passed. More importantly, everyone was worried when the party she had been planning was getting closer to its date, and she wasn't around. That's when the police took her missing status seriously. There was no way Sally Anne would miss her only sister's baby shower.

Lizzie called over to her partner. "Hey Dave, what about our crime scene guys? Are Ralph and Bob able to process the scene? And have you seen Dr. Gilligan yet?"

"Yep," Dave said and gave Lizzie two thumbs-up. "They finished right before the medical examiner showed up."

Lizzie went over to talk to the ME, Dr. Sean Gilligan. Dr. Gilligan was former military. He was a well-educated Annapolis grad and was still in great shape for a man of sixty-five. His white hair was thick and flat as a table on the top, and he kept it regulation short on the sides. He had deep sea-blue eyes and marked wrinkles on his forehead, showing his concern and his love of the outdoors. He was tall, much taller than Lizzie's five-foot-"thirteen" inches. *I refuse to be six foot anything!* There were very few men she had to look up to, so she always noticed someone tall. Sean was getting a little soft around the middle, again with the details, but he still moved in a graceful way that was odd for someone his size.

"Bowlyn, over here please," Dr. Gilligan said, motioning to Lizzie as he stood over the body.

"Without question, this is one of the most horrific mutilations of a human body I have ever witnessed. The victim was alive for most of the cutting exacted on her torso and probably the damage done to her eyes. The absence of the nipples and tears along the proximal areas of the breasts and around the corners of the eyes show bleeding after the incisions were made. That only happens when the heart is still beating. Most of the vaginal destruction was done postmortem, thank God. I can't imagine the pain she went through, and I was a POW in Nam. You're dealing with one demented and sadistic individual who enjoys inflicting severe pain."

Lizzie was horrified. Dr. Gilligan's description made the situation much more disturbing. As she looked down at the body, the skin was so streaked with dried blood that it was almost impossible to determine the exact nature of the injuries until she was cleaned up at the morgue.

An unpleasant reality of working homicide is that one dead body looks like the next. You see the same thing over and over again. But this murder was unlike anything Lizzie had ever witnessed. She was now sailing on unchartered waters. They were looking for a psychopath who was also, most likely, a serial killer. In her opinion, no one starts out killing this way with such a controlled level of human destruction. At least Lizzie trusted the fact that Dr. Gilligan was a true professional and took his job very seriously. He would leave no stone unturned, and of course, Lizzie appreciated his attention to detail.

Arcadia Lakes was beginning to feel more and more like Memphis with such a heinous crime happening in what she thought was the perfect town. Lizzie had researched places to live while she was recuperating from the severe beating that left her unrecognizable with several broken bones. Two months in the hospital and three months at the rehabilitation facility gave her a lot of time to think.

From May to September, the mayor of Arcadia Lakes gave out "Yard of the Month" awards to the nicest yard, winners receiving a $25 gift certificate and a yard sign to proudly display. Lizzie was looking for that small-town charm when she transferred from Memphis about two years ago. She needed to get her life back together, and she felt Arcadia Lakes was the answer to her problems. Until this morning, that is. What the ME described was not a hit and run, nor a burglary gone amiss, nor a domestic dispute. It was a violent act that shattered what Lizzie had hoped was an ideal place to live and, more importantly, a new healthy existence away from serious crime and her asshole ex-husband.

After Gilligan removed his gloves, he readied himself to leave the scene to head back to the crime lab. It was Lizzie's turn to examine Sally Anne Myers's forlorn body.

"Okay, Dave, let's go over the body before they bag it and send it to the lab. I've got the initial examination findings from Gilligan."

After being in homicide for six years, the past three as a senior detective, Lizzie had been called to dozens of homicides and had developed "special radar" about crime scenes. Honing in on the dead body, picking out details, and staging the scene were her forte, but she wasn't prepared for this. She was hit with a wave of compassion while a chill raced down her spine. It could have been her lying there. She scanned the tall, blond, and athletic yet lifeless and destroyed body. No one ever thought Lizzie looked like a homicide detective. A model maybe but not a cop. She was going to find this killer no matter what.

Dave and Lizzie worked perfectly together. Dave's gruff manner was always offset by Lizzie's diplomacy and sensitivity. At crime scenes, it was another story. It was only nine in the morning, and Dubowski had already started pacing, his signal that he saw everything there was to see. He was anxious to get cracking at what they had found out. Dave's walking back and forth drove Lizzie crazy. She liked to take her time, think through every possibility, turn over every leaf, cigarette butt, footprint, whatever elusive piece of evidence it took to break the case. She didn't want to miss anything that might let a killer go free. She projected that she might be ready to leave the country club before lunch time, around eleven o'clock. Dubowski created a nice worn path on the putting green. He was thinking he should take up smoking again, but when they got back to the station, he'd opt for a stale Crispy Crème and the remains in the coffee pot.

As Lizzie analyzed the body, her empathy waned, and her cop instincts took over. She took out her notepad and started piecing together the sequence of events. Sally Anne was so young, her hands were clenched, her mouth twisted in pain. Her entire life had been ahead of her. She had her own business and was well liked in town. Now, she was a slaughtered corpse, defiled and mutilated. Detective Elizabeth Bowlyn knelt down to take a long hard look at what had once been Sally Anne Myers and prayed to God that they find Sarah Jenkins before she looked like this.

Chapter 3

Sammy Rogers was late to work again. She always hated it when her mornings get off to a bad start; the whole day goes downhill fast after that. Her stocking had a run and, she spilled coffee on her white brand new Burberry shirt. It was a disaster. On top of everything, she only had fumes in her gas tank, forcing her to stop for gas. Her blond medium springy curls bounced into her eyes while she filled up. She was next-door cute, a petite thing with a giant personality. Sammy always had a smile on her face, ready to help anyone or give them her last dime. She finally finished at the pump and hurried to the office.

She pulled her red Mustang convertible into the parking lot of Protection International Team. They nicknamed themselves the Pit because they always felt that they had to pull themselves from the pit of hell. It was really a covert group of former Rangers and Seals with questionable government funding. Not standard FBI, technically they were, but they weren't in the FBI building in DC. They were off the main line in a nice, quiet, nondescript three-story brick office building. It was the perfect job for her, and it showed. She became the office manager even before she graduated from college with her degree in criminology. Sammy's three older brothers completely smothered her and refused to let her take on active duty. So by working for the Pit, she still felt able to help find the bad guys. She was technically FBI too and had Quantico training to prove it, but she knew she'd never become an active agent. For now, she would be backroom only. On the other hand, working at the Pit could be a pain in the ass because all her brothers worked there also, continually watching over her.

"Late night again?" her brother Peter asked.

"No. Just a sucky morning. You name it, it went wrong," she answered.

"Did you bring muffins?" Paul snickered. Sammy did a quick double take to make sure it was Paul asking and not his twin brother, Peter.

"When would I have time for muffins?" she said, followed by a humph.

"I don't know. You always bring muffins. Sorry," Paul whined.

"Now, children, let little sis get settled, listen to the messages. And then she can get the muffins," Scott Rogers chimed in, causing her to scream.

With Sammy's frustrated yell, Bryan Feldman came out of his office to see what the commotion was about. He was fit, forty-seven years young. He just had the slightest grey tips to his sideburns, and his jet-black hair fell in soft waves around his face. One really nice quality about Bryan was his smell, fresh crisp linen, a scent that was manly, clean, and sexy. It was that contrast of soft and hard that made him uncommonly handsome. The man was in peak form, a flat stomach, and well-defined abs. His muscled thighs were noticeable even underneath his fairly loose chinos. These features made him look like a thirty-year-old. At times like now, he felt more like their father than their boss.

"Is there a problem out here?" Bryan questioned.

"No!" they answered in unison.

"Good."

"Hey Paul, I need you and Rafe in my office as soon as he gets in. We have a new assignment, and I want to go over it with you."

Rafe was another key member of the Pit crew and often worked with Paul on assignments. Bryan had sole control over who was hired, who got security clearance, and who did what jobs. He reported directly to the Director of the FBI.

"And Sammy, get back to work. Playtime is over."

Sammy was the youngest of the four Rogers siblings. Her build was tiny, like her, mom's but she had the same piercing blue eyes like her late father. Scott was the oldest, a bear of a man, six-foot-seven and a lean two-hundred-and-fifty pounds, and the spitting image of his father. He's all muscle and knows how to use it. A former Army Ranger, Scott was always in the heat of the action, second-in-command to Feldman. He left the service and followed Feldman into the FBI. Now, he's working with his family in the Pit. Paul and Peter were the twins, also former Rangers, and followed their older brother's footsteps. After they graduated at Ranger school, Bryan snapped them up.

Peter and Paul are twins but only in looks. To be more precise, they're mirror identical twins. Peter has a dimple on his left cheek, Paul the same dimple on his right. Paul is a righty, and Peter does everything lefty. It was the only way their mom could tell them apart. With most people, they could switch and pretend to be the other, and most often, it worked until one threw ball or had to write something. Personality wise, they were opposites. Paul was the boisterous one and Peter more circumspect.

Sammy picked up the phone. "Protection International, how may I direct your call?"

"It's your mama, Sammy honey. I need to speak with Scott. Is he in yet?" Sharon Rogers said with a thick sweet Southern accent.

Sharon stood at five feet, and even Scott the bear looked up to her with affection and respect. She was a real dynamo, widowed at thirty-two. Her cop husband died a hero. She raised her kids with a strong hand and a big heart.

"Yes, and he's driving me crazy. I've had the worst day so far, and the brothers are making it worse!"

Sammy always referred to her brothers as a collective unit, never individually. For years, she wanted a sister so it could be "the sisters" against "the brothers." It wasn't until she figured out that you needed a daddy before you could get a sister. Then she stopped asking for a sister and started asking for another daddy. That didn't go over too well.

"Oh, darlin', don't let them get to ya. They always know how to push your buttons. It's in the brothers' handbook on page 47. Ya just have to ignore them. Go 'bout your business without another thought to 'em." Sharon always referred to the imaginary "rule book" when trying to smooth things over between her kids.

"It's so hard because they gang up on me. It would be different if only one made a smart-ass comment, but they all have to chime in with something. Sometimes I really can't stand the brothers!"

"Now, sweetie, you know they only do that 'cause they love ya, and don't swear when speaking to your mama!"

"Sorry, Mama. I'll put you on with Scott. Thanks for listening to me gripe. No one else here will listen."

"Well, honey, that's my job! It says so in the mama handbook on page 63, and you know how much I love my job! Cheer up, sugar doll. Ya know we all love ya, that's all that really matters in life."

"I know, Mama. You're right. Hold a minute for Scott."

As Sammy transferred Mama's call, she thought more about what her mother had said, and deep down, she knew that they only did the incredibly annoying stuff because they loved her. Sometimes though, she could do without so much loving, like every time she went out to a hot new nightclub and would happen to meet a nice guy, somehow the brothers would show up and send every guy fleeing. It's bad enough the twins are six-foot-four and pure muscle, but they're at least thin. Scottie is three inches taller and tacked on another fifty pounds of muscle. He's a freak of nature. Well, not really, her dad was the same way. That brief image made her smile. She was only three when her dad died, and the two things she remembered most about him were the bear hugs and butterfly kisses he gave her every night at bedtime.

Even if asleep, Martin Rogers would wake up his kids and cuddle and talk to them about their day. He'd kiss them and put them back to bed knowing their daddy loved each of them in a big way.

Rafe Dominguez was one hot Latino. He was probably the shortest of the crew and stood at only five feet, nine inches but was all sinewy muscle. He earned the name Hot Pants because he always put jalapeño peppers or some kind of hot sauce on his food. Even on assignment in the middle of the South American jungle, he was spicing up the bugs he would have to survive on. No one wanted him to make the meals. There wasn't enough water in the jungle to drink when he cooked. It was safer for everyone involved if he stayed away from the kitchen, especially if it was on the sand with rocks, bugs, and coconuts.

"Rafe, buddy, Bryan wants to see you and Paul in his office once you're settled, like now, pronto."

"¡Muy bien, chica! So tell me," Rafe continued in perfect English, "do I have time for my coffee?" He may have been born in Puerto Rico, but he was raised in New York and had absolutely no Spanish accent.

"No, not really. Because you're late. Speaking of which, get your butt into Bryan's office before he starts bellowing. I hate that man's bellow."

"Okay, chica."

"Stop it with the 'chica' bit, it's annoying."

Rafe started laughing on his way into his office. He only had an older brother but felt Sammy was the sister he never had. Goofing around with her always made him feel part of the Pit's extended family.

Rafe didn't have it too easy growing up. He left Puerto Rico with his mom after his father deserted the family, and they went to live with his aunt in NYC. Rafe has an older brother, Ricky, but they don't speak, and maybe it's better that way. When Rafe was seventeen, their mother died from breast cancer, and his brother never even came to her funeral. Rafe put himself through college, ROTC, and joined the Army. He made it into Ranger school and met up with Paul Rogers. They trained together and were assigned to Feldman's Ranger unit. They had some great experiences and other times, not so good. Through it all, they became a family and would do anything for each other. Rafe put his jacket over his chair and listened to his messages. He went out into the main room for coffee.

"Sammy, what happened to the muffins? Did those guys already eat them up?"

"Ugh, what is it with everyone and muffins today? No muffins. Suck it up and get to Bryan's office. Bad start to my day. I warned you about the bellowing, so go."

Just then, the last two members of the Pit walked into the common area, hearing that mini outburst about the muffins, decided they had to get in on the action to drive Sammy crazy. Michael Freeman was a former Navy Seal. He and Christian Eriksen were the only non-Rangers of the group, both being Seals. They have been working together as a team for the past eleven years. Both men at thirty-five were in peak condition, training every day at Mark's sister's gym.

"Oh, damn, no muffins. What's the deal, Sammy?" Christian asked with a huge smile on his face, knowing what the outcome would be before he said anything. Michael just stood there next to him, his white smile a sharp contrast against his coffee colored skin, his broad shoulders moving in time to his laughter.

"I know you just heard what I said. Go jump off a bridge or something and leave me alone!"

Chapter 4

T he sun was in its last moments of daylight, showering the sky with every hue of orange, with deep purples creeping around the edges. Beautiful, breathtaking sunset, if you're into that Kodak-moment type of thing, and he truly was. It was the divine gift from God to end the day, and he allowed himself a few minutes to take the sight in. He had to prepare for an evening of saving souls, and he didn't want to keep God waiting.

He went around the back of the tidy colonial home, looking to make sure no one saw him. He was as average as average could be. He was wearing a nondescript uniform, his fine straight hair parted off-center and tucked behind his ears. He brought his tool case, filled with the items he needed to prepare for the evening. He quickly popped out the window pane in the basement, opened up the window, and was inside her house.

"Harlot," he hissed through his teeth as he watched her in the bar night after night leaving with a different man. She was a whore, tempting men to fornicate with her. God's divine message was clear to him: go out and teach the world of his ways. Thou shall not commit adultery, and she was a married woman in the eyes of God. There was no divorce in the eyes of the Lord, and he didn't believe in it either.

He prepared the bedroom to receive God's cleansing. She would never check under her king-sized brass bed to find the rags caked with hydrocarbon jelly from sterno cans. There was no smell to give them away, but they worked like magic to make the fire burn hotter. She would never notice the other minor accommodations he made to the room like the piles of newspapers under her dresser and the magazines behind her drapes, also smeared with the hydrocarbon jelly. Each carefully positioned to facilitate the flames and attain his goal. *Create pure souls to enter heaven.* She would never pay attention to the sweet smelling pillowcases laced with a little something to put her and whoever she managed to bring home to a nice deep sleep—they'd be too busy with each other to notice that. While he finished his preparations for their final evening on Earth and in sin, he thought about what a good deed he was doing. *Their souls would be saved and purified by fire.* He was happy. Everything was as it should be.

Chapter 5

Seth Roberts trudged up the stairs of his condo. He was frustrated, and since it was early in the afternoon, he didn't feel like going back to his office. The police weren't saying anything; his interviews were flat. The same old info, just rephrased. He knew there was a huge story in the making, right in front of him; he could feel it in his bones. This could be the chance he has been waiting for. All those years of night-school journalism coming full circle: "Serial Killer in Perfect Town America" as his byline. Columbia, South Carolina, was a city but not like NYC, LA, or DC. He wanted a Pulitzer, to be taken seriously, to be a respected journalist like someone from *The Post* or *The Times*. He put his keys and change on the shelf hanging in his front hallway. He looked in the mirror at his face. *Not bad*, he thought. The goatee was just starting to show some grey around the edges. His bright green eyes had dark circles under them from too many late nights. He rubbed his short brown hair, sighed, and turned around to go further into his condo. Typical cluttered male place. His dining room table turned office, with stacks of papers and, of course, the predictable empty pizza box. He couldn't be bothered to walk up to his actual office and then back downstairs for a drink or food. It was just easier to set up shop next to the kitchen. Less steps. He was all for efficiency, and besides, he was lazy by nature.

After popping himself a cold one, he sat down at his table, opened his laptop, and typed in his password. He opened his e-mails and started reading. There was an assortment of paperless e-bills;

he opened those and quickly reviewed them. He'd go online later to pay them. Using his mouse to scroll down farther, something caught his eye. "SETH ROBERTS, PULITZER PRIZE WINNER." That piqued his attention. He opened the e-mail and began to read the text. He noticed that there were pictures attached to the missive.

> Dear Seth,
>
> May I call you Seth? I've never written to someone like this before, so I'm not sure how to start out. I think that we'll get real familiar with each other bcuz I'm your ticket to that Pulitzer you've been wantin to win. Yes, sir, I'm gonna get you that prize. You don't no me, and don't worry, there's no way that the cops can catch me. I'm smarter than those morons. Just thought that you'd appreciate my handy work. The film I just made and uploaded is starring Sally Anne Myers. That's who I left for the cops to find at the Forest Lake Country Club this morning.
>
> I saw you out in the crowd. I decided right then and there that I wanted you to see my first Goregasm! film starring Sally Anne before the general public. I think you'll love it, and it'll put us both on the map. Check out this website: *http://www.flurl.com/video/10136750_ comments.htm*. We'll be in touch.
>
> Yours, Carver

What the hell? This couldn't be for real. Seth immediately clicked on the link and started watching. He was shocked but simultaneously mesmerized and unable to veer from the screen. In between the graphic scenes, there were taunting words, pictures of the girls in their daily lives, and before-and-after stuff. Holy shit, this guy has been stalking them for days.

This was some seriously messed up shit. There were also other girls, older footage that was montaged into his current work with Sally Anne.

He had to think about this carefully. This is something that the cops should see, but he didn't want to lose such an amazing inside scoop. He figured that he would write his article for the morning addition, and the cops could figure it out from there. He sat down, opened a new file on his computer, and, after a few false starts, felt the story start to unfold. His fingers were moving frantically over the keyboard, and he started writing to make his deadline, all the while thinking about national coverage.

Chapter 6

Rafe walked into Bryan's office. Bryan was sitting on a chair behind his mahogany desk. Pictures of nieces and nephews, of the guys on missions in the desert and in the jungle, and of his parents were lined up three-deep along his credenza. Paul was seated on a chair next to Rafe.

Bryan proceeded to explain to Paul and Rafe the situation with an old enemy, a sect of the Russian Mob that was abducting children and teens and selling them into various types of slavery. Originally, this was the assignment that almost ended the lives of Scott Rogers and his partner, Mark Lewis.

There was a new lead, and Bryan wanted Paul and Rafe to follow up on it. Feldman mentioned how he was in the process of making a deal for information. Apparently, some big time, very famous politician from a red state, Senator Parker Stevens, was caught buying child pornography, and the worst kind, a snuff film, one where the child is killed during sex. Senator Stevens wanted to get away with his reputation intact and did not want any mention of the tape to leak out. He was trying to cut a deal with Feldman to make everything go away: no jail time, no fines, and his reputation saved. The senator would retire from public life due to health issues, and he would end any contact with kiddie porn. Feldman would be keeping a keen eye on Stevens from now on. It all sounded neat and tidy, but they hadn't gotten any viable leads in nearly three years. New information had just surfaced. Bryan began the briefing.

"This information we've collected has to do with a website that the senator subscribed to, one run by our group of the Russian mob. An innocent web surfer would assume the site was under construction, but to inside users who know the password-protected areas, it's a full menu to buy kids. It provides a *Map Site* so users can choose the ethnicity of the child. It has a *Kids World Store* so you can order up a child by age, hair, and eye color, even choose a body type, thin and athletic or pudgy and cuddly. If that isn't nauseating enough, the site offers a *Furniture Section* that includes bondage devices made for smaller bodies. *Kids World* online magazine is for like-minded individuals. It allows chatting about the latest advances and how to avoid detection from authorities. It has a *Live Auction* Section, where there are pictures of naked children, cute little bios artfully written, so the buyer knows exactly what he is getting. Bidders are e-mailed a password and told what time the live auction will begin.

"I don't want to involve Scott and Mark in this quite yet," declared Bryan. "It's too personal for them. I don't want them going off half cocked. I wanted to make sure we have a viable lead first. You guys remember when the assignment went bad. Both Mark and Scott were almost history. Mark still has a limp from the bomb explosion."

After the background details, Bryan went on to describe the next steps.

"We're still in the negotiation phase. The senator has updated us on what's going on, but we haven't analyzed the website yet. He'll release his password when we come to a final agreement. I hate dealing with pedophiles; they're the worst of the pond scum. Please meet back here at 3:00 p.m. We should have that password by then, and I want to move forward quickly on this assignment. Any questions?"

"Yeah. After we get the password, can I facilitate the scumbag's 'medical condition' by breaking both his fucking legs?" queried Rafe. "Which reminds me, are we offering the scumbag any protection?"

"We're protecting him. Or should I say watching him, for a period of time. I can't disclose that exactly until the deal is finalized," said Bryan.

"Boss, I have another question. Actually, a request." Paul raised his hand like a school boy. "My college roommate contacted me about a serial arsonist loose in his county, right outside of Philly.

He wanted to know if I could help him out. I can still work on this website case as well as the arson. I'm looking at maybe three weeks or so. You remember Rob Loyd? Really sharp dude. He graduated at the top of his class at the Pennsylvania State Police Academy, which was no surprise considering he was magna cum laude from Drexel University. He got his master's degree from University of Pennsylvania in Chemistry along with all his other certifications. I think he's the only forensic chemist in the state."

"Yeah, I remember him. He helped us analyze the bombing that almost blew up Mark and Scott," said Bryan. "Take your time to do a good job but hurry back as soon as things are resolved. I need you here when you're done. I'll have Peter help Rafe now. Get me the file and contact information about what you'll be doing and then leave your contact info with Sammy. I want to make sure I don't get burned."

"Very funny, boss." Rafe snickered.

Chapter 7

It took a while, but Melanie Richards was back on track, or should we say back in the sack. After a long divorce process, she didn't want a heavy relationship. Just good sex. It was amazing how good hard sex was to come by.

"Hard" didn't mean "good." She giggled to herself.

She decided that the best way to get what she wanted was to try and try again. That meant going out to the Roxy, her favorite bar. The drinks weren't expensive, good music was always playing, and she knew the bartender really well. She always found someone new to entice. Melanie dated regularly after being dumped by her husband of only four years. Luckily, they didn't have any children, which would have made a difficult divorce even worse and dating much more complicated.

Melanie started her night off "shimmying" to some Madonna playing loudly in her car on her commute home. She slipped into her club routine as easily as one would slip into a comfortable pair of slippers. As she entered her bedroom, she double-checked the outfit that she painstakingly picked out the night before. It was a black lacy mini skirt with a wide leather belt coupled with a white cashmere snug-fitting top. The skirt was just short enough to show a bit of tummy between the belt and the bottom of the top. Her ankle boots with three-inch heels and her black sheer stockings finished the look. She hated pantyhose but splurged on Wolford stockings. It was actually better because if she got a run in one leg, she only had to discard one stocking, not both. That helped since the hose was really expensive. *But worth it,* she thought.

She put in a Backstreet Boys CD and started getting ready, her favorite part. She ran through the shower with a quick body wash, keeping her hair dry since she had it done that morning. She bopped happily to the music, singing a tad off key. She applied her makeup carefully, a little heavy on the mascara and eyeliner, but she was intent on making her eyes pop. Lipstick was carefully applied then lip liner in a bold maroon and topped with a shimmery gloss. She wanted to make it look like she had soft, kissable lips. She swayed with the music as she checked out her body in the mirror one last time before she bolted out the door. "Not bad," she whispered with a sexy tone. She was ready for the night and all the action that was ahead. Melanie turned off the CD player and danced to the music in her head as she headed out the front door, adjusting the door's decorative wreath yet again.

With her looks, men were very attracted to Melanie, and she was happy to bring them back to her simple colonial home in suburban Philadelphia. Located only ten minutes out of Center City, it was a short trek home from the bar. The city location also made it easy to find a rather endless supply of men. As Melanie and her date approached her saffron-colored door, Melanie had to be careful not to knock off the flowered wreath. She had double front doors, and the wreath hung right in the middle, between the two. The wreath banged every time she opened the door, but she loved how inviting it looked, so she put up with the fuss.

Melanie and her new date, Sam Phillips, walked through the front entry way into the living room. Melanie went right over to a fully stocked bar, which impressed Sam immediately. Her house was set up just the way she wanted it now that she was divorced. She figured that one more drink and a little bit of talking was the perfect segue to the bedroom. She made herself a rum and Diet Coke and opened a Corona for Sam, stuffing a lime wedge in the top.

"Nice touch," said Sam. "The piece of lime in the beer, I mean."

Sam was a decent guy, and they hit it off immediately. It didn't seem like he had an agenda. Melanie definitely wanted to get to know him better. He was only a little bit taller than her five feet, six inches, and he had classic good looks, obviously well-groomed. He had a cleft chin, defined brows, and bow-shaped lips. *Perfect for kissing,* Melanie thought.

She was also taken in by his vibrant green eyes and that impish, let's-do-something-naughty smile. She was always a sucker for a perfect smile and great eyes. Now that she was a little tipsy, she couldn't wait to jump his bones!

They sat on the couch talking for a while as they finished their drinks. Sam put his empty bottle and her glass on the coffee table, saying they should get down to "business." He smiled that great smile and asked Melanie to come a little closer with a boyish manner. She giggled softly. She hadn't giggled like that since high school. They made their way to the bedroom, littering the floor with clothes as they moved. Of course, Melanie was going to let Sam remove her lace bra and panties.

Chapter 8

He was driving around Arcadia Lakes, proud to show off his new Chevy Silverado. He headed down the main street to the Peter's Hardware to pick up supplies to fix Mrs. Furhman's front porch. He left Arcadia Lakes after high school, got into construction in Charlotte, drifted to Durham, but ended up coming home. Things didn't work out too well for him there.

"Hey, Mr. Peters. How are you this morning?"

"How ya doin', son?"

"Never better. I need some supplies for Mrs. Furhman's front porch. I'll grab what I need and then be off."

"You're such a good boy. How's your grandma doin' these days? Still part of that bible group?" Mr. Peter's said with genuine affection.

"Yep. She still likes goin' and havin' tea with the ladies."

"Well, if ya need any help, just holler."

Mr. Peters went back to looking around the store, talking to his usual gathering of men who came in daily to talk about anything there was to talk about. They had been meeting in Peter's Hardware for about fifteen years. Customers were in the store picking up orders, looking for supplies, or just plain spending time talking.

Travis Johnson came up to the front of the store to pay for his order, not saying much to anyone. He quickly left the store and drove away in his truck.

"He's a strange duck, that one. Never says a word more than he has to. Not very social. Never liked him much. Never a friendly kid," Peters said as he glared at the truck pulling away from the store.

"He's harmless. Just had it tough with his pa gone," Sam Morton said.

"I guess."

Chapter 9

Mark Lewis limped into the Pit office. His leg still hurt like a son of a bitch. He was a nice-looking man, with short dark hair and strong shoulders. His handsome, intelligent face had a grimace on it from the pain radiating up his leg. He guided himself around the corner of his dark oak desk to sit down; his cane got stuck, and he fell into his seat.

"That was graceful. I can see why we called you Ghost."

He looked up and saw Rogers standing in the doorway.

"That was a long time ago. My leg's worse today than usual. Probably overdid it at PT. Now, I'm paying for it," winced Mark as he gently rubbed his thigh.

He thought back three years ago, when he and Scott were working undercover for a joint FBI and Interpol operation. They were trying to infiltrate a Russian child slavery ring. They almost had the sons of bitches, but they were sold out. They were literally blown away right along with their cover. A bomb was planted in the meeting place; they were only three minutes late which kept them away from the strongest part of the blast. Everyone else at the meeting was killed instantly. A chunk of muscle was torn from Mark's leg, and Scott had some internal injuries. Both knew how lucky they were to be alive. After months of recuperation and physical therapy, they were finally ready to rejoin the team.

Bryan Feldman was there with the rest of the Rogers family right after the blast. He made sure his men were safeguarded in the hospital and afterward and made a personal oath to destroy those bastards. Three years later, they still barely had any new leads.

Scott looked at Lewis and noticed he was staring at the floor.

"Where did you go, Lewis?" asked Scott.

"Back to the past for a few minutes."

"Don't worry. When the time's right, we'll find them."

"Yep, that's what we always say, but what about those missing children being sold to scumbags? What type of hell are they living, if they're even still alive?" Lewis said with his hands folded in his lap and his shoulders hunched over.

"Yeah, the world is fucked up. What can I say? Speaking of missing girls, a couple of days ago, the news reported that a woman's body was discovered in Arcadia Lakes, a small town in South Carolina. She was a beautiful, athletic blond in her twenties. The poor girl was not only raped and tortured to death, but the whole thing was also videoed and released on the web. It was on one of those uncensored sites that shows all the perverted and disgusting shit. I had to check it out. It seems that this could be serial," Rogers continued. "He was way too comfortable with that knife while he was slicing and dicing her."

"No, I didn't hear anything about it. And lovely description there. Man, you're heartless. Maybe my cousin Lizzie can fill me in," said Lewis. "She's a senior detective out of Columbia with the State Police and the first female to make detective in the SLED. So this would probably fall under her jurisdiction. I'll check out the latest and then give her a call. We might be able to help her out."

Scott Rogers left his office thinking about Lizzie. He met her a few times, hot as hell, legs up to the sky. There were virtually no women tall enough to meet his eyes, and he almost could with her. She was a killer blond with gorgeous tits and curves that could make a man cry. She wasn't a diva either. She was just off limits, married to some hard ass cop.

Lewis used the Pit's landline to make the call, keeping it friendly but professional.

"Detective Bowlyn, please." Lewis waited patiently for her to pick up.

"Bowlyn" was the answer, quiet but confident.

"Lizzie, it's Mark. I've heard the news this morning, and there's quite a mess going on in Arcadia Lakes. Media frenzy start yet?"

"Can't walk outside the office without getting attacked. I think the reporters are multiplying as we speak," she agreed. "They're worse than cockroaches."

"Seriously, if there is anything that we can do to help, let us know. We've got all the cool new toys here. Rogers and I can hop on a plane and be there in under an hour. I know it's not standard operating procedure for us to ask you, you need to come to us, but you know how good we are."

"No modesty there. Thanks, but that's not my call. It's already getting political. Let me think about it and let you know. It would be good to see you again. How's Remmi?"

Mark's younger sister, Remmi, was a total spitfire. She ran her own dojo/gym for women. It had a snack bar filled with nutritious snacks, juice bar, and a New Age bookstore attached to the gym. That was so Remmi, a free-spirited health nut. She worked long hours to make her gym an extension of her personality. She put in an area where the guys could come and work on their skills, mats that were set up in the basement for them to wrestle or exercise on.

"I'll keep in touch. Did you look at that freak's posting? I'd really be interested in your take on it. I'll e-mail you the link, if you don't have it, or you could just Google it. But beware, it's the lowest form of nasty," said Lizzie.

"Scott saw it earlier. I'm sure that I can find it through him. Talk to you soon. Bye, kiddo. Be careful."

"Love you too, Mark."

After Mark hung up the phone, he started searching for the facts on the murder in Arcadia Lakes. He found articles on all the major news venues; CNN, ABC, *The Times*, and *The State* website had breaking news. That site seemed to have the most information and seemed to have it posted first thing this morning. *Interesting.* Lewis wondered if the editors had inside information. It was something to think about. After reading a few of the postings, he decided to look at the actual film.

He sat staring at the screen for a good five minutes, processing what he was looking at in an FBI manner. That kept him from feeling sick to his stomach. It was apparent that the woman being tortured was cognizant of what was happening. She was screaming, whimpering, pleading for mercy, pleading to die. Whoever the guy was clearly enjoyed the process. *A little too much,* thought Mark.

Even when the poor girl finally died, the bastard kept at it, stabbing, cutting, and defiling the body. He continued ramming her body, punching her head. This sicko was playing to the camera, thrilled at being the star. He also had shots of other girls, not nearly as artfully photographed. Mark couldn't be sure, but he counted at least four different girls abused and tortured in this video. He wasn't positive because no other bodies had been found.

"The balls of this sick bastard, to display the body from so many angles. He wants the authorities to find out! He wants everyone to find out. Announcing his craft to the world and projecting a confidence that he's untouchable. God help the other girl who is still missing."

Chapter 10

He enjoyed listening to all the gossip at the drug store, enjoyed that everyone was talking about him, even if they didn't realize it. Apparently, all they could talk about was the dead body the police found a few days ago on the golf course. *Hmm, imagine that.* Next, he was off to the diner to grab a quick bite to eat. He heard the same thing: talk, talk, talk, all about finding poor Sally Anne Myers. Some were saying she was butchered and what kind of sick animal could do that to that beautiful young woman. *Yeah, wonder that.*

He maneuvered his tall lean body out of the booth, pushing on the table with his too-long arms. His thin, sandy blond hair hung down, loosely brushing the top of his shoulders. He paid in cash at the counter for his pot roast special and was on his way. It was amazing. Not one person talked to him or even looked at him. That's why he left after high school. He was like the invisible man. Invisible but infamous, which was okay with him.

He couldn't believe that he was driving near the area of the golf course where Sally Anne was found. He just couldn't help himself. Being here again helped him relive two nights ago. As he got closer, he actually got a hard on. He rubbed his crotch and got a full erection. He could still see the crime tape blocking off the area; his adrenaline surged; his heart pounded out of control. He edged his way to the end of the block and then made a right onto Mrs. Furhman's street. He was thinking about the rumors circulating about how Sally Anne met her maker, but nothing came close to the gratifying horror of the actual event. He smiled as that tingly feeling surged from his crotch all the way up his spine. He couldn't wait to start filming Sarah Jenkins. Another masterpiece in the making and more fame for him. But before filming resumed, he had to have a talk with Susan Starks.

He abducted Susan while she was jogging near Forest Lake. It had been a snap. She was so predictable, doing laps the same time, same place every day, rain or shine. He was waiting behind a massive oak tree which had to be over two hundred years old. His hands were sweating, and his heart almost exploded out of his chest. He thought for sure she could hear it beating.

As she passed by his hiding spot, he grabbed her and quickly stuck the chloroformed towel over her face. She was breathing hard from her run, and she was so light that struggling was useless against him. His arms were sinewy and muscular, nearly twice the size of hers. He easily carried her to his deluxe Chevy and shoved her under the tarps and construction material that was always left in the back bed. She would be quiet for a while, he figured about four hours. Even so, he gagged her.

No loose ends. Damn, I'm smart, he thought brazenly.

That would be enough time for him to be able to get supplies, breakfast, and then start work on the porch. He'd take a lunch break and check on Susan. His stomach was full of butterflies; he was so pumped. He couldn't wipe a silly crooked grin off his face. He was so stoked for what was on the horizon. He finished work early on Mrs. Furman's porch, so he decided to head home and put in some valuable time on his computer.

He sat in front of the computer thinking. It wasn't always like that, free to do what he wanted; he worked for a jerk, never having time off during the day. He played with the girls but ran into trouble, and he had to leave Charlotte quickly. He just started his activities with the girls, and before he perfected his act, he almost got caught. He learned from his mistakes. He's so much smarter now: never leave them alive.

"When life gives you lemons, make lemonade," he reminisced sardonically. "That's what that shriveled up old bat used to say over and over again."

It was that saying that made him come home and stay with granny again. She always thought she could save him, so he wouldn't turn out like his good-for-nothing daddy. She would take him to church every Sunday, him in his little shorts with the matching button-down shirt with a clip on tie, all proper for "seein' the Lord." After church, they'd go to the diner, get lunch, and then head to Lieber Correctional Institution, a maximum security prison in Columbia. His father, Billy Joe, was in prison for beating his wife and her lover to death. He had come home from work early one day and found them having sex in the bedroom. In an uncontrollable rage, he took a Louisville slugger he kept hidden beneath the bed and smashed both their heads in. Granny still loved her Billy Joe, and she would tell her grandson every Sunday on the drive home, "If it weren't for your whore of a mother, your daddy wouldn't be rotting away in prison."

Good ol' Granny. She'd still be goin' to see that dumb ass every Sunday if he hadn't died years ago. But not me. I won't have nothin' to do with old Billy Joe. And there ain't no way I'm gonna end up rottin' in jail like him, he thought to himself, pushing his hair back behind his ears.

Breaking away from his rare lapse into memory lane, he shook his head and moved the mouse to start creating and editing his latest work of art.

Chapter 11

He stood hidden outside, watching the progression of lights going on and off throughout the house. Then he waited for the bedroom to darken.

"Soon," he mumbled quietly.

Soon, they would be ready for the cleansing fires of purification. He knew what they were doing in the bedroom and looked away from the house in disgust. He could hear the moans in his mind, echoes from long ago. He waited for over an hour for them to finish their unholy act while the chloroform silently did its work. They'd be happily "in lust" and fast asleep within minutes.

He made his way to the backyard of the colonial as soon as he was confident. Not only were all the lights were out, but the two would also be in deep sleep. On a previous night when she was out carousing, he loosened the glass on the basement window. It was a nice big window she had newly installed to allow more light into the basement when she did her workouts. He was in the house in less than a minute. He moved with stealth through all the Christmas decorations that were boxed and stacked around like a maze. Using a small Maglite flashlight, his presence was nearly imperceptible as he made his way into the main part of the room where she kept a few pieces of exercise equipment. He went up the stairs to the living room, avoiding all the creaks that might alert the sinners. He doubted they could hear him anyway, but he was careful just the same. He opened the door at the top of the stairs and stepped into the living room. This was almost too easy.

As he continued to make his way around the room to the sofa, he made sure he kept as quiet as a church mouse. "Patience is a virtue," he muttered to himself, and he was definitely virtuous.

To that end, he would cleanse those who weren't. He waited in the dark living room until 3:00 a.m. There weren't any sounds or movement, and it seemed safe to venture upstairs toward the bedroom. He avoided more creaks and the sporadic placement of discarded clothing, knowing it wasn't laundry. He opened the bedroom door and instantly knew everything was going as planned.

The couple was asleep, naked, loosely holding each other. The words "filthy harlot" silently spewed from his lips as he worked quickly to push them closer together like they were having sex. Then he used duct tape to keep them positioned as a unit, the way he needed them. He opened the window just a crack to ensure that there would be enough oxygen to feed the flames and give the fire added life. Next, he got the gasoline he had hidden earlier in the spare bedroom and began dousing the bed and the curtains, spilling the last of it on the floor, making a trail to the door.

He took one last look at the sinners entwined on the bed that had been thoroughly prepared for their funeral pyre. Everything was ready; he could hardly wait. He struck the long match against the wall and held it close to his average face, enjoying the sweet smell of the sulfur that filled the air, and looked into the bright guiding light that shone in the night. One little match and all the power it had—it was a beautiful thing. He stood in the doorway and lit the wet streak of gasoline that led out of the room. He watched with gleaming eyes as the blue flames rose higher, feeding hungrily from the fuel surrounding the bedroom. The snap, crackle, and hiss of the fire were his favorite parts. The heady smell filled his lungs, and the reaching flames joyously danced up the wall to a tune of its own making. He dashed out the front door and left the flames grow larger and upward toward God, taking the two lust-birds with them.

Fire. It was such a wondrous gift to man, a perfect means of purification. The Lord spoke to the profits of the Old Testament. Now, he was speaking to him through the flames, just like he did with Moses on the mount. Only now, it was his turn to bring God's message to sinners today. God showed him that it was his destiny to rid the world of sinners with the fires of hell. Through the flames, those worthy would be reborn and gain entrance into heaven. He was the Servant, a modern-day prophet. His message was clear: sin will be punished. *Only through the purification of fire would God save their souls from eternal damnation.* He was saving their souls as God wished. He nailed a hand-forged crucifix to the front door, one of several he had carved. It was his calling card so all would know that a servant of God had saved their souls. As the silk flowers were knocked down from the front door, the saffron paint stood out in the moonlit night. He nodded on a job well done and walked away humming "Amazing Grace."

Chapter 12

L izzie met up with Dave Dubowski in the hall on her way to the South Carolina Law Enforcement Division Chief's office. This was not going to be a fun discussion, and she was looking forward to it like a root canal. The media frenzy was surrounding the old-fashioned, regal brick building, accosting anyone who entered or left the building. The Department of Justice was a typical southern state courthouse, located in the heart of Columbia. It had ten floors, housing state offices, courts, chief's offices, and the DA's office. Large white columns, a la Tara, were shining brightly in the sunlight. Everything one could want to fight for justice was under one roof, kind of like the Macy's of law enforcement. The district attorney was on eight, holding cells on nine; SLED offices were on two; and in the basement was the morgue. However, they were on the third floor in the chief's office. Chief Walter Montgomery was a walking contradiction, almost a caricature. He had a deep voice and larger-than-life personality wrapped up in a little body. He was only five-three but weighed about two hundred fifty. He was reminiscent of that old Southern gentleman, the Colonel Sanders type with glasses and a thick, white, bushy moustache. He always wore a bolero, and his uniform was starched to perfection, tautly covering his huge belly which protruded like a shelf, obscuring his belt buckle. He was waiting for homicide detectives to report what the hell was happening.

Surrounding the County of Richland, with a population 360,000, twelve detectives covered homicides. One of them was Lizzie. They shared a thirty-five-foot squad room, lit by harsh fluorescent lights. Since Lizzie was a senior detective, she had a choice spot with her desk by the windows. Her area was neat, a dog crate tucked discreetly underneath her desk; her inbox was overflowing with manila file folders, but no other papers were on her desk. As she stood in the hallway outside Montgomery's office, she was thinking about all the stuff she could be doing, like going down to the morgue to get the autopsy report. Instead, she was on her way to get chewed out for losing control of her case. Media frenzy always worked against her. They made it seem like nothing was getting done and wanted instant arrests. She started knocking on the thick door. She heard the chief yell, "Come in and make it snappy!" She and Dubowski entered the office and stood by his desk, watching the man struggle to get to his feet.

"You see this?" he said, tossing a copy of *The State* across the desk to Lizzie. The headline, in bold stark letters, read, "Abduction Turns to Murder at Country Club." Walter continued to read the article with a sarcastic tone. "'By the stunning view from the fourth hole, the body of missing twenty-three-year-old Sally Anne Myers was found naked, curled up as if in an offering, on the green near the pin. She had been brutally raped and tortured for hours before she finally died at the hand of a sociopath. He has a penchant for tall blond women and is known to this reporter as Carver.'"

"What? Did we invite this reporter onto the green for a personal tour of the crime scene? He knows the name of the victim, the killer's nickname, and has the crime scene mapped out pretty damn well. Maybe I should call him, this Seth Roberts, and ask him if there are any more leads on this so-called Carver since my detectives can't get off their collective asses and give me anything. I want to know why this guy got more information three days ago than we have today!" The chief ranted on.

Lizzie and her partner were silent.

"Give me something I want to hear!" he roared.

"I can give you a 900 number that will tell you whatever you want to hear for three dollars a minute," suggested Dubowski.

"Do you think this is a joke, Dubowski? You want to wise crack yourself out of a job?"

"No, sir. Sorry, sir. That was completely inappropriate. Please accept my apology. I guess that's just my way of coping with the horror of the situation, sir."

Dubowski was like that, always trying to break the tension with a laugh. This time, it was pretty hard to achieve under the circumstances, but he almost always got a smile from the peanut gallery.

"Well, cope on your own time and not in my office. Not in front of my face. I want you to get everything we can on this Carver person, and you two might as well start with that know-it-all reporter from *The State*. Be in my office by 9:00 a.m. tomorrow. We need to lay this thing out carefully. This is national news now, and I, for one, do not want to get caught with my pants down and look like a buffoon or some Southern hick unable to do the job. For now, Bowlyn, it's all yours. Start a task force, take up to six guys. I know this is only one murder so far, but from what I saw on that video, looks like he's killed a few others mixed in on that tape that we have no bodies for. Get someone to try and identify those other girls in the video. We may be able to pinpoint some other missing women. Why he's changing his MO from snapshots to full feature films, I have no idea, but I want you to figure it out. Don't just stand there with your mouth open collecting flies! Go on! Get out of my office and get to work."

"You got it, Chief," said Lizzie, as she had so many times before. Dubowski followed suit.

Lizzie and her partner used the stairs rather than the elevator and, within a few minutes, were back at their desks. Lizzie's sweet puppy Mandy was still waiting patiently in her crate. She hopped out of her crate and onto Lizzie's lap after she sat down at her desk. Mandy could always tell when Lizzie was stressed and put her tiny paws on Lizzie's chest, giving her a lick on her cheek.

"I'm going to take Mandy for a quick walk . . . and to clear my head. Be right back, Dubowski."

Lizzie returned to her desk fifteen minutes later and immediately started putting together a plan. She would definitely need some help. First, however, she had to go to the morgue and talk to the ME to find out what evidence the lab had uncovered so far. The crime scene was a dump job, so she really didn't think there would be much there, but hope springs eternal. She walked across the dingy squad room to Dubowski's desk. After a short conversation about what they had, they decided to find out what was going on with the autopsy.

Even though it's a depressing environment, and you'd never go out of your way to visit it, the Crypt held a certain appeal. Cops always congregated there. The coffee was good and hot, and because without dead people, homicide detectives would be out of a job. Besides, there's nothing like the sharp smell of formaldehyde first thing in the morning to clean out the sinuses. The depressing sheen of the ancient grey tile walls added to the drudgery of walking down the hall. But since that's where the autopsy was being done, it's where they needed to be. Hopefully, after having the body for a few days, Dr. Gilligan would find something conclusive so Lizzie had somewhere to start in this case. Of course, they wanted to find the killer but also avoid the wrath of Walter Montgomery as well.

The morgue had certain rules. When Dave and Lizzie arrived, they were escorted into Dr. Sean Gilligan's office, which was off to the right of the main autopsy room. He was wearing his doctor's white lab coat covering kelly-green scrubs. His "S. Gilligan" was embroidered in red above the upper left-hand pocket. Lizzie always thought the thread should have been green to match the scrubs, or black. Anything but blood red. The first thing striking about Sean was his size. Again, Lizzie always noticed anyone taller than herself. The next thing was his commanding presence. He obviously lived by the credo "once a marine, always a marine." As they walked in, Dr. Gilligan gave a weary but nice smile, showing a small amount of his straight white teeth and a hint of a dimple on his left cheek. It seemed like he had been up most of the night working, and Lizzie hoped he had some answers.

"I've been expecting you" was the only small talk out of Dr. Gilligan. He immediately got on with the rest of the report. "It was standard autopsy preparation, Y cut, organs removed, weighed. You remember Autopsy 101 or do you need a refresher?"

They both gave him a blank stare, which he took to mean *Yes, continue on.* "I just finished the preliminary. Just have to wait on labs before I post my final report. I think it will be easier to explain as I go over the body. You up for that now?"

Lizzie nodded anxiously. Not because she couldn't stomach it but just desperate for a lead.

"Be prepared. Even for me, this was bad. I've never actually seen anything like this, but I've read about it in trade magazines."

He led them through a series of automatic compression doors, automatically opening and closing around them, leading them into the heart of the Crypt, the large refrigerated room where the dead bodies were stored within the walls, each body placed in a sliding tray with its own individual door. The morgue was able to hold up to 16 bodies at a time. Autopsies were performed in the center of the room on the cold steel table. There were gurneys around the room, one holding their victim, ready to be put back into her assigned refrigerated slab.

Lizzie was no neophyte. She had seen her share of dead, even dismembered bodies, but what she saw nearly made her pass out. This was far worse than seeing the body on the golf course. The mutilated corpse of Sally Anne Myers seemed barely human. She lay naked on the gurney, her face frozen in the horrifying moment of death. It was the same face that Lizzie had watched on her computer and then saw haunting her nightmares. In these terrible dreams, Lizzie saw Sally Anne's stark ghostly figure suddenly joined by other dead women she had seen on the Internet, scarred and mutilated, ganging up on her, pleading that they find Carver and make him stop hurting them.

Lizzie scanned Sally Anne Myers ravaged body, a freeze frame of grotesque horror and the sad proof of a demented killer. In all her years in homicide, Lizzie never turned away from a victim, but she turned away now. Dubowski touched her shoulder. "Hey, I've been doing this for over twenty years, and even I have to turn away."

She picked up the folder on the gurney next to Sally Anne as Dr. Gilligan started catalouging her wounds. Most of the stab wounds around the breast were only superficial to the breast tissue. They did not puncture the main underlying organs. Her eyes had been forcibly pried from their sockets, and Lizzie replayed that vial scene from the video in her mind. There was severe trauma to her genital and anal area. Not only was she repeatedly and violently raped as evidence of spermicide and condom lubricant, but she had been sodomized by a jagged object as well. Again, the video replayed the horror of Sally Anne's torture and her screams of pain and whimpers when it was too much.

"As you can see right here, this is the killing wound where the blade pierced the juncture between the sternum and the ribs, rupturing the AV node. It's like smashing the hard drive of the heart's electrical system, causing an electro-myocardial malfunction. Technically, she died of cardiac arrest and not exsanguination."

"What, like she had a heart attack but didn't bleed out?" Dubowski asked

"Yes. That's what happens when you get stabbed directly in that spot of your heart. The heart just stops, no longer moving blood through the body or blood out of the wounds. Either your killer has medical knowledge, or he's very practiced in precise and instant death, like military training, a slaughter house, or a hunter. Death is on his terms and only when he is ready. This also leads me to believe that this person has killed before, definitely more than once, maybe more than twice because there were no hesitation wounds. If this were a first time kill, I would expect to see some hesitation, experimentation with the knife. I see nothing but precision cuts and deliberate stab wounds. Based on the interior pooling, I'd say she was lying flat when she received the killing stab wound."

"Well, duh. Doc, didn't you see the video of her murder on the Internet?" Dubowski asked.

"There's a video of her murder? My god, I had no idea! Why didn't you tell me about it earlier?"

"It's been all over the news, local and now national. It was leaked by a reporter from *The State*, so I thought the whole world had seen it."

"Sorry. I've been a little busy down here doing the autopsy, not sitting back with my cup of coffee watching the news. I can barely imagine what this poor woman went through, let alone watch it in progress. Sometimes I think I should have just been a veterinarian."

They finished up with Dr. Gilligan, getting his final summation, and then they showed him the link for the video. He sighed and said that he would alert them immediately if he noticed any contradictions to his report after viewing the video. This was one movie that he dreaded to watch.

Chapter 13

He set up the cameras for the final scene and would burn the action directly on a DVD. This way, all the images would be easier to transfer to his computer and released through the website he had used before. He also changed his production plan. Instead of a short, like the Sally Anne flick, he wanted to make it longer with more action, closer to a full-length feature. He already had a lot of good footage. After three days of playing with Sarah Jenkins, he decided that this final scene could be at least two hours. *Of sheer pleasure*, he thought.

As usual, watching his performance with Sarah Jenkins got him really turned on. He instantly had a full erection, and his penis pushed outward, stretching his Levis, in an uncomfortable way. He just unzipped them and threw them to the side of the room. He was watching the part where he used a single-edged blade to cut off her nipples. When the girl saw what he was doing, she screamed louder, and oh, how the blood drizzled over the sides of her huge breasts like fudge flowing over a scoop of ice cream.

He made a lot of small slits around her tits. How clever and creative he thought he was. Adding to the beauty of the scene, the little cuts made a tributary so that more blood flowed into the valley between her breasts. She wouldn't look at the camera or his eyes. He wanted her to look, she kept refusing. So he popped one of her eyes out of the socket with his finger. She wailed on that one.

It infuriated him when she was disobedient. Not again. It would not be tolerated. She would do as she was told for the big climax. He didn't even realize that his hand was inside his Jockeys rubbing his penis until he came. He had just been determining how he would finish off Sarah Jenkins. He'd show that bitch or that bitch was the show. Again, how fabulously clever he was, a movie mogul! His movie was approaching the one-million-viewer mark.

He took a deep, satisfied breath and wiped himself off and put his pants back on. Everything was in play. Arcadia Lakes will never be the same. All those boring little people doing the same thing day after day will continue talking about him. They had such simple, shallow lives with simple, average dreams. Not him. His dreams were soaring. He was flying high on the top of the world.

Susan Starks heard terrible screaming. *What the hell is going on!* she thought as her heart raced and sweat collected above her bow shaped lips. Earlier in the day, she could feel the room moving and bumping along, so she figured that she must be in some kind of trailer or mobile home. The ride wasn't smooth enough for a mobile home, so she figured a caravan trailer of some type. It also must be fairly large since there seemed to be two connecting rooms. Right behind the door to her very small room is where the screaming was loudest.

After that horrific screaming for what seemed like hours, Susan finally heard soft whimpers for over an hour. Then there were only sobs after a long silence. *What just happened to that girl? I wonder if that was Sally Anne or Sarah . . . and if I'm next.* A million thoughts flooded Susan's aching head. Listening to the screaming and sad aftermath made her sick to her stomach. Susan felt some relief when she heard the start of an engine. He was leaving again, but the trailer wasn't attached. Maybe they wouldn't die. Maybe there was hope that someone would find them. She was disgusted by lying on the soiled mattress. The stench was overwhelming. He came in to feed her, but she still had to relieve herself on the mattress. He would not untie her for any reason. She had long since stopped feeling her limbs, and the dull ache was a constant reminder of her horrific situation.

He parked outside the supermarket and started taking pictures of the checkout girl, Saddie Mae Reynolds. "Hmm . . . Sally Anne, Sarah, Susan, and now, Sadie Mae. They just keep getting sweeter and sweeter," he hissed. He loved being in his hometown because so many girls were tall. Maybe it was because the high school had such an outstanding basketball team. In his mind, his victims had to be at least five-nine because it looked so much better on film when he could see a long body strapped onto his "examination" table. Having blond hair was a must as well, and the lighter the better. Dark hair hid the blood too much and didn't have the visual impact that clotting blood had on blond hair. It looked so fantastic, dripping and matting those golden highlights.

Sadie Mae Reynolds was going to be the star of his fourth production. For now, he had to get back to the trailer and finish his second film. It needed the perfect lighting, early evening, to enhance the last moment of life in Sarah's face, right before it went slack with death. Maybe evisceration while he was firmly pounding into her ass, legs high in the air. That would be the perfect ending, climaxing while she died, bleeding to death. A nice slow ending with a lot of rough sex. He imagined his hands buried in her intestines, unwinding them from her body like a long rope that needed detangling. He would jab her liver, severing it from the main artery or her femoral artery to hasten death so it would occur simultaneously when he ejaculated. "This is your big part, Sarah! Now scream for me!" It was a notation he considered to be a professional director's cue.

Chapter 14

Diane Benson looked at the blackened structure before her. It had once been a sweet, small colonial home just like the ones on either side of it, owned by a young woman who was finally coming out of her shell after a wearisome divorce. That's what the neighbor had said. Now, it was her tomb.

Diane was a "freelance profiler" that was the official title the Reno police had given her. On an unofficial leave of absence from the Reno police, she had been traveling around for nearly three years, following any and all leads that might finally put the arsonist who killed her mother behind bars. Luckily, Diane still had enough money in her trust fund to allow her to keep this search a priority in her life. She tapped all media sources to figure out where this creep might strike next. That's when Philly became her latest destination. She hoped for a chance to look at the scene and the evidence to find out if it was the same guy. She had to know if it was him, the one who called himself the Servant. Hopefully, he had left something significant behind so he could finally be identified.

The Servant carefully planned and started the fire that killed Diane's mother, Fran and Fran's live-in girlfriend. Fran Benson was widowed and had lived quietly with Beverly Truman for the past twelve years, and everyone accepted their relationship—they didn't feel the need for a man justify that relationship. The town's residents as well as visitors loved them and would frequent their gift shop located in Kampos, Nevada. Fran and Beverly showcased local pottery, blown glass, and hand-carved sculpture. The store and its owners fit beautifully within this perfect, sheltered town. *How could such a horrific murder happen here and to such a nice couple?* Diane thought while her eyes welled up. What could possibly be the motive for an arsonist to pick this town and this couple for his crime? Probably the same thing that drew her mom here in the first place: peace.

She wanted to get closer to the site to see if it was the Servant's work. She needed to see if he nailed the carved crucifix on the door. She needed to know how the bodies were positioned and if the lovers were drugged. She was so frustrated. Taking a leave of absence sucked since the police wouldn't let her get close enough to talk to the professionals on the scene. It was difficult making new contacts with police outside of Reno. She didn't have any credibility with these guys, and most likely, they didn't want to listen to a bunch of theories without supporting evidence.

"I think I have important information about what is going on," Diane said to one portly officer hovering in front of the yellow crime scene tape.

"A detective will be out to talk to you in a while," he answered in rather bored tone. She had heard that before.

Diane just stood there waiting. She knew this had to be the work of the Servant, but she had to prove it. Trying to get someone to believe her "evidence" was another thing. In Reno, they may have thought she was a freak, but at least they believed what she said. This time, Diane just hoped whoever was coming to talk to her would have an open mind.

Paul Rogers walked through the charred remains with Rob Lloyd, the fire inspector for the Philadelphia and lower Merion Counties. Rob was in his early forties, a tall, lanky six-one with thick sandy blond hair and hooded brown eyes. He was in his turnout gear, stepping over debris on the burned floor. He always had a smile on his face except for times like these. This would be yet another fire attributed to the unknown arsonist who was targeting homes in the Philadelphia area. They were desperate to find this guy. How he had gotten into the homes is unclear. Whether he was amicably invited inside because he was known to the victims or snuck in undetected remained a mystery. No one had been left alive to question, and the neighbors knew nothing, so a lot of holes remained in the case. Rob needed help solving this, and he thought that Paul Rogers, his former college roommate and current FBI special division agent, would be the perfect addition to their team. Rob and the others wanted to stop this recurring and senseless waste of life. They knew this guy was smart and very calculated. He only left evidence he wanted the police to find. Rob started giving Paul the background.

"Thanks for helping me on this one, Paul. There have been three fires in the past eight weeks, and all seem similar: same positioning of the bodies, same drugged pillowcases, and same carved crucifix on the front door. At the first scene, we didn't know what to look for, and the crucifix was thought to be the homeowners. After the second fire, when crime scene techs got done with their analysis and photographed the crucifix, one of our agents remembered seeing the cross before. The fire chief was alerted to watch for any other crosses left on the front step, door, or porch. So far, we have quite the collection. We found three crosses, clearly hand-carved and pretty much matching the one tonight. I think this is fire number four, in the Philly area that is. They're getting more frequent, and we have no idea why they're being set or who's setting them. Although there is a religious connection, we don't know what it is. We don't believe it has anything to do with the Ku Klux Klan. We can't find anything to connect the victims. They lived in different towns, different economic brackets; some were married, some single, some divorced. We are at a loss and need to come up with answers. I need your help."

"I'll do everything in my power to nail this bastard. Sully, our computer expert, will help me find other fires that fit this MO, and I'll try to find some things to tie together. Let me know what the crime scene techs say."

"Sir," said the bored officer pointing toward Diane. "That girl is still waiting to talk to someone. She claims she has valuable information and needs to speak with a detective or someone in charge. She's been waiting over two hours."

"Let's go talk to her now," Rob said.

Rob and Paul walked out of the blackened house over to Diane. Paul took a look at the cute red head and liked the springy curls that formed around her face like a halo. In that instant, he'd wished he could have taken a shower since he reeked of smoke. She was about five-five, with small waist, slim hips, and clearly in shape. Of course, Paul's eyes glanced at her chest first, but he couldn't really tell much since she had on a loose-fitting nylon jacket. She was wearing sneakers, jeans, and looked concerned and a bit impatient. They walked over and introduced themselves, flashed their IDs, and apologized for the way they smelled. They decided that it would be easier to talk in Rob's temporary office set up with the local homicide detective unit than stand outside. Inside, they could also talk with the detectives who were going to be assigned to the case.

"Do you want to follow us in your car, Ms. Benson, or would you rather go with one of us?" Paul asked.

"I'll follow. This way, you don't have to make an extra trip back here."

"We're off. Rob, you're the leader," Paul said with a smile.

Chapter 15

At the offices of *The State*, the newspaper of Columbia, South Carolina, Seth Roberts's frantic brain was just barely staying ahead of his fingers. The afternoon deadline was a mere hour away, and he was desperately trying to get all the information from the second and third e-mails along with another video into his article. This time, it was another girl, Sarah Jenkins, who'd been missing for three weeks. She was also being raped repeatedly, tortured, but still alive. The sicko was keeping her alive, a "tune in tomorrow" type deal. His e-mail states, "Had enouf? Not until I say so. This isn't the end, it's only the beginning!" The guy definitely needs to learn how to use spell check.

Seth had done background on Sally Anne and put together a tragic, heart-wrenching story about her along with a description of her horrific final moments of life. For the next unfortunate victim, Seth worked on another headline grabber. This bit was about Susan Starks. The other reporters were trying to piece together what little information the cops were willing to part with. He was so much farther ahead, and it was also his best writing in a long time. His writing rut had now ended. Everyone was enthralled by his pieces, and he was in a total writing zone. After he finished the article, he continued doing research on Sarah Jenkins. He paused for a moment, thinking that the girl would most likely be dead by morning.

At the paper, editors, graphic artists, proofreaders, and even temps were all congratulating Seth on his fine work and how he had become somewhat of a celebrity. *Man, what a change and a good feeling,* he thought. The national news desks were contacting *him* for information, asking if he wanted to go on TV and talk about what was going on with the investigation and any insight he had on the perpetrator. People who scarcely acknowledged his existence two weeks ago were instead stopping him and shaking his hand or patting him on the back. Even the owner of the paper made a special trip in to find out who he was and tell him he was doing an excellent job. He was really putting the paper and website on the national map. Success felt good and long overdue.

Chapter 16

Lizzie called her cousin, Mark, to discuss a few more particulars about the murder of Sally Anne Myers. Since they were family, she felt like she could talk to him like the brother she never had. She was much closer to Mark and his sister, Remmi, than normal cousins. She was lonely growing up, and she would spend a lot of time at their house, hanging out and eating dinner. Her mother wasn't great in the kitchen, so she loved to go to her cousin's house and learn how to cook and bake from their mother, Lizzie's dad's sister. She and Remmi would end up with more flour on themselves than in the recipe. They would have so much fun eating their creations and cleaning up the kitchen afterward, giggling the whole time.

She told Mark about all the media attention and how it appeared she had lost control of the case. Part of her plan was to include the FBI, but past partnerships fell flat. She had worked with the local office in Memphis during a rash of murders that were threatening tourists around Graceland. The FBI cut her department out of the investigation, and when they were finally allowed to say something, if they thought it had any merit, the Feebies took the credit. Mark said that Lizzie would remain the lead, and his people would assist her in any way she needed. He told her that they were not standard FBI, that they were able to play it a lot looser than regular agents, which was definitely a relief to her. The Pit was a special division within the bureau, and they had a lot of wonderful perks. Mark and the Pit also did outside contract work, almost like a private firm. It was all government-related, just some rather confidential sources of large funds covered all their expenses. They finished their phone conversation, and Mark limped out into the main office and past Bart Jeffries.

Jeffries was the newest member of the Pit team. He had been a former Ranger also but not part of Feldman's platoon until the last six months of their active duty. He was the youngest member, only twenty-five. He had flowing glossy black hair, almost feminine in its beauty, but he was definitely all man. He had a wolfish upper twist to his lips and considerable charm that really worked in his favor. His sharp, intelligent grey eyes twinkled when he smiled. He walked into Tom Sullivan's office, the resident master techie, and glanced around the large beige room, which looked like a cyclone had just hit it. Tom Sullivan was a cool hand. He had street smarts as well as super intelligence and always fast with a joke and the right answer. He was six-two, of prime American male, with long solid legs and broad shoulders. His butt rested against the edge of his desk with his back to the door. Sammy always swooned over Sully, calling him an uber chick magnet, and it was true. He didn't flaunt himself, but he had a natural hunky apple-pie appeal. He was the Pit's resident computer genius, who sat behind the junkyard that was his desk. "Man, what a mess! How do you find anything in here, Sully?" Bart asked.

"I have a system. I can locate anything. I know where everything is. Call it creative filing."

"Yeah, but *how long does it take* to find it? You need to put your office on a diet. I bet you have crap in here from the old office, and that move was four years ago."

"I like my office just fine."

"That's like a fat person saying their happy being fat. They know that it would be helpful to change their diet and exercise more, but knowing those stellar facts doesn't make the pounds fall off in awe."

"Are you insinuating that I need to work out, go on a diet?"

"No, idiot, it's a metaphor. You need to drastically clean this disaster area you call an office. Does Feldman ever make it in here?"

"No, it gives him a headache."

Chapter 17

Rob, Paul, and Diane made their way to the police station, and it only took about fifteen minutes to get through to Center City from the crime scene. The three-car caravan pulled into the large public garage and parked near each other on the third level. Paul got out of his government-issued Tahoe, Rob practically lived out of his Dodge Durango, and Diane exited her very sensible Toyota Corolla. Cars can tell so much about a person.

The threesome made their way through the crowded squad room with its dirty beige walls and desks crammed together in the center. Stacks of file folders littered the tops of every desk and filing cabinets surrounded the perimeter. Clusters of detectives were talking. Some held mugs of coffee, and others sipped from soda cans while discussing open cases. This was the heart of the homicide major case division, and the detectives working here were the smartest and most respected in Philadelphia.

Diane followed the two hunky men into the conference room and took a seat on the other side of the table away from the door. The room had a wall of windows looking out into the busy squad room. A long modern conference table with an assortment of neutral cloth covered chairs were the only items in the room. Diane scanned around and felt a lump forming in her throat. She looked at the two men looking at her, and she swallowed hard.

"Would you like to tell us a little about yourself and why you think you have important information about the fire?" Rob asked with a quizzical expression.

"Well, as I said before, I'm Diane Benson, and I'm originally from Kampos, Nevada. Maybe you've never heard of it, but it's a little town about four hours away from Reno, which is where I live now. I've worked with the Reno Police Department as a freelance profiler." She went on to tell them about how her mother and Beverly were killed.

"I know what you're thinking, but I'm good at what I do. Cops usually think profilers are a waste of time, but I've got a very successful track record. This particular case, or should I say cases, is personal for me, not just a way to get my name in the news." They eagerly listened to the rest of her story, and Rob couldn't help notice the intensity in her eyes as she spoke.

"As I told you, about four years ago, my mother and her partner, Beverly, were killed in an arson fire, and I'm willing to bet the same creep is responsible for the murder of the two people found tonight. My mom's fire was started by someone who calls himself the Servant. The Servant is some kind of religious freak who got his divinity education from some Internet site, a minister with the Church of the Divine Light. He is cleansing the earth of sinners in the supposed way that God would with the purification of fire. He obviously missed the New Testament part about 'thou shalt not kill' and only focused on the Old Testament 'cleansing fires' part. He believes he is readying the sinners' souls for heaven, and they would not be allowed into the pearly gates without his intervention. He feels all would know the souls he saved by his calling card, a hand-made crucifix. So far, that cross has been the only piece of evidence the police have found. It's a kind of a blessing on the house. Is this one of his homes? Did you find a cross nailed on the front door or on the front step or porch? I've been chasing him across the country for the past three years. I think I'm closer than I've ever been to finding him. Please tell me that he's here."

Rob and Paul looked at each other silently conversing as to whether they should tell her or not. After a minute of awkward silence, Rob spoke.

"If what you say is true, he's here."

"Can you pull together all the information you have on this so-called Servant, his trail, and anything else that we can use to identify this guy?" Paul asked.

"Why haven't we heard about a serial arsonist working his way across the country killing people? That's the kind of story that usually makes headlines," Rob interjected with a penetrating glare.

Diane was prepared for this question as she pulled a hefty file folder from her handbag. Rob and Paul raised their eyebrows in unison, both being quite impressed.

"It's taken me a while to track down his other fires. He doesn't stay in one place long enough. Three months max and usually sets only four of five fires within a seventy-five-mile radius. He hits small towns off the beaten path and then moves on. Most of these towns don't consider it more than an isolated incident, and it seems like they'd rather keep it hushed up, if anything. Double homicide with charred victims is not the best advertising for an idyllic place to live." Rob and Paul nodded, understanding her point.

"The local police are really reluctant to share information with me or, it seems like, anyone. The Servant rarely hits metropolitan areas, and Philly is rare for him because he usually keeps to the small towns with limited resources. Right now, if the smaller towns don't register the arson with VICAP, ATF, or their state arson database, it falls through the cracks, and it's hard to identify as one in a number of serial attacks. I go through and read all the arson listings in small local papers via the Internet and then follow up and ask the local officials if there were any of the usual MO with the fire. They generally blow me off once they find out I'm a freelance profiler. Either they think I'm trying to make them look bad for missing a serial arsonist or that I just want to make a news headline. I tried going to the ATF, and they wouldn't listen, to the FBI, but again, they wouldn't listen to me. They took my information and my file and said they would look into it. I've never heard anything since. It's extremely frustrating and exhausting."

Paul leaned against the glass wall taking copious mental notes. He thought that Sully would be able to put together something and do a state by state search of arsons that would fit this same staging and murder scenario. He looked at Diane and smiled. She was cute, spunky, and so driven to find this guy. He liked her style.

"Earth to Paul. What's going on in your head?"

"Sorry. Zoned out for a second thinking about having Sully do a state by state arson search," he stammered, trying to recover from his thoughts about Diane.

"Yeah, right. Let's move on," Rob motioned with a revolving hand movement.

Paul picked up on Rob's cue and made a request from the adorable freelance profiler.

"Ms. Benson, can we have this folder to copy and could you forward what you have electronically so I can send it off to my people? Since I'm FBI, I can assign agents to the case and start the ball rolling to nail this killer."

"Sure, but first, please, just call me Diane." Then she pulled out a flash drive and handed it to Paul.

"Everything that I have is on that. You can download it and then give it back to me when you're done. Of course, I do have a copy." She gave Rob and Paul her card, and then she stood up to leave. "If that's everything, I'll keep doing research and wait for your call."

"Will do," said Rob.

"Thanks for everything, Diane. This has been very helpful. Oh, by the way, I'm sorry about your mother and her friend," added Paul.

She smiled at them and shook their hands. Upon leaving the conference room, she glanced back over her shoulder at the two men. Giving a small wave, she turned and left the squad room.

"What do you think?" Rob asked.

"She's damn sweet and has eyes I could get lost in. Nice bod too. I'd love to take her out to dinner and see where it leads."

"Not that, you idiot! Use your other head! What do you think about what she said? Moron," Rob said in an irritated voice

"Jeez, calm down. I was only kidding. I think she's definitely done her homework and has got some valuable insight into this case. Once I get Sully on the job, he'll probably be able to find out more than she's got on this flash. But it is a good place to start. I will also need all your files."

"While you're at it, you should have Sully check her out with the Reno police to see if she's legit. You are FBI-trained, you know."

Chapter 18

After leaving the Crypt, Dubowski and Lizzie walked up the stairs back to their offices on the second floor, mostly in silence. They were thinking about the second missing girl, Sarah Jenkins, another beautiful tall blond. She worked as a landscaper while earning her degree in landscape architecture. She helped one of her neighbors decorate their yard, and it won "Yard of the Month" that past September. She didn't have a boyfriend, having just ended a ten-month relationship. It took a few days for someone to figure out she was gone, just like Sally Anne. There were so many similarities between the two girls: their names both began with S, both friendly but no real close friends, no pets, no one depending on them or immediately missing them and calling police about their absence. They were single professionals who were their own bosses.

Detective Bob Weck from Missing Persons Unit came into the squad room asking for Lizzie. He relayed the report he had just taken over the phone about a girl named Susan Starks, a waitress in Arcadia Lakes. Lizzie knew this waitress. She usually worked evenings at the diner where Lizzie wanted to catch a late dinner and was too lazy to fix it for herself. She always told Lizzie that waitressing was temporary, and soon, she would get her license as an interior designer. Lizzie felt her stomach clench, bile starting to rise up as she pictured the chatty girl. Susan was tall, just a pinch under six feet, and blond. The killer had abducted another victim.

Lizzie knew she needed more help. This was getting out of control, and Chief Montgomery would have her head on a platter if she didn't make more progress soon. She could really use a good profiler, and her cousin, Mark Lewis, was the best. Thinking about the FBI reminded her about Mark's offer. She needed a team of hand-picked, highly trained pros. At the same time, she trusted Mark to make sure she remained the team leader and respected that this was her investigation. She decided to tell the chief first thing in the morning that she was contacting the FBI. He wouldn't have any problems; it would just give him someone else to blame.

Their priority now was to figure out if Susan was really missing or if there was a reason, any reason, to explain why she didn't show up for her shift last night. Lizzie and Dubowski went out to the parking garage and got into their dark blue state-issued Impala. Lizzie drove the four miles into town and parked the Impala across the street from the diner.

They entered the diner and were met by the owner, Kathy Kulak, a very intelligent looking woman with tight lips, a rather large nose, and doe-like brown eyes. She was about forty-five and a little on the heavier side because she always said, *No one wants to eat food from a skinny cook. All the good ones are fat.* Kathy recalled how Susan was supposed to show up for the dinner shift at 4:30 p.m. yesterday, didn't call and didn't show, not like her at all. She was incredibly reliable.

"Her mom and I were good friends, so I look after the girl. I gave the local police a key to Susan's place, and they went over to check her apartment but didn't find anything weird. All her stuff like her clothes, purse, car, and luggage were still there. I know she woulda told me about a trip or something. I'm worried about her. She'd always say she was gonna help me fix up the diner when she got her degree," said Kathy as a few wrinkles formed across her forehead.

The local police technically couldn't contact the county until she'd been missing for 48 hours, but they wanted to check out the situation anyway, especially with all the crazy things that had been going on. Kathy was the first one to report a concern, and after an initial investigation, the police called Missing Persons.

Lizzie and Dave got the key to Susan's apartment. They wanted to check it out for themselves and be extra thorough. It was bright and cheery, complementing the owner's personality. The living room was immaculate and attractively decorated in vivid accent colors, with a predominance of warm, neutral walls and furniture.

A festive painted cabinet contained a small TV and a DVD player. Behind a pale orange curtain was a large window showing the tidy yard. A beige linen sofa was scattered with various orange and yellow floral-print pillows, and chunky chartreuse chairs flanked the fireplace. There was a funky velvet cube that served as a coffee table, with magazines artfully arranged on top. Her computer sat on a small desk, and Dave noticed some homework she had been doing. The computer would be taken to the lab for a more complete examination. She had a definite flair, and she wanted to start her own business. Her dining area was neat with a variety of different colored and shaped candles arranged in the middle of the table. Her retro-yellow kitchen had older appliances but was clean and tidy just the same.

They agreed with the local police that no signs of a struggle were evident, so she most likely was not taken from here. They decided that she must have been abducted while jogging, part of her daily routine that she did alone. They still weren't sure which day because Susan had three days off from the diner and could have been kidnapped the morning before her evening shift or during those other days. No one has seen her for a few days. She had no siblings, her mother had died from a brain aneurism, and she wasn't that close with her dad.

Lizzie was more than worried. Looking through the victim's closet and seeing a pair of size 10 ½ shoes didn't help. She had a bad feeling, and her instincts were rarely wrong. She was not going to sleep well tonight with more nightmares on the horizon.

Chapter 19

L izzie and her partner went to Chief Montgomery's office at nine in the morning to report their findings. Or their lack of them. Again, they were met with more bad news. Another video was on the Internet. The chief agreed with Lizzie's idea to bring in the FBI. They needed help, and they needed it now. Lizzie mentioned Mark and started saying how he was an elite part of the FBI, and she would make the call as soon as she got back to her desk.

Dubowski asked Lizzie if she might join him for a chili-cheese dog over at Mike's "Dog in the Hand" stand where heartburn was guaranteed to take your mind off your troubles. But Lizzie was anything but hungry, thinking about the horrendous ordeal that Sarah was being put through. "Who is this bastard? Where does he keep these girls? He tortures and films one and grabs another with such ease? At least for today, she's still alive. I've got to make this shit stop."

Lizzie sat down at her desk and patted her palm against her forehead, hoping to jar a new idea loose. Dubowski could tell she was frustrated but knew enough to give her some space. She was sitting there, silent, still forming the image in her mind of the girls tied up, being tortured. She hated this cruel, inhuman bastard more and more each day. She hated her feelings of total helplessness. She finally refocused her thoughts and started telling Dubowski about Mark being FBI. They really needed help if they were going to solve this before anyone else died. Dubowski agreed that bringing in the feds was a good idea and believed her cousin understood the importance of allowing Lizzie to stay in control and call the shots.

Another bonus was that Mark could get them access to all sorts of cool technology. It was just as critical to have a staff of highly trained experts who knew how to use it. Lizzie and Dave would have access to all the databases, the advanced FBI labs, and Mark would be able to get through any red tape to process their evidence. She truly felt that Mark wouldn't come in and take over the investigation. He would work with them, not around them.

Chapter 20

Mark and Scott met at the Hartsfield-Jackson International Airport on the outskirts of Atlanta. They parked their government-issued Tahoe outside the private hangar that housed the Pit's new Gulfstream G650. The two had just finished another very lucrative project. As a company, the Pit did phenomenally well making a lot of money taking on odd jobs off the FBI's clock. They were able to travel in luxury, which was a great perk for the field agents. Mark and Scott walked into the airport's waiting area and saw the flight crew heading toward the plane.

After a few last checks, the flight attendant reported to Lewis and Rogers that everything was ready for takeoff and that they should be in the air within 20 minutes. They followed her up the steps into the jet and sat down in matching taupe leather swivel seats. With their seat belts fastened, they settled in for a comfortable flight. A cup of hot java would be served shortly, along with a snack tray of warm foods. The weather was sunny and cool, cooler than normal for April, but perfect for flying.

"What are your thoughts about all this?" Lewis asked.

"The bastard is really ballsy, dumping a body in the middle of a golf course and posting a video online. He obviously likes national attention and is getting it. I'll ask Sully to try and trace the URL. Maybe we'll get lucky and get a lead on our guy. I can't see that happening, but it's worth a shot. What did Lizzie say about what they found on the body?" Rogers asked.

"Basically, the body is clean: no evidence, no trace, no DNA. We should run the autopsy results through VICAP to see if we get a match. I can't believe this is his first victim. He seems like a highly evolved killer. He's controlled, has all his torture tools available right next to the table where he's torturing the girl. He is very careful about not leaving any evidence, so it shows he's done his homework watching TV crime shows and reading trade journals."

Lewis couldn't stand all the crime shows. They make for great TV but give the bad guys too much information about how to cover their tracks. "I don't think he's well educated. There were too many spelling errors on his video and e-mail, but he's clever and intelligent. Probably a high school dropout or barely squeezed by with a diploma. After carefully looking at the video, you can see he's got some serious muscles and has big, calloused hands, probably from manual labor. I'm also guessing he's employed with a construction company or maybe he's part of a utility road crew.

"I say all the other typical serial killer profile fits: twenty-five to thirty-five years old, single, white, male, above-average intelligence, poor school performance, strong addiction to pornography, sexually frustrated, socially inept, family issues, missing dad, mother absent, the standard. Most likely was a bed wetter, set fires when he was a kid, or started abusing small animals. Let's go through the list of types, each one has their own reasons for killing. He's not a visionary serial killer. I doubt there are voices in his head telling him what to do. I don't think he's the missionary serial killer type either. I can't see what mission or responsibility he has to the world to rid it of tall busty blonds. I also don't see him as a gain serial killer. He's not doing this for money, so he has to fall in the last two categories. Either he's a thrill serial killer or a power seeker killer. He could just enjoy the experience of killing, or it could be the total power he has over his victim's life or death, or a combination of the two. What about you? Anything I missed?" Lewis asked.

"Nope," Rogers said. "I think that covers about everything. Basically, it's the textbook stuff that covers just about any number of people in the boondocks of South Carolina. They've got some mighty strange people there."

"Strange people are everywhere, and there are boondocks near New York City, so you can't generalize like that. We'll have to work on refining the profile when we see the body, talk over the evidence, review the videos, and ask Lizzie what they've found out. Hopefully, they've discovered something since we last spoke."

"I like the part about discussing everything with Lizzie." And a huge grin appeared on Scott's face.

"You were always sweet on her. Hey, you know she's not married anymore."

"Damn, that's good news. How long has it been?"

"Nearly three years. She should be over Matt by now. I'm not sure, but I think he treated her pretty bad by cheating on her."

"What an asshole! She's a goddess with brains, a body to die for. Some people are just too stupid to live, and he is one of them. Of course, that's better for me," Scott chuckled.

Time moved quickly, and they were landing in Columbia before they knew it. After finding the car rental area, they picked up a black SUV and loaded it with their bags. They brought enough stuff for a week's stay, maybe two. They weren't sure if they would be there longer than that, but they could always get Sammy to send more necessities. They truly felt that if they were going to break the case, it would happen quickly.

The unsub seemed too bold to escape apprehension for long. If he did, he was just that good, and they might never catch him.

They arrived at the Calhoun Building in Columbia about a half an hour after they left the airport. Mark called Lizzie from outside the building while still in their black Chevy Tahoe right outside in the parking lot.

"Bowlyn."

"Hey, Lizzie. Mark. Okay if we stop in and look over what you've got?"

"Where are you?"

"Parking lot."

"Wow, really? That was so fast. Yeah, come on up. I'm on the second floor, keep walking straight toward the windows in the back. You can't miss me."

"We'll be right there."

Mark's leg was still giving him problems, so they made their way slowly through the crowded squad room. Lizzie was talking on the phone but held the receiver once she saw them coming toward her. She had two chairs in front of her desk, and she motioned for them to sit down.

Rogers all but stopped breathing. Lizzie had long blond hair to her slim waist. Her eyes were a beautiful shade of light blue that rivaled the color of the sky on a crisp autumn day. She had perfectly straight white teeth, overall making a dazzling impression on him from across the squad room. He was suddenly lost in her smile. It was the kind poets wrote sonnets about. And those eyes. So stunning he could feel himself being swept away, floating as if on a cloud. Words flew through his mind. Words he hadn't even thought about since one of his college literature course. *Breathtaking, mesmerizing, exquisite.* The litany of words broke only when Lizzie had spoken. Before he turned blue from lack of oxygen, he took in a deep breath and tried to focus on something other than his poetic reflection and desire.

"Rogers! What the fuck! Pull yourself together, man. Shit! Get your head in the game and out of your pants!" Lewis spit out in a hushed undertone.

"Sorry, boss. What can I say? It's been a while."

"It sounds like you've got nothing," she said into the phone.

Bob Martin, Chief of CSU, replied, "I've got tons of partials on the flag that was in the fourth hole, but unless we can match them up to someone, they're basically useless. Ran them through AFIS, and it came up clean, no hits."

"Did you dust the body?"

"Of course I dusted the body after setting it with crazy glue fumes. Nothing. No stray hair, no print, no fluids. Someone was very, very careful."

"Any footprints around the body? It rained early the night before we found her. We should have some impressions," Lizzie asked trying not to raise her voice, being conscious that Mark and Scott were within earshot.

"No impressions other than long, wide marks. Maybe he walked on wood planks. No footprints other than the cops first on the scene and the joggers who found the body. Sorry, Lizzie. I know this isn't the news you wanted."

"Thanks, Bob. Please keep at it anyway," she muttered disappointedly and hung up the phone. She was hoping for some kind of lead, some place to start.

"Sorry, guys. I didn't mean to be rude, but that was the chief of CSU, and I wanted to see what he came up with. I'm really glad you're here." And with that, Lizzie gave Mark a big hug and Scott a firm handshake combined with a friendly smile. Then Mandy gave a little bark to let Lizzie know she should be introduced as well.

"Who's this cute pup?" asked Scott.

"Oh, this is my little girl, Mandy. She keeps me sane."

Lizzie looked up and caught Scott's piercing deep blue eyes as he bent down to pet Mandy. She could drown in those eyes, but she was currently drowning in a more unpleasant way. "I don't know if you caught any of my conversation, but we've got nothing. Are you brimming full of ideas to help a girl here?"

Lizzie briefed them on what little they had, and Mark and Scott gave her the profile options they determined. Next was to go to the office of Mr. Seth Roberts and find out what the deal was with him being the first to break any kind of lead. It seemed he knew more than anyone else thus far. Mark suggested to Lizzie that they meet with the task force later.

Chapter 21

Diane sat down to another Lean Cuisine dinner. She was tired of living like this, out of a suitcase and microwave. She wanted to get into the Servant's head *before* he killed someone so that he could finally be caught, and her obsession with finding him could be put to rest. She was thinking about a really weird vision she had last night but just couldn't make it fit with what she already knew about him. She saw a very young boy with sandy brown hair, wearing cute little feety pajamas and holding a teddy bear. His mother bent over and kissed him, saying that he had to stay as quiet as a church mouse and that if he was a really good boy, he might get a new daddy. She laid him down and then tucked a light blue "blanky" up to his chin, smiled, and closed the coffin lid. Diane shot up out of bed in a cold sweat, breathing heavily and shaking. "What the hell was that about?" she said to herself as she recalled the images. Was this something the Servant was dreaming about himself or some kind of symbolism? She shivered at the thought. Diane heard a knock on the door which shifted her concentration. She suspiciously approached the window. She saw Paul Rogers standing outside and opened the door to greet him.

"Hi. This is unexpected. Did something new happen with the case?" she asked, praying he wasn't going to tell her there was another fire.

"No, I just wanted to make sure that you were okay and see if you had any additional information. It's not unusual to experience stress after seeing death like that," Paul said with an understanding look on his face.

She looked directly into his blue intelligent eyes. He must have realized that she was just gawking when he finally said, "Would you mind inviting me in? It's still cold outside in April here at night."

"Oh my god, how rude of me! Of course, come on in." His face lit up with a huge smile, and she was lost again.

"I'm just sitting down to dinner. Would you be interested in Turkey Medallions with Cranberry Stuffing or Sliced Turkey with Sweet Potatoes? Fresh from the freezer to the microwave. Sorry, it's a rather limited menu, but I can only stand turkey frozen dinners."

"I didn't mean to intrude on your dinner. I already ate, but if you don't mind, I'll join you with something to drink. Do have anything in that tiny fridge? Or should I just hit the vending machine I saw by the main building?" Paul offered.

"I've got beer if you're interested."

"I'd love one."

She motioned for Paul to sit at the table by the window and then turned to get the beer from the refrigerator. He followed her as she walked, loving the way her ass looked in her jeans, the long legs, the curve of her waist. She turned with a sweet smile, twisting off a cap and handing him a Stella Moon.

"Hope you like this brand of beer. You just don't seem like the Miller Lite type."

"You got that right. And by the way, this happens to be my brand of choice." They both chuckled at the coincidence.

"How about I give you the grand tour? It'll take all of two minutes . . . literally," Diane said.

She moved her hand as she gave the tour, standing in one spot. "Here, you've got this great table and a picture window overlooking the parking lot. Nice huh? A lovely nondescript sofa and a TV make up the living room. A mini stove top, a mini fridge, and a microwave make up the mini kitchen. And a desk and bed are my bedroom two feet away from the kitchen. What do you think?"

"Looks like you're all set," Paul replied. "It's almost as homey as my apartment."

"Trust me, I'm sure your apartment is a bit bigger, better defined rooms, and definitely more inviting than this place. Then again, it's better than other places I've stayed in, so it's home for now."

"Don't you ever miss home?"

With a really sad look on her face, she answered, "There's nothing left for me back in Nevada except memories, not all of them good and more painful ones than not. Enough about me. What about you? Do you like living out of a suitcase?"

"No, I miss my family too much. I'm one of four siblings, close together in age and close in relationship too. Sometimes too close. In fact, I'm a twin," Paul disclosed smiling.

Diane's face brightened up immediately. "No way! You're a twin? That's so cool. I always wanted a twin. I swear! Hell, I'd have been happy with a brother or a sister. But it's okay. My mom loved me to death, she was the best. She really was my best friend."

"I feel that way about Peter, my twin brother. My older brother is Scott, and my younger sister is Sammy. We gave my parents a lot of grey hair. One time, when Mom was pregnant with Sammy, she needed to pick up her prescription sunglasses. Peter and I were sitting on the third bench seat facing out the back window of our Volvo station wagon. Scott was riding shot gun without a seatbelt . . . which was okay in those days. My mom couldn't find a parking spot, so she just pulled up in front of the optician. Well, since it was really hot out, Mama comes around the back of the car, lifts up the hatch so we wouldn't bake, then gives Scott strict orders that he and the twins must not leave the car. Here comes the good part . . ." Paul says as he holds back a chuckle. "Mama is standing half in and half out of the shop door asking for her glasses. As she tells it, the next thing she heard was hysterical laughter from a street crowd, pointing and staring at the three of us as we're pissing out of the back of the station wagon. My mom yells, 'Boys, put those away right now!' Peter had to go to the bathroom, so the two of us joined in to see how high we could arch the piss!"

Diane was laughing so hard tears were streaming down her cheeks. "That is hysterical! I can just picture three angelic little boys, dropping their pants and lining up pissing out of the back of the car. I think I have a cramp in my side from laughing so hard."

"Can you stand to hear more?"

"Of course! Be my guest!"

"Another time, my parents had just gotten a huge brand-new rear projection TV for our family room. My dad set everything up, and my mom rearranged the furniture so that the TV was the focus of the room. They put on Frosty the Snowman. Somehow I got my hands on a two-pound bag of confectioner's sugar." Paul paused briefly waiting for Diane to respond, which she did.

"Let me guess. Here comes the good part?"

"Now, just a side bar to this, the week before, I got my hands on the huge container of baby powder, and it was 'snowing' in the basement. My mom made it really clear that I was never to do that again, so I didn't. But I'm smarter than that. Remember, we're watching Frosty, and it never snows in Atlanta, so I figured that we needed to have snow. The day before, we had waffles and were shaking powdered sugar on them, so I figured that would work. I ripped open the top of a new big bag and started covering the TV, along with Scott and Peter. Peter would always suck his thumb while hugging his lion, named Beezey. He was covered, sucking his thumb, looking at Beezey, and just shook the sugar off, looking around at the growing 'snow' on the ground! Thumb never left his mouth."

"I hate to ask, but what happened next?"

"My dad walks in and starts cracking up. He yells for my mom to come into the family room, and she starts freaking out about the sugar ruining the new TV. He just kept laughing, and she said it was his turn to 'shovel' and clean up the 'snow.' She cleaned up the last snowfall, and now, it was his turn. Dad quickly stopped laughing."

"Do you guys still drive your parents crazy like that?"

"Well, kind of. Mostly, we drive my mama crazy since my dad died years ago in the line of duty."

"I'm so sorry. I didn't mean to bring up any sad memories," she said.

"S'okay," Paul said in a more Southern accent after the second beer. "I just came by to see if you had any other information or had any other leads that you might have forgotten to give us."

"No. Nothing that I can put my finger on just yet. There may be something, but I don't understand if it fits with this case or not. I'll know more in a few days," she said as she thought back to her weird vision about the little boy and the coffin.

"Well, I'll see you around. Maybe we could go out for lunch or dinner some time. Would that be okay with you?"

"Yeah, I'd really like that."

Chapter 22

Lizzie grabbed her prized Burberry anorak. It looked like it was going to rain any second, and she didn't want to be cold and wet. Hell for her was being cold *and* wet (and on a boat; luckily now, there was no boat). They hustled down the stairs and into the Tahoe as fast as Lewis could move. They made their way through the congested streets, hitting almost every light between the SLED and *The State* office building. The rain fell harder and faster, and the streets emptied as most people sought shelter.

They got lucky and parked close enough to the building to dash to the front door of the newspaper offices. The reception desk was managed by a very well-endowed brunette with peekaboo cleavage. She perked up, in more ways than one, when she spotted the two hunks approaching. Scott inquired about Seth Roberts, and she told him that Mr. Roberts could be found at the Crime Desk in the News Department located on the seventh floor. She directed them to the elevator bank with a perfectly polished nail and said if there was anything else that Scott needed, he should ask for Stephanie. His eyes sparkled as he smiled and thanked her.

"I think she likes you. You should get her number," Mark joked.

"No thanks. I like my girls with brains." Scott smiled while he looked directly into Lizzie's wide eyes. She could feel her face flush, and she quickly pressed the "up" button at the elevator bank.

They arrived on the seventh floor as instructed and had no problem finding Seth Roberts's office. They knocked briskly at his door.

"Come in."

With an extended hand, Lizzie said, "Mr. Roberts, I'm Detective Bowlyn with SLED. Special Agents Lewis and Rogers of the FBI. We'd like to ask you a few questions regarding the Myers murder. Is now a good time?"

"Not really, I've got deadlines. Could we do this tomorrow?"

"I should have made myself a bit clearer, let's start over. We are here to ask you a few questions. It can be here or at the department building, your choice, but it will be now. I was rhetorically asking, not really expecting you to answer anything but yes. So may we sit down?" she said while sitting down.

Mark sat next to her, and Scott stood behind Lizzie in the doorway of the cluttered office. She could feel the heat radiating off of him. She had to mentally kick herself to get back on track.

"How did you know it was Sally Anne Myers when we weren't sure it was her? How did you describe the scene like you were there? Were you there and didn't report it, Mr. Roberts?" Lizzie asked.

"No, I saw the pictures. I received an e-mail to my work account with pictures and with the video link."

"I'd like full access to your account to try and trace the e-mail, or I can get a subpoena and take the computer, it's your choice," she stated rather coolly.

"Look, this guy's a sicko, but I'm happy he picked me. Finally, my writing is getting exposure and hopefully national recognition. That said, I still want this guy caught. I'll give you whatever you need, but give me a little consideration too. How about an exclusive from the lead detective when he's caught?"

Lizzie gave him a dirty look. Seth cringed, knowing he just stepped over the line. He looked through a bunch of papers on his desk and handed a few to Lizzie. "He contacted me twice. Here are copies of the e-mails."

"Looks like you were ready for us," Scott said, lightly brushing against Lizzie to glance at the emails.

"Of course! I'm not an idiot. I would hope that you were smart enough to figure out the killer contacted me since I was the one to break the news about the video. Give me a little credit."

Lewis took out his phone and contacted Sully back at the Pit. He gave all the information from the e-mail, account information, password, and tracking numbers at the bottom of the e-mail. Sully said he would get right on it and have the information shortly, an hour at the most. They finished up their interview with Seth Roberts and headed back to the department.

"That Seth Roberts is a bit of a douche bag if you ask me," Scott whispered to Mark. Mark nodded in agreement.

Chapter 23

fter getting settled into the conference room, which would be their makeshift offices and where the task force was meeting twice a day to basically talk about nothing, Mark and Scott got to work. They were there for about an hour before four other members of Lizzie's task force walked in. Dave Dubowski made the introductions.

"This is Leland Griffin. Everyone calls him Griff. He's been in homicide for the past ten years and has had a number of really good busts, taking some really bad guys off the streets." His brown eyes crinkled in the corners, his bright white teeth contrasted nicely against his coffee-colored skin. He was a single dad with two young children.

"Next is Craig Finnegan. Craig was VICE before he came to us four years ago." Mike smiled and reached out his hand to shake hands. Craig, a medium-height man, his head shaved, had a light shine to it, shook hands and smiled at Lizzie; his brown, almost black, eyes shone brightly. He was a family man with four kids at home.

"Meet Jeff Peer. He's been a detective for only three years, and this is his first in homicide. He came directly from the academy and has been working his way up the ranks at lightning speed." Jeff also shook hands firmly, and his pale skin was marked by millions of freckles. He smiled at them, his green eyes bright and alert, offsetting his glowing orange hair. He was tall and skinny, and Mark thought if a nice big wind came along, this kid would go flying.

The last person they met was Paulo Santos, a Miami transplant with a very pronounced Hispanic accent. His dark Cuban looks were very captivating. His dark brown eyes were almost hypnotic, and he moved with the grace of a large, exotic cat. He came to Columbia after he met and married a girl who was going to the University of Miami, and they moved back to South Carolina when her mother died so she could take over the family bakery. He always brought in the freshest, most delicious pastries for the squad.

After the introductions and other small talk finished, Lizzie asked Mark to get started with the working profile for the unsub. Mark sat where he was, elbows on the table, his hands clasped in front of him.

"The term 'serial killer' was invented to describe a specific type of criminal. The definition is clear enough. There has to be quality, quantity, and a time element: 'three or more separate events in three or more separate locations with an emotional cooling off period between homicides.' That's straight from the FBI Classification Manual. It's meant to separate a serial killer from a mass murderer."

"What's the difference?" Peer asked.

"A mass murderer is the guy who goes to work with two fully loaded semiautomatics and blows away fifteen coworkers. Serial killers usually kill one or two at a time, and there is always a ritualistic way about the killing, always a sexual component or the killing is a substitute for sex. Recognizing this fact, some experts stress the sexual component behind the motivation for the kill, defining it as the act of ultraviolent deviants, who get extreme pleasure from inflicting extreme harm on their victims. Serial killers will keep killing until they are caught or die. Some serial killers seem so normal—that's the scariest thing about them. Underneath that mask of sanity, they are profoundly disturbed individuals. Apart from the obvious characteristics like sick minds, twisted desires, and a compulsion to kill again and again, it's hard to generalize about them."

Mark collected his thoughts and started presenting his profile of the murderer. "Our Carver goes about his work with unbridled savagery. No empathy at all to the begging of his victims. It seems to get him off when they begged for mercy he doesn't have. He burns the victims with a blow torch or with acid. He cuts off chunks of skin and taunts them with it. He has eviscerated his victims. His filming is much more sophisticated. He's put up a few of his earlier films that he made for himself and incorporated them into his current films. He has killed more times than we first suspected, and he has honed his craft.

"He has no qualms about using his own voice. He feels superior and believes we'll never catch him. After watching the video feed several times, I feel he is very deliberate, cunning, and rarely, if ever, makes mistakes. We're not dealing with some whack job who has gone mental or has some kind of damage to his frontal lobe. He is absolutely not *psychotic*. He is a psychopathic sexual sadist who has above-average intelligence and is able to function well enough in society to act appropriately and maintain a normal persona. He is a highly organized killer. He is white, male, late-twenties to midthirties, and most likely had an absent father and dominant female figure. He takes his hatred of that female and transfers it to the women he is torturing. More than likely, he dropped out of high school not due to lack of intelligence but motivation. We suspect he is a loner, unable to form lasting relationships, and is therefore unmarried or divorced. He's a big guy, so my guess is he does manual labor and some kind of construction where he can come and go as he pleases.

"Those weren't gym muscles he was sporting in the video. His hands seemed hard and calloused, from what I could see when he did a close up of his hand holding the knife. These are my initial thoughts. I've spoken for a long time, any questions?" Mark Lewis asked and looked around the table.

Lizzie was in awe and extremely proud of her cousin. He was so articulate and professional. In addition to being an FBI agent, he also had his PhD in psychology, making him the go-to guy for the loonies. For the first time since the onset of this case, she felt hopeful that they would have a chance of finding the killer.

"Thanks, Mark," said Lizzie. "This gives us a great start. Our next challenge is figuring out how he moves around the town without detection or suspicion."

They discussed that fact in more detail, and she handed out assignments. First, she would have Mark put in the parameters of the crime through VICAP and see if there were any hits. The general consensus around the table was that this was too good to be a first-time effort, so there had to be some beginning trials somewhere else, so hopefully something would come back as a hit.

After about thirty minutes, about five thousand crimes came back as a match, so they decided that they needed to refine their search, and that brought back two hundred hits. They divided up the pile of possible matching crimes between the seven working the task force. Scott touched Lizzie's hand while giving her a stack of paper, and she pulled away as if scalded.

Scott suggested that they needed a more comprehensive study of the victims. He complemented Lizzie on the study they had started, but to know the unsub, he has to really know his victims. Lizzie understood and directed Griff and Santos to get more information about the girls, friends, activities, hobbies, and school. They were to leave no stone unturned in this investigation. That left Peer and Finnegan to look over the VICAP results with Mark and Scott. They started putting the results into different piles on the table by location, then by torture methods, then by how the victims were discovered. It was slow going, but progress was being made.

"Lizzie, chief wants you in his office ASAP." It came an unidentified yell from the squad room. Lizzie headed to the third floor. She decided to take the stairs because the elevator was slower than molasses, and he did say ASAP. She ran up the cement stairs two at a time, ignoring the institutional green cinder block walls and strong smell of industrial cleaner. She came out of the stairwell to a very pissed-off chief.

"PD is on the scene. Second body was found. The media has already been alerted to the scene, and it's a goddamn zoo. Worse, is that four days—*only four days*—has gone by, and we have another body and another missing girl! Jesus Christ!" He spit the words out, and Lizzie could smell the chief's coffee breath. "I don't like what's happening here . . . or should I say *not* happening! I want you and Dubowski there five minutes ago. I'll be over soon. CSU is on their way. I want that scene buttoned up tight. Move it!"

"Crap!" Lizzie uttered to herself. She hated her ineffectiveness. She couldn't save Sarah Jenkins. She headed back to the stairwell to get her crew together so they could head to Arcadia Lakes and see what had been left for them.

Lizzie and her team drove up to the crime scene where pandemonium had clearly set in. Several police vehicles were parked with flashing lights and personnel standing around waiting for something to do. The press was surrounding the police vehicles, perched and ready to pounce as soon as a cop got close enough to the yellow tape to hear one of their questions. Not that there would ever be an answer. Photographers were snapping away, and the cameras sounded like mini fireworks popping on the Fourth of July. Reporters were calling Lizzie's name, but she just ignored them and continued past the crime scene tape.

Lizzie and Scott made their way quickly to the body. Mark and Dave took a while longer. Scott held a hand in the middle of Lizzie's back to politely guide her along the uneven terrain, and Lizzie didn't object. Peer and Griff were standing off to the side while Bob was taking impressions near the body. Ralph was putting plastic bags over his clenched hands to try and preserve any trace evidence.

Sarah had been found propped up leaning up against a large oak tree. She was naked and covered in blood. There was so much that it was hard to make out her features. Lizzie could smell the blood that coated Sarah's body. It was a strong copper scent, like someone shoved a bunch of pennies up her nose. It made it hard to breathe.

Upon closer inspection, Sarah's eyes were closed but sunken in, probably damaged or removed. Her face was not as contorted like Sally Anne's. She looked almost at peace, with her swollen lips slightly parted, her mottled skin shining in the light. Underneath her was a plain blue cloth. Could have been a sheet. Ralph, the first CSU technician on site, was folding the cloth over again and again to preserve the scene. Bob Martin, Chief of CSU, arrived shortly after, along with Kurt, the forensic photographer. Kurt took pictures from every possible angle, his slight brown ponytail tucked into his shirt. He wore his baseball cap backward so it wouldn't get in the way. Ralph had trouble getting back on his feet—bad arthritis in his knees. The extra sixty pounds he carried on his five-seven frame didn't help his situation either. Bob walked over to Lizzie and started describing what they were able to find. Some impressions near the body looked to be a fairly small foot for someone thought to be over six feet tall. Bob estimated a men's size 9 shoe. There were other disturbances over by the body, and Ralph was dusting the sheet and was able to pick up a couple of useable prints.

Two dozen or so onlookers had gathered at the crime scene, gawkers who wanted a "look see." It was such a strange sight. The area was full of new life. Spring had started, and flowers were growing everywhere; buds formed on all the trees that didn't already have leaves. Then there, in obvious and sad contrast, was the dead body of this young woman. In the middle of all this budding life was the end of a beautiful life. She looked at Sarah, so young and with such a promising future ahead of her. Lizzie had to make some progress soon—to save the next victim, to save her own soul, and, lastly, to save her job. The chief would be arriving any second.

"Dubowski, get the locals to start canvassing the crowd to see if anyone saw anything. Who discovered the body? I want to talk to that person."

"It came in on an anonymous tip. I'll ask Daly to start organizing and asking questions."

Chapter 24

He stood there watching. He fit in with these people so well. Everyone in town knew him to be a shy, quiet, good boy. He thought for a moment. *If I placed one of those single want ads, it would read: "Polite, strong, good-looking single white male seeks tall blond to appear in major motion picture. Must like power tools and knives."* Ha! If they only knew what he was really like, they'd shit in their pants. He continued gazing around at the action. All the lights blazing and so many cars parked every which way, helter-skelter.

One of the cops came up to him touching his shoulder, jarring him out of his slight trance, and said, "Hi, son. Did you happen to see anythin' here today? Anythin' unusual? Anyone who didn't belong, like a stranger to the area? This is horrible, terrible thing that happened. Don't know what the world is comin' to."

"Sorry, officer. I just saw all the lights flashing and got curious. If I see a stranger or somebody weird, I'll let you know."

"Thanks, son. Be careful, ya hear." The cop walked away, bowing and shaking his head in disgust.

He knew. Ha! And they didn't. It was only going to get worse. They'd never figure it out. He was invisible to the police and was going to keep it that way. He stood right in front of them, and they had no idea. *Such morons!*

Chapter 25

aul slowly picked up the eight-by-ten color glossy photograph while scanning the pile of evidence, his methodical mind's attempt to place the facts in order. *Too many missing pieces*, he thought to himself. With a swipe of his hand, he moved aside several slips of paper and fixed his gaze on the disturbing snapshot of Melanie Richard's blackened body. The bodies in all four fires were found entwined like they were in a lover's embrace. He wondered if that was a recurring position of the victims found dead in the other fires across the country. He couldn't wait to get the information back from Sully. The autopsies from these four fires showed that the victims were all drugged prior to the fires being set, with the cause of death due to smoke inhalation related to the fires. At least they didn't feel the pain of the fire or know the fear of being trapped within the flames. It was better that they were drugged. He wondered if the murderer did it out of mercy or efficiency. Maybe both. The bodies of Melanie and her lover were coated in a methanol gel so that they'd burn hot and fast. The two were burned beyond recognition, and dental records had to be used. For the time being, they had tentative IDs on the two most current victims because of the cars in the driveway. Paul remembered the overwhelming stench of charred human flesh and hair throughout the house when he and Rob did their walk-through. He hoped that with this new information from the pseudo-profiler, Diane Benson, he would be able to make swift progress and nail this guy.

The telephone rang, and Paul picked it up. "Rogers."

"Howdy. It's your friendly neighborhood computer geek checking in. I took a look at those files that you sent me last week, and I started a database, checking to see if the ATF has any info about these fires. Then I started a program doing a state-by-state arson listing. In addition to that, I ran the stats through VICAP. Sorry it's taken so long. Feldman has me working on five things at once, all important. I also ran a background check on your Diane Benson of Reno, Nevada. She's got quite an interesting background. How'd you meet up with her?" Sully asked.

"She was at the scene of the most recent arson here. What's so interesting about her? She said she worked as a profiler for the police there," Paul said.

"If by profiler you mean psychic, then I guess that's what she does. The guy I talked with, a Detective Marshall, was totally wigged out by her. Said she was a freak. They don't really think too much of her out there. For the first two years, they listened to what she had to say. They did investigations on her because she 'knew too much to not be involved,' whatever that means. They used her when the information she had lead somewhere and they had nothing. Somehow she, how did he say it, 'just knows stuff she had no business knowing.' She helped find a kidnapped kid and solved three murders for them with nothing more than her 'intuition.' They say she's a loner and kind of becomes obsessed with cases. They haven't seen her for a while. Anyway, that's what Marshall said about her," Sully said.

"Are you talking like voodoo shit, premonitions, seeing the future, seeing the past, shit like that?"

"I'm not sure. He just said that she knew things that she shouldn't know if she were innocent and had nothing to do with the crimes. She said that she saw things and gave them leads to get the bad guys. He admitted that when they had absolutely nothing, somehow she just knew details. It's impossible to explain, but she did get results. I think he feels a little guilty about suspecting her. With so many cops, it's black and white and nothing in between," Sully said.

"I hope that doesn't mean she's like that little boy in the *Sixth Sense* or like one of those TV psychics that can tell your future by calling a 900 number," Paul joked but now wondered what to make of the helpful little cutie.

Chapter 26

Lizzie took stock of the activity, carefully assessing the situation as she always did. It was structured chaos—everyone scurrying about like ants but with a purpose. It just wasn't coming together. Carver was so meticulous which made evidence scarce. *We need a decent lead we can work with besides Seth Roberts. We've got some fingerprints on the sheets at least.* Lizzie couldn't wait to get back and check the prints against AFIS and the county records. She had a nagging feeling that whoever was doing this had to be a local resident. She looked out over the calm lake, where she had often taken a kayak for some peace and quiet. Thoughts of tranquility were fleeting as she watched Bob Martin and his CSU techs finish up. Bob waved her over, an indication that it was okay for her to examine the body.

In general, the body seemed to be in better shape than Sally Anne's but gruesome just the same. Sarah's face, her lips a deep shade of blue, revealed just minor swelling around the mouth and eyes. Her hair fell in soft waves around her face, hardly any blood. How odd. However, her legs were covered with many more stab wounds than Sally Anne's lower half.

Thankfully, Dr. Sean Gilligan, the ME, was able to leave a private dinner party to accompany Lizzie. They both knelt down and started their own examination. Lizzie noticed the strange placement of the legs and the ligature marks on the wrists and ankles. This indicated that she must have been tied up for a long period of time, and she bloodied herself trying to pull free from the restraints.

"She's better in some ways, worse in other ways. She has a lot more stab wounds, deeper and more penetrating. If I had to guess the cause of death, it would be exsanguination. See this large stab wound to the upper leg here?" Sean pointed with an extended rubber-gloved finger. "That's where the femoral artery is. Those gashes look like the knife practically went through her leg. I hate to ask but do we have a corresponding video yet?"

"I'm sure it exists. We just haven't seen it yet. He had the video posted just after Sally Anne's body was discovered. It will probably be up as soon as we get back to the office."

Mark and Scott stayed away from all the commotion dealing with the crime scene. They watched the professionals do their job and decided their time would be better spent back at their temporary office going through victim studies and searching the VICAP printouts.

Mark put in a call to the Pit to find out about the traces from the e-mail or video uploads. So far, everything came back clean. It was a bogus free live.com account that the e-mail had been sent from, the first and only e-mail from that account. The videos had been uploaded using free Internet access, a Starbucks and Panera Bread Restaurant, as well as the Columbia Public Library. None of those places had video surveillance where he was situated. Unfortunately, Sully hadn't yet worked his magic, but it just made him more determined.

Chapter 27

He came into the room wearing a mask from one of those scary movies. Susan started shaking in her binds. He looked into her light brown eyes and said, "Pretty, they'll be perfect when I pluck them out of the sockets. Bet you can't wait for that, right? It looks so cool on video, you're gonna be my latest masterpiece."

He took a rubber tourniquet and tied off her arm, injecting her with a hypodermic needle. She tried to pull away and resist, but he just knelt on her arm to keep her still. She felt the burn creep up her arm.

"I'm trying something new with you. I want to see what happens when you're stoned, so I shot you up with some junk. Know what that is Susan? It's heroin. A nice girl like you bein' a junkie. Who woulda thought?" he said with sarcastic malice.

She felt the first effects of the drug hitting her system. She felt a rush of euphoria, even though she was scared out of her mind. It made it seem like a dream. She started to nod off; he untied her binds. Her arms and legs felt like they weighed a million pounds. As much as some part of her brain was screaming for her to try and escape, she couldn't help but enjoy the rush.

He picked her up and carried her into the "performance room," as he called it, and placed her on a table. It wasn't an autopsy table; rather, it was more like an examination table found in a gynecologist's office. It took him over a month of painstaking craftsmanship to build it. Part of the table included a short chair with places to position the feet and spread the legs wide open. He affixed her to the table with leather hand restraints at her wrists and at her elbows. Next, he secured her legs; one set of leather stayed at her knees and the other at her ankles. He was talking the whole time, but she couldn't follow what he was saying. The drug made everything a blur.

Getting this one into the chair was far easier than when the girls were struggling or unconscious. He was excited to see how much she would be able to handle now that she had some dope in her system. He hoped that it wouldn't diminish her screaming, which was the best part, as well as the mesmerizing way the blood flowed out of the cuts, of course. He started with her legs, making thin cuts on her thighs with his straightedge. She cried out and then moaned, and he got excited. He slapped her breasts and pulled her nipples hard. She cried out with the sudden sting of his actions and then moaned again, as if she was enjoying it. This was a whole new effect, and he kind of liked how it was going. The absolute terror was not in her eyes, but she was definitely scared. He liked playing with Susan. A lot.

Chapter 28

He was so glad the investigation was started for Melanie Richards. He'd been waiting more than a week for the article to hit the newspapers where headlines confirmed that the fire was arson and that police were looking for leads. The Servant was satisfied and felt that he could move forward. Although the most euphoric part was the actual cleansing itself, the Servant liked the process of finding the next sinner almost as much. He could never start the search until his last "soul saving" was discovered. That was God's rule: one at a time. The job has to be finished properly and completely. Rules kept the order and controlled the chaos. The greater the chaos, the greater the chances of discovery, and that wouldn't do at all. God needed him to follow the rules so that his mission would not be interrupted by the police.

The Servant never left a trail for the police to find because he had a heavy travel schedule required by the company that employed him. He pulled his computer, a top-of-the-line Lenovo ThinkPad W701ds, out of a neoprene case. He was able to get such an expensive piece of technology because he works for Hughes Network Business Systems, which sends him all over the country to handle serious network glitches. His main client is Walmart, which links all the company's operating units in its regional offices, stores, and distribution centers to the corporate offices in Bentonville, Arizona. When the network goes down, it means thousands, maybe millions, of lost revenue. The Servant is the go-to guy whenever one of the Walmart stores has a major problem with the company's network. *The perfect job.* They basically fund his mission, allowing him to do all his personal stuff on the road via a laptop. Everything was at his fingertips, fingers that were anxious to do God's work.

The Servant had his next victim in sight. He closely watched the woman in the bar while he nursed a club soda set on a small scarred cocktail table. He picked the Towne Tavern for a couple of reasons. He was actually comforted by the stale smell of cigarette smoke, and surprisingly, this bar still allowed smoking. Also, he wanted to be incognito and liked sitting in a dark corner while making observations. No one noticed him beyond the faded and peeling wallpaper or the photos of various soccer and football teams screwed into the walls. There were tons of old skis and sleds, footballs and football helmets, college banners, and used jerseys. A giant moose head, positioned directly over the greasy mahogany bar, had little white Christmas lights wrapped around its antlers. Clearly, it had seen better days. The Towne Tavern was a housekeeper's nightmare, and neither a vacuum nor Windex had been used in it for well over 20 years. All the more charm, apparently.

He felt the fizz of the club soda trickle down his throat. Occasionally, he would have wine—even Jesus drank wine—but that was for celebrations, like during the Last Supper. It wasn't okay for *her* to drink the way she was, drink after drink, or dress the way she dressed, showing off her body.

Just like his mother, he thought with disgust. He was so little he should have been protected, but she could have cared less about him. He was just another accessory in her life, to be trotted out when needed and then locked in the window seat when not. She would have her men "friends" over and put him away like a blanket in a chest. He would beg his mom not to put him in that box. He would hear them in the other room, making all sorts of horrible noises, and sometimes thought they were hurting his mama. One time, he was terrified that the man was going to kill her but he jiggled and pounded on the lid until they had obviously heard him. His mama got real upset. The man screamed at her and then walked out and slammed the front door. His mother beat him so bad that night he almost lost consciousness. He learned to stay really quite after that happened. Other times, he prayed that at least they would go into the bedroom because otherwise, he could see them through the lattice in the window seat—all that drinking, laughing, kissing, and touching. *Whore*. She was the first soul he cleansed nearly five years ago.

He had plans for this next harlot, but he had to be patient. As the bar filled up, more men than women, he wondered which man would succumb to her flesh. Of course, that one would need to be cleansed too.

Striking a match, he held the small flame up to his face, breathing in deeply the scent of the sulfur, loving the flickering motion. All aspects of this action calmed him.

Weird. No cigarette, thought the bartender as he gave a glance over at the dark corner. *Seems to enjoy the match but not lightin' anything. No cigarette, no cigar, no nothin'. Ain't right.* He took a long drag on his own cigarette, wiped down the bar, flipped the Budweiser tap, and poured a draft for the next customer.

Chapter 29

Seth Roberts finally got his computer back from the police. He sat in front of it in a daze and almost wished he never written the article he titled "Dreams," about local people and their aspirations. He revealed his own lofty ambition of becoming a famous writer for the New York Times. That was how Carver had picked him, and he was thrilled . . . at first. Now, reality set in. Why was he chosen to document these horrific events? Carver thought they were on the same path to destiny. He would report about what was written in the constant e-mails, but there was no way to write about the details in the videos. Why would he want to do that anyway? They were filled with obscenely violent pornography depicting disturbing graphic torture and rape sequences. Being an editorial superstar wasn't all it was cracked up to be.

Roberts shut his eyes. He was weary and didn't want to watch this shit, but he felt compelled to look. One thing was for certain: Carver had definitely given Seth Roberts his first national byline, appearing in papers across the country, including *The Times*. He continued typing, breaking intermittently to rub his eyes. It was a failed attempt to stop the grotesque images burning onto his retinas, flashing in and out of his mind. Brutality was Carver's trademark, a current-day Jack the Ripper, only he was picking "good girls," not prostitutes.

Considering how unsettling the whole idea of a serial killer is, why does it have so much appeal to the press? He knew why. It fuelled people's desire for reading about all the sorted details. People want to see pictures and read the fine details of highly morbid matters. Sad but true. That fascination kept him in a job, so he got back to clicking away on his keypad.

Chapter 30

L izzie felt the same surging anger for the second time in ten days. She despised this son of a bitch, this monster on a rampage of human destruction. Now, he successfully abducted Susan Starks and would begin her torture. She was sure that he wouldn't stop until he was caught, and she was sure that if his pattern held true, he would be taking another girl tonight. The bastard was taunting them. They had crap for evidence, and the chief was breathing down her neck. She sat at her desk until about 11:00 p.m. She dreaded going home. Ever since she got home from the hospital two years ago, she had lived alone. She hated living alone. She was an only child but was part of an "extended" family. Her father was the police chief in a little town outside of Little Rock, and her mom was the fire chief's daughter—a great combo. She always did activities with the police families or fire families every holiday and all summer long. She was the apple of everyone's eye except her parents. One day, she just realized her parents loved each other more than they loved her. She had everything that she wanted except lots of love from them. But this deficit made her even more loving to others around her.

She loved her friends, even her stupid ex-husband. It broke her heart when she found out he was cheating on her. It almost killed her, literally. Her heart was broken into a million pieces, and her trust in men was destroyed. Even though she hated living alone, she was afraid to be with someone else. What if they stopped loving her? What if they broke her spirit or beat her and she ended up in the hospital again? She couldn't take any of that, so she just shot down every guy who asked her out on a date.

She decided to finally get up from her chair, shut down her computer, and woke and picked up her puppy. "Well, I do have you, Mander," she said, and the little pup gave her a gentle wet kiss. Feeling defeated, Lizzie headed out to the parking garage. Suddenly, she felt a tingle down her spine. She whipped her head around, not seeing a thing. Mandy had a low growl. She withdrew her Glock .22, still feeling like someone was watching her.

"Whoa! Lizzie, it's me! Put the gun down." Lizzie turned frantically to Scott, seeing him getting out of the SUV, arms raised in the air.

"Damn! What are you doing here after 11:00 p.m.? I thought you left two hours ago! You scared the shit out of me. God, can you hear that? My heart is practically pounding out of my chest. You just added 10 years to my life and what girl needs that?" Actually, she was so happy he was here. She wanted him to ask her to go for coffee.

"Sorry, I hung out in my car finishing up some paperwork until I saw you leave. I just didn't think it was safe for you to be out by yourself," Scott said sheepishly.

"Are you serious? I'm a cop, for Christ's sake! I don't need a babysitter!" His comment got her angry, and she didn't realize it set off other emotions. Forget coffee. She was glad she didn't take that chance.

"I was thinking you look like his typical victim. If his pattern holds, he's going to take another girl in the next twenty-four hours. I just wanted to make sure that it wasn't you! Cut me a break. Mark and I care about you. Hey, listen, we won't let you down. Do you want to grab a cup of coffee with me or even some tea so you can sleep?"

Panic rose inside her stomach. "No, I . . . ah . . . can't, sorry. I've got to get Mandy home."

"It's just coffee. It's been a rough day, to say the least."

"Thanks, but I really have to be getting home. I'm tired and cranky, can't you tell? But try me again in the future, okay?" She noticed that he was sort of crushed, but she wasn't in the mood. A hot bath and flannel PJs were more like it.

She wearily got into her car, put Mandy on the seat next to her, and started back to her house. She noticed that Scott Rogers followed her all the way home. *Sweet*, she thought. Thankfully, he stayed in the car then drove off when she went inside and turned on the lights. She opened up the back door, and Mandy raced out to do her business. It was the greatest feeling in the world to have this puppy who absolutely adored her. Mander Pander was always so excited to see her. She was unconditionally Lizzie's best friend.

She kicked off her black Tory Burch flats and headed upstairs to the bathroom. She turned on the light and looked at herself in the mirror. She had dark circles under her eyes, and her complexion was pale. She started the bath water and added some lavender bubble bath. The room filled up with scented steam that immediately relaxed her, if only for a moment. She stripped off her clothes and threw them into the hamper. She stepped into the hot foaming water toe first. But immersing her body into a luxurious bath could not wash away the horror that had filled her day. She could not change the fact that Sarah Jenkins was dead and that Susan Starks was missing.

Lizzie toweled herself off and put on some sweats. She brushed her long thick hair, staring at herself in the mirror. *Not bad. Pretty but not stunning*, she thought. She wondered if the unsub knew what she looked like. A crazy, desperate idea ran through her head. What if she could make herself a target and get herself kidnapped? She'd take precautions. Mark would know how to set it up, how to protect her. This was worth a discussion at the very least. For now, she needed to relax and eat something before she passed out.

Lizzie went downstairs to her airy kitchen and made herself some penne with pesto sauce and a frisee salad. Mander got some canned dog food so she wouldn't wander up on the table while she was eating. It was the weirdest thing: this dog acted like a cat, jumping so high that she was able to get herself onto the table and then help herself to whatever was on the dishes. She was just too cute to really discipline.

Lizzie was still hungry after the last bite of salad but not for that pint of Häagen-Dazs butter pecan she knew was sitting in her freezer. She heated up some soup from a couple of nights ago and started thinking about Rogers following her home and smiled. She didn't get a sick sensation when he was around. Instead, she felt a kind of peace mixed with uneasiness. She recalled how he gently touched the small of her back when they walked to the crime scene. She got all tingly, and the small hairs on her arm stood on end. Her heart skipped a beat every time he brushed against her, which, thinking back, he seemed to do repeatedly. He makes her feel safe. Could she have a future with him? *Whoa, girl! Start with coffee and go from there.* For the first time in two years, she was at least considering the possibility.

Chapter 31

Diane Benson woke up in a sweat, shaking and gasping for air. She looked around her dreary motel room, trying to get her bearings. The small kitchenette came into focus, with the tiny refrigerator and microwave underneath the counter and a stove that looked like it was part of a Fisher Price play set. There was a small scratched Formica countertop where she could prepare a frozen dinner at best. A small pedestal table for two was next to the loveseat, all done in early 1980. A cheap, painted particleboard armoire held the TV and three drawers for her clothes.

Diane felt a jolt along her spine and a sharp stabbing pain in her stomach, which made her bend over and clutch at her midsection. *The Servant was planning something.* She could tell! It wasn't clear, but she believed he had found his next victim and for some reason needed to wait. "No," she said out loud to herself. He has only found one victim, and he needs to find the other. He consistently goes after couples.

Images were fuzzy, and she couldn't get a clear picture. She saw someone watching, then a flame . . . and a moose head? What the hell? To get something concrete, she needed something that he touched, like the handmade cross. But that meant going to the police . . . or, better yet, Paul. She rummaged through her stuff for his contact information. She liked him. He was a gentleman, smart, and incredibly handsome. He had a gorgeous smile, and he made her feel like she had credible information. She'd like to curl up in his arms and rid herself of this whole mess. Wishful thinking.

She found her phone, but of course, it was dead, so she had to search for the charger. Finally, she called Paul's number, hoping to get him and not his voice mail.

"Rogers."

"Paul, this is Diane Benson. I need to talk to you about the Servant. I think I might know something else."

"Did you have a premonition or something?"

"What?" She froze and immediately felt a burning sensation in her ears. *He knew.* He must have contacted the Reno police, and now, he thought she was a freak too. In an instant, a picture appeared in her head about Paul talking about "voodoo shit and the kid who talked to ghosts."

"What's the matter? You don't want someone around who's involved with voodoo shit? Isn't that what you said to Sully?" she asked, defensively.

"How do you know about Sully? I never mentioned his name. How did you find out about him?" asked Paul, a little unnerved.

"Didn't you listen to what the Reno police said about me? They think I'm a nut job. I don't know how I know, I just know things. I can't explain it. It just happens. But I need to talk to you. Now. I think that the Servant has found his next victim, and I have to touch something that he's touched to get a clearer picture."

"How does that work? Does it come to you in a dream like when you're asleep?" Paul asked.

"It's hard to describe. It just comes to me, like a YouTube video clip. I don't have to be asleep although I get clearer pictures when I am actually sleeping. It's harder to focus when I'm awake. You must really think I'm a freak," she said.

"Well, you're a little freaky but still cute all the same. Let's get you that cross."

Chapter 32

"We got a match back from the fingerprints, and you're not going to like it," Dubowski said as he presented Lizzie at the door with a coffee. "It was a match for Seth Roberts."

"What!"

"He must have been the one to call in the body after he checked it out."

"I'm on my way to talk to him now. You better come with me before I murder him myself!"

Lizzie and her partner sped through all the traffic signals with their police lights flashing but turned them off once they arrived at *The State*. Lizzie asked the brainless receptionist if Seth was in but was told he had not arrived yet. She left her card at the front desk, and Dave followed her back to the car, hoping to catch Seth Roberts coming into the office. As luck would have it, Seth was just pulling in his five-year-old Mazda. She whipped open the passenger's door and plopped down in the seat next to him. Seth Roberts recovered from his initial panic, thinking he was about to be car-jacked. Lizzie looked around the car and noticed it was littered with fast-food debris.

"Don't you ever clean this thing out? The Health Department will come and condemn it."

"Detective Bowlyn, I'm sure that you didn't come here to comment on the sanitary state of my vehicle. So why are you here?"

"Somehow we have your fingerprints on the sheet that was found under the dead body. I also believe I have casts of the impressions you left with your shoes while you traipsed over my crime scene. What the fuck were you doing there? Should I arrest you?"

Suddenly Seth Roberts changed his tone. "Listen, Detective. I'm in this pretty deep. The psycho sent me an e-mail with pictures of the dead girl telling me where to find her. So yes, I visited the crime scene, and I nearly threw up. I want to break my ties with this animal, Pulitzer or no Pulitzer. It just isn't worth it! I don't want to be his go-to guy anymore . . ."

"Why didn't you contact me?"

"I did. I forwarded the e-mail that I got at three o'clock in the morning, and then I went to the oak tree where he said the body would be. I called it in, anonymously."

"So you're my anonymous caller? Next time he contacts you in any way, please call me first thing and leave your name so I know it's not a prank caller. We need your help here, Mr. Roberts." She handed him one of her business cards.

A very disgusted Lizzie exited the car, and Seth Roberts took off, leaving rubber on the asphalt. She told Dave what Seth had said while returning to the office. She parked on the street and couldn't help but check out the newspaper stand filled with sensational headlines that announced the latest work of a deranged, sadistic serial killer. There were before and after pictures of Sarah Jenkins and the latest announcement that Susan Starks was missing. Clearly, the papers were trying to attract readers from cable news and filled their pages with frighteningly specific, horrid details. It went far beyond the useful information with warnings of a possible serial killer to mass hysteria of an uncontrollable Frankenstein. It only made women who lived alone more terrified to leave their homes. Network stations had their crews buzzing around the department steps, hounding anyone they thought might know something. Tragic photographs of beautiful young girls were the lead on every evening news show, highlighting that there are no clues and no suspects.

The unsub was picking his victims with precision. He knew specific things about their lives and exactly where they would be and when. She had gone over this again and again. They had to find some common thread. The only definite thing she felt in her gut was that the guy was a local.

Lizzie sat down at her desk, took a deep breath, and gave Mandy a pat on the head and a treat. Then she started watching the latest video. She was watching the unthinkable and horrendous images coming across her screen, and she started trembling. Finally, twenty minutes later, the video was finished, and she closed it out so that only her screen saver, a tropical waterfall, was visible. She needed a break, and just before she was about to stand up, she saw Scott Rogers walking into the room.

He looked over at her and smiled one of those dazzling smiles that made her melt. She couldn't help but answer with a smile of her own. Then he did something totally unexpected. He lifted her out of her chair and gave her a big hug. She was so surprised that she didn't even object. Although it was a nonsexual action, Lizzie felt a detonation of passion rip through her body, and she nearly wet her pants. She had never felt passion to this extreme, even with her ex-husband.

"You needed a hug." Scott looked deeply into her eyes.

"You know this could be seen as harassment."

"Want to write me up? Here's a pen."

"No," she gently pulled apart from him. "You're right . . . I needed that. Thanks."

He had some of the VICAP sheets that he felt were the best matches and wanted to discuss them with her over coffee.

"Relax. I'm not asking you to go away for the weekend," he said. "Just coffee."

They went into Café Mavé and sat down. She ordered her usual English breakfast tea, and he had a decaf mocha latte.

"What's the point without the caffeine?"

"Oh there's some caffeine, I don't want to get edgy. I'm hyper enough without the extra kick. Ever wonder how this place makes any money? Coffee shops are everywhere, different names, all competing for the same two dollars."

"You are so random. What's with the small talk? You said this wasn't a date, so where's the list?"

"Can't we just take a moment to talk about something other than murder and mayhem?" said Scott in a light-hearted tone.

"No. I don't mean to be rude, but after passing the newsstand and watching the video, I need some answers fast. Before the bastard kills another girl."

"All right then. Let's get started."

He handed her about fifteen sheets with the heading "Violent Criminal Apprehension Program," which Lizzie fanned out on the small round table. She knew this would be helpful since VICAP is a huge federal computer database. Local law enforcement and state police agencies from around the country complete a checklist of 186 questions about solved and unsolved crimes in their jurisdictions, and those cases get stored in VICAP. When it works, it's great. Many new cases have been solved because they related to some data, description, or pattern found in VICAP. It's not perfect. When information is entered incorrectly or misinterpreted, you can miss valuable leads. When it works right, like now, the computer system is designed to flag similarities that might otherwise go unnoticed, such as tall blonds missing in a particular age group, area of the country, and/or found murdered the same way. Lizzie couldn't wait to start comparing them.

Lizzie and Scott noticed that the VICAP information indicated similar murders to those happening now except the victims weren't as uniform. When you took into account this Carver guy's victim preference, there were eight VICAP sheets that fit the crime and the victim. Most of the homicides were concentrated in and around Charlotte and Durham, North Carolina. They decided to contact the Charlotte and the Durham police departments to see what leads they might have. They hoped the unsub was still in his learning phase and had made some mistakes.

"So do you want to have dinner with me tonight?" asked Scott.

"You're part of my task force for now, and I don't date anyone I work with. Besides, I can't date right now. It's too much. You don't live here. You're from DC, which is where you'll go to back to as soon as we catch this twisted serial killer. So what's the point?"

"It's just a friendly dinner. You need to eat and take a break."

"I can't tonight. I'm going home and I just can't. Sorry."

She got up collecting the papers and already formulating a plan about contacting the Charlotte and Durham police handling those cases.

"Man, for once I wish I were a dog. Give Mandy a scratch behind the ears for me, Lizzie," Rogers said as he followed her out of the coffee shop.

Chapter 33

Sadie Mae Reynolds was early for once. She had to meet Charlie at the store at sunrise, no later than five o'clock, because he had to deliver the bread and bakery order for the Smith's Market. It wasn't a supermarket but more like a chic market that had a butcher, three aisles of products devoted to everyday items, and, of course, fresh-baked goods. If you had to do more than that, you would go into Columbia's Walmart. This was convenient for everyone in town so that they only had to make the trek once a month for major brands. If there was something you really wanted and used a lot, the owner, Debbie, would go out of her way to stock it in the store. Charlie met Sadie Mae out back with a big smile on his face. He had been trying to get her to go out with him for months, ever since he started this delivery job after high school.

"I got big plans, Sadie Mae. I'm not gonna drive this truck forever. I just need more money for school, then I'm gonna get me a degree in architecture and build fancy buildings. Come on. Go out to the movies with me Friday night, and we'll go to Maxwell's afterward for somethin' to eat. Please . . . my poor pride can only take so many rejections."

"Charlie, I'd love to, but I'm workin' at O'Dell's on Friday. I'm in the same situation you are: I'm workin' three jobs to save up money so I can go back to nursing school. I only got one more year left 'til I get my BSN. I'd love to go, but if I'm not working, I'm sleeping.

I ain't got no time for a date. Maybe in a couple of months, after school starts."

"You've got to eat sometime, can't we get together then?" He practically pleaded on his knees.

"Charlie, I've got work, and so do you. Git goin' to your next delivery."

"We'll have a date one of these days, Sadie Mae, 'cause I don't give up that easy."

He turned around and headed for his white delivery van, climbing in and starting the engine. He waved goodbye and pulled out of the parking lot. Sadie Mae started tidying up the recycling bin. Some animal must have come and knocked the cans over again.

He stood off to the side, hidden by the morning shadows cast against the building. He watched that boy and his Sadie talking. He was waiting for her to be alone. He had knocked over the recycling twice before, and each time, she straightened up the mess. He knew she would take the time and do it again this morning. His heart started pounding in his chest as he looked around to make sure that they were alone. The only sound he heard was Sadie tossing the bottles and cans into the bin and the wind blowing down the alley. He was a little afraid to be in the alley, but the fear was natural and intoxicating.

Fear made the moment more fantastic for him. His senses were sharper, his adrenaline spiked, his heart was pounding in his chest, and his breathing was shallow and rapid. He took a deep breath. *Relax. Slow down. Enjoy this.* He was careful, and he took his own sweet time. Seeing no one else around, he slid up silently behind Sadie Mae and grabbed her around the waist with his left arm. Holding her against his body, he placed the dampened cloth over her nose and mouth with his right hand. She struggled for a few seconds, and then she fell limp into his arms. He quickly lifted her into the truck, covered her over with the tarp, and threw some building supplies on top. He was on his merry way to his home-away-from-home, his brand new Coachmen Captiva Ultra Light, the best $16,000 he ever spent. He couldn't wipe the smile that spread from ear to ear away. His heart was racing, and he was hard all over. His groin throbbed almost painfully. He couldn't wait to start what he had planned for Susan while Sadie Mae listened.

Chapter 34

Lizzie got into the office earlier than usual. It was almost mid-April and getting warmer as hot rays of sunshine streaked her desk, highlighting the stack of papers from VICAP. She had to go through the Charlotte or Durham murders and come up with ones that fit her evolved unsub. She came up with six in Charlotte and five in Durham, adding another three found yesterday, that could be precursors to the vicious murders happening in Arcadia Lakes.

It seemed like the killings started in Charlotte, so she would begin there. After calling the North Carolina State Police barracks in Charlotte, Lizzie finally got through to a voice mail for Detective Sean O'Leary. While she was leaving her contact information, Scott Rogers entered the squad room. He was rather dashing in his light blue button-down oxford, red-striped tie, and grey flannel pants. It was a picture right out of the pages of a Brooks Brothers catalog. He walked around then down the aisle looking for Lizzie, and she watched him, thinking what a nice saunter he had . . . and nice butt too! He caught her looking at him and did a full smile, dimples and all. *Oh god, he is so hot.* She quickly finished her call and tried to look busy.

"Hey, what's up? You seem distracted."

"The contact person in Charlotte is Detective Sean O'Leary. Unfortunately, I was only able to leave a message. I'll try again in an hour."

"I've got today's paper. You ready?" Scott waved the rolled up newspaper around in the air.

"No, Rogers, not really," she said dejectedly. She really wasn't ready to see the sensational headlines, further showing that the police had nothing and another girl was found dead and possibly a third was being tortured. At least he hasn't taken another girl yet. She hoped he hadn't.

Lizzie and Scott sat down in the conference room and were joined by Dubowski and Lewis. They decided that Lizzie and Rogers would go to Charlotte tomorrow, and Lewis, partnering with Rafe, would meet up in Durham. Dubowski would stay in Columbia to keep the rest of the task force moving and handle any emergencies.

Lizzie's phone rang, and she hoped it was the detective from Charlotte. Her face grew pale as she listened to the local police chief describe what had happened at Smith's Supermarket. Sadie Mae Reynolds opened up the store, received the bakery delivery, and then vanished into thin air. The recycling was disturbed, but other than that, there was no sign of her abduction.

She looked up at Rogers with her eyes wide open, gesturing for him to come closer. She whispered, "Get everyone now, there's been another abduction." She had one of the sergeants call CSU and the other members of the team. Rogers called Lewis and arranged for him to meet them at the scene. Rogers went with Lizzie to the parking garage and got into her car.

They traveled in silence to Smith's Market. Smitty's wife, Debbie, met them outside, her face streaked with tears and eyes bloodshot, her hands twisting an embroidered hanky.

"Lizzie, she's only 19. You have to find her. She's opened up the market for the past year . . . I can't believe this has happened. I should have been here with her. I feel so awful. It's my fault she was kidnapped."

"Debbie, don't think like that. This guy would have abducted her some other way. We know once he decides on a victim, he follows her for a couple of weeks. Did you see anyone hanging around? Anyone acting in a strange way?"

"Nope. Didn't see no strangers here, no strange vehicles. And I've been watchin' for anythin' weird since poor Sally Anne turned up at the golf course. I should have said somethin' to Sadie Mae because she looked like the other girls, looks like you too. Oh Lizzie, you be extra careful. I don't want to be feeling this way about you."

"Don't worry about me. I've been trained, and I can handle myself. Besides, I'm at least ten years older than these girls, so I should be okay. If you can think of anything, please let me know."

"Lizzie, hurry up and catch that maniac before he hurts poor Sadie Mae, ya hear me?"

"I'm doing my best, Debbie."

"In the end, you always catch 'em, right?"

"Almost always," she answered but thought to herself that wasn't totally accurate. The really smart ones not only didn't get caught; they're barely even noticed. She knew this guy was really smart.

Charlie drove into the parking lot and got out of the delivery van, running to Debbie. "Is it true? Did somebody kidnap Sadie Mae?" His hands started shaking and tears filled his eyes. "I just saw her three hours ago!"

"Son, did you see anyone, even if it's someone you know, any vehicles or anything out of place?" Rogers asked, getting his attention.

Charlie thought and couldn't remember seeing any vehicles nearby, only that the recycling had been knocked over again. He explained that this was the third time this week that the can was on its side and its contents spilled onto the ground. The other days, he stayed and helped Sadie Mae clean it up, but he was already running late this morning, and he didn't want to get too far behind and get into trouble.

Chapter 35

I was standing in a crowd of people. We were all looking at something, but I couldn't tell what it was. Then I saw him. He had the mask on and was following me through the crowd of people. "What are you all doing? Run! He's after us! Get away from him!" I needed backup . . . Where were they? "Dave? Mark? Scott? Help!"

I looked around and couldn't see him any longer. Must have lost him in the crowd. Out of nowhere, he lunges at me with an enormous butcher knife, cutting my arm. I scream . . .

Lizzie woke with a start at the sound of the knocker on her front door. Mandy, who was sleeping next to her, also woke up and started licking her face; she then gave a growl. She was small but a good watchdog all the same. Lizzie was sweating and shaky. Looking at her watch, she saw it was only 9:30 p.m. and that she must have dozed off. Mandy jumped off the table and ran to the door, barking in her cute little high yap.

"Who is it?"

"Scott Rogers."

"What are you doing here?"

"I was . . . um . . . in the . . . um . . . neighborhood," he said clearing his voice. It sounded more like a question than a statement. "Think you could open the door instead of us having this conversation through two inches of solid wood?"

She was a bundle of nerves. He did that to her—made her edgy and giddy at the same time. She looked down at herself and realized that she wasn't fit for company. Her hair was in a ponytail, and she had on a worn out University of Richmond sweatshirt and baggy flannel pants that she usually slept in.

"Is this business or pleasure? There isn't anybody else with you is there?"

"Nope, just me. I wanted to make sure you were okay. I brought wine," he said, hoping the offer would get him inside faster.

She unlocked the door opening it slowly. He stood there with that great smile, and she just had to invite him in. All barriers were down. She said she was just about to throw together something for dinner and asked if he wanted to stay. With that, his eyes lit up, and that smile spread across his face wider than ever. *Oh god, help her.* She looked at him as he filled the doorway, noticing that his blue eyes sparkled with warmth and a touch of impish mischief when he saw her taking in the sight. He was wearing those *damned worn-out jeans*, molded perfectly to his powerful thighs. The sleeves of his white button-down shirt were just a little loose and in no way hid the power of his muscular chest and broad shoulders. She continued to look down his legs, and she noticed his scarred Doc Martens boots that made him all the more manly and sexy—*the icing on the cake.*

"I guess you must be really hungry, or thirsty, or both," she said, and they both laughed. It felt really good to laugh, and she couldn't remember the last time she thought anything was funny.

They headed back to the kitchen, and all the while, Mandy was doing her usual "happy dance" of jumping in the air, licking his fingertips, and hoping that Scott would pet her. He set the wine down on the counter and asked for a corkscrew and some glasses. "I hope you like sauvignon blanc. It's nicely chilled." He poured an ounce of wine into their glasses. He swirled his glass around, brought it to his nose, and said, "Excellent bouquet. Not too flowery, with apple and pear notes. Cheers!" And he clinked their glasses and looked into her eyes when he did.

Lizzie put a large pot of water on the stove to boil. For the sauce, she started sautéing the ingredients she had already prepared: diced tomatoes, fresh basil, chopped zucchini, and yellow peppers. She lowered the heat and let the mixture simmer. She would toss in a couple of tablespoons of ricotta and a couple of handfuls of shredded mozzarella in a few minutes. Scott wasn't the only one licking his lips.

"Um . . . Your dog, or should I say pseudo-cat, just jumped up on the countertop. I've never seen a dog do that."

"I'm really bad at disciplining her because I think it's so cute when she hops up on the chair and then walks on the table to try and share my dinner. I never tell her no."

"Well, she does have that adorable puppy fur ball thing going for her, and she knows how to use it. I hope you don't mind me inviting myself over for dinner. I was in the neighborhood anyway and thought I'd stop by to make sure you were okay."

"Again with 'in the neighborhood.' Really? You're staying in a hotel two towns away on the opposite side of Columbia from here. I let that comment slip the first time. You want to try something else?"

He just smiled and filled her glass with a couple more ounces of wine. He checked out the sauce and said, "That looks good and smells fantastic. The cat-dog isn't sharing any of my dinner tonight!" They laughed again.

"It's nothing special. Just something I was throwing together before I fell asleep on the couch. Thanks for waking me up. I was having a restless sleep anyway."

"I'm forcing my way into your dinner. I really just wanted to check on you, make sure you were okay."

"With a bottle of wine?" she asked with one raised eyebrow.

"Well, I couldn't show up empty-handed."

"Come on, let's sit while the sauce simmers and drink our wine." As she walked to the counter, she grabbed knives, forks, spoons, and plates and arranged them on the counter. He walked over and turned the radio on to some easy-listening station. They sat down on the stools and watched the pasta boil and the sauce simmer.

"Admit it, you were expecting me. You had the food already prepared. Or are you going to tell me that this is the way you always cook? Do you always make enough food to feed an army?"

"I really do cook like this. I love to cook, and I like having leftovers in the fridge. My mom could barely boil water. She hated cooking, and it showed. She burned most everything, turning it into shoe leather. Mark's mom, my Aunt Nancy, was a great cook, so growing up, I would spend a lot of free time cooking with her and Remmi. She taught me how to bake too. Maybe I'll let you try my oatmeal raisin cookies later. Well, anyway, one night, my mom had made dinner and asked me and my dad how it was. I, silly me, thought that she would want the truth, so I said, 'Not your best

effort, Mom.' She must have been hurt because she immediately
said, 'Well, smart ass, if you think it's so darn easy and you can do
a better job, be my guest! You're welcome to it!' So from that night
on, I made all our family meals, through my four years of high
school and beyond. My dad died of a heart attack my senior year at
college, and Mom died three months later of a broken heart. I was
the only child with parents that never really wanted a kid. They
just wanted each other."

She went over and checked the pasta, then poured it through
a strainer in the sink. She put raspberry vinegar and olive oil in a
large bowl and added some raspberries, walnuts, and feta cheese.
She gently tore romaine lettuce into bite-sized pieces and then
tossed the salad ingredients. She placed the pasta onto a platter
and poured the steaming sauce over it.

"Can I do anything? How about I set the table?

"Sure. And you can come over here and grate the parmesan
over the pasta while I get some rolls out."

Sarah McLaughlin was singing in the background about being
in "the arms of an angel." With that incentive, Scott pulled her into
his arms. "Let's dance?" he asked with a wicked glint in his eyes.

"I don't dance."

Scott stopped in his tracks. "You don't dance? How can you not
dance? My mama says that all girls love to dance. That's why she
taught all her boys how to dance proper like."

"Well, I have two left feet . . . metaphorically speaking since
obviously I have a right foot. And I was always several inches taller
than all boys at dances, so no one ever asked me. That's why I don't
enjoy it . . . I don't do anything I don't enjoy."

"Well, you'll enjoy me. I'm taller, and we're not in school. And
you know?" He paused slightly. "You're really cute when you
babble." He smiled, and she just melted into him. Before she could
argue, he pulled her tighter into his arms. As much as she hated
to admit it, she wanted to be in his arms, to be held close by him.
At first, they sort of just stiffly swayed back and forth. Then she
put her cheek on his shoulder, and they glided around the kitchen
relaxing together in each other's arms.

When the song ended, he looked into her eyes and said, "Now,
that wasn't so bad, was it?" He took her hand and led her over to
the table. Ever the gentleman, Scott pulled out her chair first, and
they sat down, smiling at each other.

"I'm glad you were in the neighborhood." she said

"So am I."

They ate every morsel of pasta and drank every ounce of wine. They both felt good, and the wine allowed them to talk openly about their childhoods. Scott had so many hilarious stories about himself and his brothers and sister growing up. Lizzie's side was hurting from laughing so hard.

"That was not the funny part cuz Mama and Pa didn't realize how sick she was. We all got onto a plane and went on this big vacation down to Disney World. Sammy started throwing up on the plane, and Mama noticed she was really hot. We ended up in the emergency room of Arnold Palmer Hospital for Women and Children. Mama had to stay with Sammy, and that left my pa with the three of us. I'm six, and the twins were three. My pa was a great man, but he wasn't always on top of things when we were real little, caretaker-wise.

"He took us to some Cinderella parade in the Magic Kingdom, and the next thing we knew, Paulie was runnin' up and climbin' between the reigns of the Clydesdale horses, pullin' at Cinderella's coach. There was a collective gasp from the crowd. Well, Petie and I didn't want Paulie havin' all the fun, so we started to climbin' on the back of Cinderella's carriage. I don't know what Pa was doin', but he certainly wasn't watchin' us. He's just enjoyin' the parade and all the characters and musicians goin' by. Finally, he realizes that the parade has stopped and that it was because of his kids, so he's runnin' and pullin' us off the carriage and apologizin' to everybody he sees." Scott kept talking a mile a minute.

"Right after that fiasco, we were wrestling while Pa was waiting in line for some food. We got all tied up in a pretzel, and Paul and I tripped Petie, and he fell and chipped his tooth."

"Let me get this straight," Lizzie interjected. "Your mom is in intensive care with your little sister, and now, your brother has a chipped tooth?

"Yep. Mama says that her only break from being with Sammy in ICU was to take Pete to an emergency dentist. I guess you could say our whole vacation was one big emergency!"

Scott continued. "Anyway, a security guard came over to find out what all the commotion was about, and we blamed it all on Donald Duck, sayin' that he came over to us and somehow ran Petie over. They never thought that three cute little kids would lie to get out of being grounded at Disney World. So from that point on, we had a private tour guide who brought us to the front of all the lines for the rides. He got us the best table at the restaurant and even dinner with Mickey Mouse. My mama would kid around that Pa made a great dad, but she'd have fired him in a heartbeat if he was the babysitter."

"You know, your Southern accent really comes out when you talk about your family and being a kid. I can't believe you guys. You were nuts! Your poor parents."

"Well, for most of my life, it was just my mama. Pa was shot during a bank robbery. He wasn't even on duty that day. Just happened to be there, making a deposit. One of the robbers shot three people—they all lived—but then he and my pa got into a gunfight. Pa was wounded but still killed one robber and disarmed the other one by shooting him in the hand. My dad died a week later from complications." Scott's voice softened and cracked a little. "I was only eleven. Mama had it real hard, but she was never sad in front of us. There was always a silver lining, and she always had a smile on her face. She just said that Pa was so good that God needed his help, and he now had to live up in heaven with him. We believed her."

Lizzie just stared at him as tears welled up in her eyes. She didn't realize that his dad had died so young.

"On that note, I'll be leavin' you now. Sweet dreams princess. I'll see you tomorrow at the plane, and we'll be in Charlotte by midmorning." He placed a small chaste kiss on her cheek and walked out the door. "Make sure to lock up. And remember: this was *not* a date."

Chapter 36

Paul stared at her from across the desk. Diane was naturally beautiful. She didn't need a lot of makeup or a fancy hairstyle to enhance her looks. She made his heart beat faster and his mind wander to places that it shouldn't. Plus, it didn't help matters when he noticed her toned, flat stomach and the sparkling tiny pink stone that was piercing her navel. Did she even realize how perfect she was? Her blue T-shirt was just short enough to rest about an inch above her form-fitting blue jeans. She had short hair that fell to her shoulders in ringlets, and it was the most gorgeous color of red that he had ever seen. But it was her intense green eyes with flecks of gold in them that really got to him. There was an exotic tilt at the corners that made it seem like she was always happy. Once the nylon jacket came off, Diane's ample chest didn't hurt either. Paul also felt some kind of connection that he couldn't explain. He had an urge to protect and take care of her. This combination of sensations made him glad he was sitting behind the desk to hide his growing erection.

"Are you just going to stare at me or are you going to ask me questions?" Diane asked, smiling at the fact that he seemed surprised when she caught him staring.

"I just want to go over how you see such pertinent stuff. Can you add anything from the other night?" Paul asked.

"Well, you have my file, so you already know about most of my 'skills.' I connect on some cases. Not all but some. I can't force it.

I usually need to touch an object that is part of the case, which is why I need the Servant's cross. It's different for each case. Sometimes I identify with the criminal, other times with the victim. I even feel it physically. It's not a fun time. Once I connect, I see images. Sometimes things in the past that lead up to the crime. Or possibly the outcome of the crime before it actually happens. Occasionally, I get images of what is happening at the very moment that I am connecting. I've been able to help the police, but they usually only come to me as a last resort. You've most likely read the derogatory remarks in my file. So even though I help them, they don't like using me to solve cases. They won't try to understand my ability and think I'm a freak or, at the very least, somehow involved in the crime."

Paul continued to ask questions and knew that she was telling the truth. Diane was happy to answer them and relieved that someone with clout was actually listening to her. She also liked that he was such a hot guy with a sincere and strong manner.

Chapter 37

L izzie got up the next morning glowing. She had an incredible time with Scott Rogers the night before, and she was kind of disappointed that he didn't try anything like kiss her senseless. She got back to the matter at hand and packed an overnight bag just in case they had to stay over. She was hoping that they might put some pieces together and acquire evidence that would give them a major break in the case. She sent a text to Detective O'Leary's cell phone to say that they would land sometime around ten o'clock that morning and that they would be to his office about an hour later. She dropped Mandy at her neighbor's house since she might be gone overnight.

She met Scott at the Columbia airport in one of the smaller hangars that housed the private jet he pretty much had at his disposal. She walked into the waiting room and saw Mark sitting there with a hot cup of coffee.

He saw the look of desire appear on her face as her eyes zoomed in on his cup. "Help yourself, it's over there."

"Thanks, I need at least three before I'm functioning in the morning." Lizzie said.

Rafe walked out from the hangar with one of the pilots. "¡Buenos diás, mis amigos! ¿Comó están?" Rafe said with a big smile.

"Rafe, meet Elizabeth Bowlyn of the South Carolina Law Enforcement Division, homicide senior detective." They both extended a hand and gave each other a firm handshake. "Lizzie, this crazy Puerto Rican is Rafe Dominguez, one of our team members."

"What's up for today? I'm up on the case. Just need to know what you want me to do," Rafe said in an eager way.

"I think it would be best if we head to Durham and Lizzie and Scott go to Charlotte. Then we can compare notes on the return flight," Mark said.

"Sounds good to me," said Rafe.

Mark walked over to the coffee machine, his limp barely noticeable through his hunky stature and otherwise fluid movements. He made a cup with her. "So how are you doing? Sometimes it seems like it's hitting you harder. Is it because you empathize with the victims? You know, you also resemble them in many ways. You're not afraid of this guy for yourself, are you?"

"No, although Scott thinks I might even be a target. I just feel so useless. It's like we're running around in circles and not getting anywhere. We've got nothing to go on, and he keeps kidnapping girls and torturing them. I just have to stop him," she said as she stirred milk into her coffee cup.

"My aunt used to say that if you seem to be going around in circles, maybe you're cutting too many corners," Rafe added.

"I know how you feel. Scott and I still never closed that Russian mob case. Part of my anger has to do with all the deaths from the bomb, as well as my own injury. But worse is that young girls are still being abducted and sold. It's terribly frustrating and all-consuming. You can only do your best and hope God will help you out a bit. I pray every night for those girls."

"Agent Lewis, we're ready for takeoff. Please have your group board the plane," the pilot said to them.

They boarded quietly, found their seats, and settled in for takeoff. They talked about the case some more. Scott kept peering over his paperwork at Lizzie from across the cabin. She smiled demurely, then looked away, embarrassed.

Chapter 38

The jet made its first stop in Charlotte. Then Rafe and Lewis
continued onto Durham. Lizzie and Scott gathered their
overnight bags and were met by a local FBI agent. He said
he was at their service and would drive them where ever they
needed to go. Lizzie was most anxious to meet with Detective Sean
O'Leary, so they headed to the State Police Barracks in Charlotte.
They hustled into the black Suburban. Sitting in the rear seat,
Lizzie felt the air leave her lungs as she watched the back of
Rogers's head move as he chatted with the agent. She started
daydreaming what it would like to be alone with him, naked. As
the car stopped in front of the State Police Barracks, she couldn't
believe how fast the time had flown.

They went into the nondescript three-story brick building and
spoke to the sergeant on duty at the desk about their meeting with
Detective Sean O'Leary. The sergeant placed a call and said that
he would be right down.

A tall, good-looking man with warm, coffee-colored skin walked
into the waiting area and looked around. He went over to the
sergeant and was directed to them.

"Wow. Wow! You're not at all what I expected. You're . . . aah . . .
like a live Barbie doll!" O'Leary immediately realized that he said
the wrong thing by the look on her face.

It didn't faze Lizzie. She got that all the time, and she came back with her own dig, "You're certainly not as Irish as I thought. Where are the red hair and freckles?"

"Sorry, I have this problem of my mouth disconnecting from my brain, and my filter stops working. My saying the first thing that pops into my head drives my partner crazy."

"Yeah, I have one of those back in Columbia. Dubowski's the same way."

After the awkward start, they started talking about the case, and they started talking comfortably. On the way up to his office, he brought Scott and Lizzie up to speed.

"There had been a series of murders about two years ago that had to do with young women, blond, well-endowed. First, there were two rapes, women beaten up pretty bad. We got a description and two composite sketches, kind of similar, but not a dead-on match. So we thought it could have been two different guys. Then the murders started. The first victim was strangled. At the time, we thought that he did it by accident while raping the girl, but we soon realized that once he got a taste for death, we were watching the evolution of a serial killer. He wasn't nearly as fancy as your guy is now. I'm not convinced it's the same guy, but I don't know all the facts of your case."

He led them to a glassed-walled, sparsely decorated conference room with about eight different boxes. They were cold cases but still considered open, all leads exhausted, and the suspect still at large. O'Leary went on to explain that they almost had what they thought was the killer, stopped in a road block, but was unfortunately let go.

"Ashcroft felt horrible for months after that. He had only one of the composites. He ran across a guy that made the hairs on the back of his neck stand on end. Said he had dead eyes, but he was bald and didn't look like the composite. Later that night, when he got back, he saw the other composite up in the squad room, same dead eyes. We put out the description of his vehicle, an old Ford F-150, but there are tons of those around here."

They started with the first box, each taking out a manila file folder. Inside were a series of glossy 9x12 crime scene photos, all graphic, stark, and gruesome faces and lifeless bodies. The crimes were years old, but twisted bodies of the girls made the horror jump off the photo. There was no staging, no posing of the body; these girls were just dumped with their bodies contorted at odd angles.

O'Leary held a manila folder, gripping it as if he could wring the unsub's neck by proxy. No one should be left out like trash. No one.

They were looking at grisly crime scenes, girls who had their lives stolen from them by a deranged killer. They almost looked the same except the method of death was becoming more efficient. His first was strangled, his second had deep lacerations on her throat, and the third and fourth were stabbed in the heart. Victim number five was alive the longest after being abducted and had cuts to her femoral artery and deep stab wounds to her liver. The sixth was unlike the others and could have even been murdered by a different killer, but Lizzie didn't think so. It was a rush job, like he didn't have time to torture her, just bash her face in and crack open her skull. Lizzie recreated the scenario in her mind: the police were closing in on him; he didn't have time to play; he had to kill her because she might have identified him; he had just enough time to dump and run.

They had some evidence from the rapes like partial bite marks and saliva from the bite marks but no evidence from the dump sites. With a suspect, it's evidence, without one, it was nothing. *Maybe even worse than nothing because it gave them false hope.*

Chapter 39

He planned and executed his crime so perfectly. He was already bigger than Dahmer or Bundy. In fact, he nearly fell over when he went into Best Buy and saw "Serial Killer Still at Large" on nearly every HD TV in the store. That was a real high.

He'd been planning to kidnap someone since, well, as long as he could remember. The "who" factor changed constantly throughout high school but never the objective, which was always crystal clear in his mind. He's been fantasizing about abducting and torturing girls for years. Now, he's actually made it to the pinnacle of his imagination, perfected his art.

The news reports provided a clue as to what was really going on. He saw all the pictures of the girls on the nightly news programs or on the front page of the papers, and they all started with *his* story. So this is what it was like to be famous. He liked being famous. He liked it a lot, smiling as he walked out of the store.

He watched as dusk turned to night. He felt the different hues of darkness as each gradually descended around the trailer. It was eight o'clock. Time to get on with the night's entertainment. "Let's do it!" he said as he walked into the room with Sarah. Mask in place, he started the cameras rolling. "Action!"

Chapter 40

Over their morning coffees, Detective O'Leary stayed with Lizzie and Scott for several hours, going over all the information, re-reading witness statements, and trying to fill in any holes in the investigation. O'Leary had to leave at two o'clock in the afternoon for a briefing on one of his own investigations. He came back down to the State Police Barracks later at around five-thirty and had some good news, not about the killings.

"Hey, I don't know about you two, but I'm just about ready for a decent hot meal and a drink. I took the initiative and made us all a reservation over at Murphy's Tavern. A traditional Irish pub down the street from where you're staying. You'll be able to walk it no problem, so feel free to tie one on."

O'Leary went on to say that he would meet them at Murphy's because he had a meeting that evening with an informant about a possible drug deal going down, and he would be there after that. The three of them wrapped things up, and Lizzie and Scott made their way back to the hotel.

Murphy's was a fun place with great Irish music lending to the welcoming atmosphere. The bar was clearly the main attraction with dark wood tables scattered around. Lizzie had never been to an Irish pub and definitely not to Ireland, but O'Malley's is exactly what she always pictured an Irish pub should look like.

"Let's start with a pint of Guinness, then some wine with dinner. It's on me!" said Scott.

"You're my kinda guy!" said O'Leary.

"Mine too!" said Lizzie and then blushed when she realized what she said and what she meant were a little bit different.

They ordered off the menu and enjoyed their pints while they waited for their dinner. They tried to sort out all they learned from the files and where that left them with their investigation. They were pretty sure this was their guy, and they believed he was now living locally in or around Arcadia Lakes.

O'Leary ordered another bottle of wine, and for the first time that day, Lizzie felt relaxed. She was glad for the company and chance to brainstorm while listening to the Gaelic music wafting from the speakers. She was also aware of Rogers's long legs next to hers under the table, his arm brushing up against her arm, and the now familiar cadence of his voice as he spoke, flowing as smoothly as the wine down her throat.

Scott excused himself briefly to contact Sully at the Pit offices and ask him to do a DMV search of all Arcadia Lakes residents for the past ten years and find out if any of those cross with DMV from Charlotte for the past four years. They wanted to see if any left and came back and if any residents lived in Charlotte. Hopefully, there wouldn't be too many names that matched. After they finished their hearty meal, O'Leary left to tend some other business, and Lizzie and Scott were thankful for the fresh air and walked back to the hotel.

"How about joining me for an after-dinner drink?" Scott said with enthusiasm. "I'm just not ready to sleep. We covered a lot of ground, and I still feel like chillin' a bit longer."

Lizzie and Scott sat on the patio finishing their drinks, and they chatted some more about their childhood memories, Lizzie egging Scott to reveal a few more tales. Lizzie could feel a tingling sensation throughout her body. This was the first time since her apartment that they had been alone together. There was only so much time to be filled with the case. As much as they tried to ignore the chemistry, the sexual tension between them was growing, and it was a losing battle as far as Lizzie was concerned.

They sat there not saying much, and Lizzie got that tingling feeling again across the surface of her skin. Occasionally, his knee would bump into hers, and that was enough to turn her on. She moved closer to him as if being pulled by an invisible force.

"I think it's time for me to head up to my room. See you tomorrow, Rogers."

"We've been partners long enough that I think you can start calling me Scott. You call Mark by his first name."

"That's different. He's family. I'd feel silly calling him Lewis."

"Do you want to know what I feel like? I feel like it's hard to keep pretending that there's nothing happening between us."

"I know, but I just can't," she whispered. As much as she wanted him, there was something within her that she just kept holding her back.

"What does that mean, Lizzie? 'I know, but I just can't'? Can't what?"

"It means that I'm feeling this thing between us, but I don't know how to handle it. I've got some issues that I have to get over first."

"Do you still love him?"

"Who?" she asked.

"Your ex."

"God no! No! It's not that at all! But it does have something to do with what happened between us. I don't want to do this now. I'm heading up." Every nerve in her body was on alert.

"Okay, but we *will* discuss this later." They walked to the elevator and rode up in silence. Their rooms were across the hall from one another; she turned her back on him as she slipped the key card into the slot, the light turning green. She was very aware that he was doing the same thing across the hotel hallway with his key card. "Night, Lizzie."

"Sleep tight, Rogers."

She closed and bolted the door behind her, breathing heavily with a mixture of relief and regret. She kicked off her shoes and draped her clothes on a chair and started the shower, steam immediately filling up the small white-and-blue-tiled bathroom. She stepped under the hot spray and let it pound on her head. Lizzie consciously used too much shampoo so that her body was covered with soft, luxurious bubbles, which she used to her advantage. Wishing it was Scott's fingers instead of her own, Lizzie cupped her breasts and moved down touching her slim stomach and between her inner thighs. Once the shower ended, Lizzie wrapped herself in the soft white robe that had been provided by the hotel and lay down on her bed, exhausted but not yet sleepy.

"Oh, great! Now I can't sleep. Why can't I sleep? Because he is driving me crazy! No one—and I mean no one—should look that good in a pair of pants! *Hot damn.* His legs are solid, his butt amazing, his chest broad and strong . . . and that smile! Don't get me started on his smile. I can't tell you how good it felt to just have that muscular leg pressing against mine . . . *Too damn good!* Oh, what we could do together!" At that point she was almost considering another shower—this time a cold one.

There was a knock on the door, and she quickly grabbed the ends of her terry belt and tied them tightly around her waist. Looking out through the peephole, Lizzie saw Rogers standing there with his shirt unbuttoned and untucked and holding a toothbrush tightly in his hand.

"Who were you talking to? Were you on your cell?"

"You caught me, jabbering to myself," she answered trying to hold back the redness rising in her cheeks.

"You know, they say that's the first sign of insanity."

"Only if you answer back." She looked up into his eyes and smiled.

"Then I've been crazy since I was about, oh, two. I've been having conversations with myself since I learned how to talk. I'm quite an interesting girl, in case you haven't noticed."

Lizzie broke out into a wide grin, and Scott's heart was beating like a marathoner's.

"Of course, I hear exactly what I want to hear. Never an unkind word, no arguments. I'm a brilliant conversationalist," she said with a wink. "So why are you roaming the halls holding a toothbrush with your shirt unbuttoned? Trying to catch the Tooth Fairy with your manly chest?"

"I was wondering if you had any toothpaste, Lewis took my dopp kit, and I don't have any. The hotel has a nice basket of useless soaps, shampoo, and a shower cap but no toothpaste."

"If you put on the shower cap, I'll give you some toothpaste," she said with a girlish giggle.

"Sure . . . as long as you don't take any pictures!" Lizzie liked that he was so agreeable to her goofy suggestions. "I've got some toothpaste in the bathroom. Be right back." Lizzie tripped over her shoes, and Scott caught her, pulling her into his arms, staring into her light blue eyes. Next thing she knew, he was kissing her, and before she knew what was happening, she gave in to her desire. He lowered her onto the bed in the dimly lit room. Only the bathroom light provided a small glow. They started exploring each other's bodies. She ran her fingers lightly over his soft chest hair while he whispered her name over and over again. He opened her robe, putting his lips to her full breasts and caressing her nipples gently. A bolt of pure pleasure shot through her body, and she was moist in just the right spot. Then, in a moment of panic, she sat up and covered herself with her robe, throwing cold water on the scene.

She uttered in a barely audible voice, "Please, no. I want to, but I'm just not ready."

Immediately, like he was burned, Scott jumped from the bed. "Lizzie, I'm so sorry. I thought this was what you wanted. I didn't mean to force myself on you. That's not me. I'm so sorry."

"I do want this as much as you do, but I'm not ready for it now. We work together, but not this, not now. I can't explain it right." Tears started falling from her eyes. "I'm sorry. When I can, I'll do my best to explain and hopefully help you understand why I can't just let go and be with you."

They got up early the next morning, ate breakfast, and then headed to the airport. Scott was careful not to push Lizzie, and she appreciated this immensely. It really seemed like he cared about her. The ride back to Columbia was another steamy ride of suggestive looks but few words. Lizzie dashed to the parking lot, got into her car, and drove off as quickly as possible. Lewis made his way to their car, stopped, and looked hard at Scott.

"What?" asked Scott, shrugging his shoulders in that universal questioning mode.

"Did you sleep with her?"

"What? Me? No way! Why would you think that?" Scott said, clearly uncomfortable.

"Oh, I don't know. Maybe because she was quiet as hell and as nervous as a cat in a dog pound the whole ride back. I was afraid the plane would catch fire the way you two were looking at each other. You look at her, then she looks away, or she was looking at you with longing when you wouldn't see her. Then as soon as we land, she's out of here like a bat out of hell. Listen, dude, just don't hurt her okay? She's like a sister to me. I don't care how good a friend you are, I'll beat the shit out of you if you damage her any more than she is. She had a really rough time getting through the divorce."

"Believe me, hurting her is the last thing I would ever do. I'm nuts about her."

Chapter 41

"Hey, Paul, can you come over for dinner tonight? Sue's having some associates, secretaries, and a few others from the law firm over for an impromptu barbeque. Even the lawyers who fought the case might show. Since she's the office manager, she wants to thank everybody for all the research and paperwork it took to win such a huge civil suit this afternoon. A $300,000,000 judgment to be exact. They are ecstatic to say the least," Rob said.

"Man, that's a hell of a lot of zeros. What time and can I bring a date?" Paul asked.

"Wow, you work fast. Who do you have in mind? You're not seriously considering that crazy psychic, are you?"

"She's not crazy. She really knows stuff and proved it to me the other night. Unless she bugged your office, she could reiterate parts of our conversation. Like when I talked to Sully about that movie where the kid spoke to ghosts, you know the one. Bruce Willis was a shrink who didn't really know he was dead 'til the end of the movie? What was it called?"

"*Sixth Sense*," Rob said in a monotone.

"Yeah, that's it! She *knew* that Sully and I thought she was like that kid in the movie seeing freaky shit."

"He just saw dead people. He couldn't see the future or read people's minds like she apparently says she can."

"So can I bring her or what?"

"Yes, you can bring her. Just don't say anything to Sue. She might freak and think it could wig out the kids."

"How are the not-so-little buggers? Still having problems at school with the girls switching themselves? I remember when Peter and I would pull that. For the most part, we got away with it if the person we were trying to fool wasn't really observant."

"The girls just learned that they could switch, and no one really noticed, so they got bolder. At first, since Tina likes math and always gets As, she would go to *both math classes*. They're in middle school now, so they have separate classes. Tammy is better at English, so she went to *both Language Arts classes*. Somehow they made it work. It was fine until they started taking each other's tests. We had to have a sit-down with the principal because he said that Tina was cheating off of Tammy's English assignments and that they cheated on a take-home test. Tammy didn't realize that she got the same answers wrong on both tests, so Tina got caught for cheating when really, Tammy cheated on herself. *Are you following me?*" said Rob as he realized his story might be kind of confusing. "Of course! I'm a twin! Been there, done that!" Paul said proudly.

"It was pretty bad, but Tina and Tammy definitely learned their lesson. I suggested to the principal to let the girls make up their own work and put them in the same classes at the same time. I actually thought it was rather ingenious of me," Rob said, praising himself by patting his own back.

"Well, anytime you have twin questions, please feel free to ask. I've always enjoyed being a twin. It was really cool growing up and having people gawk all the time. I loved being the center of attention. Peter, not as much."

They continued to work on the case throughout the day, trying to sift through all the files that Diane brought with her, the files from the flash drive, and then the files from the three fires that had occurred in the two counties in the past eight weeks. Paul rubbed his eyes. It was tedious work looking at the same information over and over again and not finding anything that pointed to a suspect.

"I got nothing. How about you? Paul asked.

"Nothin'. Have you heard from Sully again? Have any new fires been reported that we can lump in with what we've got so far?" Rob asked, hoping for a clue.

"I called him earlier today, and he said that he would try and get back to me tonight. My brothers are working on that Internet slasher guy. What's he calling himself? Oh yeah. Carver. Sully is running data through his mega computers for that as we speak. We're running on his alternate system. He says it's slower but will hit all the same databases, so the info will be top-shelf."

"We'll I guess we're set for the night. Let's head out and over to the barbeque."

"Yeah, looking forward to it," said Paul as he gave a quick wave goodbye. He thought he might just show up at Diane's motel and ask her over to the barbeque rather than call her. It seemed more personal, and he wanted to drive her so she wouldn't have to worry about directions.

Paul parked next to Diane's car in the motel lot, shut off the engine, and sucked in a deep breath. He hadn't seen her since he was here the last time after he had spoken to her and knew the extent of her abilities. He really, really liked her. Of course, he thought she had a dynamite body, but what turned him on the most was her fantastic smile. It made him crack one just thinking about the way her face lit up when he was telling stories about his childhood. She was the whole package. *If she was only a little bit more normal.* Maybe if she was a regular kind of girl, he wouldn't like her at all. He looked up and wondered how long she was standing at the window watching him think. He waved his hand and smiled at her as he got out of the car.

"I wasn't sure if you were going to get out of the car and actually ask me out to dinner or if you were going to change your mind and head over without me."

The hair stood up on the back of Paul's neck. "Did you actually know I was going to show up here and ask you over to the barbeque? I swear, I can't help it. It still startles me that you know what's going on without me saying anything. It is kind of creepy."

"Yeah, it's creepy that. Rob called and invited me to dinner at his house and said that you would be picking me up. Did I miss something? What's so creepy about me waiting by the window for you to arrive?" Diane asked somewhat annoyed, standing with arms akimbo.

"Oh no . . . Sorry, my fault. I thought that you were reading my mind or something," Paul's faced turned crimson. "I didn't realize Rob had called you ahead of time and was . . . well . . . sort of shocked that you already knew I was coming over to ask you to go with me to his house. My bad."

"No worries. I'm ready to go, and I'm starved! Anything but a frozen turkey dinner sounds fantastic."

Chapter 42

The Towne Tavern was nearly finished preparing for the dinner crowd, which prompted her to check her watch. *Oops! It's already past six.* Luckily, she was invited to an informal outdoor get-together, so they wouldn't care if she arrived a few minutes late.

The Servant followed her to the outskirts of town to her little house, the same place last night. He was displeased to see that she left "Happy Hour" sober and alone. He thought for sure that this was the night she'd get drunk again and lure another man home to her bed. Salvation would have to wait. During the past three weeks, he noted her regular routine: straight home from work, quick dinner, shower, and then go out to the bar and flaunt herself *just like the rest of them.* He would save her and the poor bastard she trapped into sinning.

He was an ordained minister, thanks to the Internet. He was officially chosen by God to tend to his flock. It was late and time to pray.

> *My lord of the highest power, oh righteous savior, I am your servant, and you have put me on this earth to do your work. I believe in abolishing sin. I believe in entering your kingdom without sin. I believe in cleansing every sinner's soul until the day I die. Oh, my lord, you are the almighty. Lord, I ask that you bless this cross. I carve it in your name*

to let others know that you have redeemed the wicked. Protect me in my mission to glorify you through the actions that must occur to receive eternal salvation. Praise be to you, oh lord.

"Soon, my sorry little souls. Soon, salvation will be thine," he said, then switched off the light.

Chapter 43

"So what specifically haven't you told me?" Remmi Lewis asked her favorite cousin.

Lizzie could barely respond. As she held the phone to her ear, she could feel a hot blush rising in her cheeks. Her ears started burning and ringing. She was so glad she was on the phone so her cousin couldn't see the glaring red color on her face. She was sure hives would be appearing next all over the upper half of her body.

"So what went on between you and Scott? I just got off the phone with Mark, and he said the looks you two give each other, he's surprised all those papers that you have around your desk haven't caught on fire."

"There's nothing to tell," she uttered into the receiver as she simultaneously shrugged her shoulders.

"One thing about cops, they make bad liars, and I can tell you're lying over the phone. How pathetic is that! I would have thought you were better at it the way you interrogate all those criminals. Your technique must stink."

"What? Do you have a new job at *The Inquirer*? Because I don't want to deal with inquiring minds right now," said Lizzie with a snappy voice. There was an uncomfortable silence. Remmi *humpfed* a couple of times, and then Lizzie finally gave in and started talking . . . and didn't stop. She told Remmi everything: coming over, the impromptu dinner, dancing in her kitchen, which immediately elicited an "I thought you don't dance cuz you're too tall and awkward!" exclamation from Remmi. She went on about how her heart was fluttering when she sat next to him on the plane, the almost sex in the hotel room, and her and her inner doubts, which led her to the next part.

"Remmi, I never told you about this, but when I went on the leave of absence from Memphis, it wasn't because of the pressures of the job I told you in my letters. There was an incident where Matt beat the shit out of me. I was in intensive care. My jaw was wired shut for two months to allow all the fractures to heal."

"Oh my god, honey, why didn't you tell us? We're your family, we love you! We would have been there for you."

"I didn't let anyone know. I was embarrassed and humiliated that my husband was the one to do that to me, especially since I'm a cop and should be able to defend myself. I never saw anyone while I was recovering and never told the family. Matt did feel horrible afterwards and pleaded guilty to felony assault and battery. He's doing five to ten in the Federal Correction Institution in Memphis and should be out soon on good behavior."

"Honey, you have to tell Scott about this . . . at least some of it. You'll never be able to move on if you don't. I've known him for years, and he's such a sweetie. So gentle. He would never do anything like that to you. Ever."

"I think I know that. It basically took every bit of self-control that I had not to strip him bare and jump his bones on the plane coming home."

"It might have done you some good!" Remmi laughed. "I can just see things getting pretty hot, steaming up the windows in your squad car."

"I don't know," said Lizzie. *But she did know.* She wanted Scott with a severity that frightened her. She wasn't sure if she was ready for another "relationship." It scared the crap out of her that she could be that vulnerable again. Her confidence had been shattered, and mending it was harder than she thought.

Chapter 44

It was another late night, and Lizzie was by herself again. She really hated being alone. That was one of the main reasons she was so happy in the beginning when she was married. So nice to have someone to cook for and snuggle with when a scary thunderstorm struck.

It had been a whirlwind romance, and in just three months after she met Matt, she was saying "I do" in a small ceremony that included just family. That made her think about the first time she met her ex-husband, Matt Bowlyn. He was all about flash and swagger. Heads would turn whenever he walked into a room. Women gasped, licked their lips, sat up straight, and stuck out their chests. When people first saw him, they just stared; he was that stunning and commanded that much attention. With his dark brown wavy hair and sexy brown eyes, he was your typical Hollywood action star, gorgeous face, tall rangy frame. He was a better version of George Clooney. *Imagine that!* His dark eyes could undress you on the spot yet had a depth and sincerity that were instantly convincing. Even eighty-year-old ladies were enthralled. Matt had an excitement about him that drew her to him like a moth to a flame and clearly to her demise. In retrospect, she realized that she had been wrong about him. Painfully wrong. He wasn't her hero; he was just a man. A very flawed man at that.

There were so many things she let slide because she was in love, but in hindsight, all the signs were there. She thought back to her first year of training at the academy. Matt scrutinized everything she did and said, always making her feel like she was on a tight wire, balancing on a razor's edge. Lizzie quickly found out that Matt thrived on adrenaline and ego. *But oh, what a hot body, and that handsome face!*

Lizzie remembered the first day of the police academy, and she couldn't take her eyes off him. How was she ever going to be a cop if this hunk was in the class distracting her? As she stood there with her mouth open, all she could think about was how awesome this man must look naked. Mr. Tall, Dark, and Handsome must have known what she was thinking because he gave her a knowing smile that made her blush scarlet. When their eyes met, he gave her a full body scan, slow enough to check her out completely but not long enough to be lecherous. Afterward, he gave her his approval with an appreciative grin. *This guy was trouble,* she had thought. *He'll probably break my heart.* In the end, he broke a lot more than that, but her heart was the hardest part to heal. *How deceiving looks could be.*

What had happened? She felt a hollow sadness for the man that Matt had been the first couple of years they were married. She wondered if he had ever really been that loving and caring man or if that was simply what she made him into, something no man could ever live up to. She had been so blinded by his good looks, personal style, and self-confidence. Lizzie thought back, wondering how she could have overlooked the fact that he wasn't the hero type but, rather, more the narcissistic type. During their basic training, Matt went after her aggressively but in a good way. He was outrageous, always flirting with her and always making jokes with a sexual connotation. He only had eyes for her . . . or so she thought.

Even their first date was amazing.

"I don't think so. No way," Lizzie said hesitantly.

"Come on, babe, it's just a bike! Not the space shuttle, not dangerous. I've been riding since I was seventeen. Had my own dirt bike. Let's go! Just hold tight," Matt said with a deep voice that made her melt like butter. *God, he was so sexy! And such a bad boy,* she thought as he straddled his Harley with a big old smile reaching ear to ear. It was a beautiful motorcycle, fast, smooth, great lines, revved and ready to go—just like its rider. Lizzie loved the way his faded jeans molded perfectly to his body with a black leather jacket and Ray Bans. He was right out of a James Dean movie, only better. It was a gorgeous day, and she couldn't wait to go on the picnic Matt promised to take her on. She wondered what surprises were hidden in the wicker basket strapped onto the back of his bike. This was going to be the perfect date.

"It's Sunday, babe, and the weather is perfect. I've got good food, good drink, and I'm hoping for some perfect company to share it all with! And that would be you. Come on, Lizzie, you could use a little fun after that week of training. I know I could use a break."

"Fun . . . That sounds really good . . . Sure, I guess I could use some fun right about now," she had said, and she climbed on the back of his big bike, prepared to infuse a little excitement into her life.

"Okay! Hang on, little girl. Daddy's gonna take you on the ride of your life! You ready?"

"Would it matter if I said no?"

Lizzie remembered how Matt just laughed and kick-started the bike. As the motor thundered to life, she squealed as it jumped forward, clutching Matt's waist, hanging on for dear life.

"You did that on purpose!" she yelled into his ear to be heard over the loud rumble of the engine.

"Yes, I did, and I'll do it again to get a hug that tight," he admitted. "Just hang on to anything you like. You won't hear me complain," he added with a smirk. Matt goosed the throttle again, making her hold on even tighter. Lizzie screamed and wrapped her arms around him with a death grip, burying her face into his strong back, the smell of leather making her never want to let go.

After about an hour of traveling along the highway, Lizzie became more relaxed riding on the motorcycle, now immensely enjoying the changing landscape. Matt was taking it easy now, and she felt safe and comfortable with him. The road changed from highway to a winding country road, which led to an open field on the side of a forest. She recalled what he asked her once they had stopped.

"Seriously, you've never ridden on a motorcycle before?"

"Nope, that was my first time. It was definitely exciting . . . once the fear factor was gone. Actually, it was exhilarating, if you want to know the truth!"

"Well now, I'm honored that you made your virgin ride with me, and it was so enjoyable."

That was a loaded statement, if there ever was one. She glanced into his searching eyes before he turned back to the bike for the basket and the blanket. He was so prepared; everything was lovely. Matt led Lizzie up a path through the woods and helped her over a couple of fallen logs. She thought that he was just doing it so that he could keep touching her. Finally, they turned a corner, and she was mesmerized. It was a moment she would never forget.

"Oh my . . ." was all she could muster up because it was the only thing that came to mind when she saw the idyllic sight before her.

"Yeah, I thought that you'd like it. My parents used to take me camping here. My mom always said it was a special little piece of heaven. I hope you agree."

Lizzie didn't like it; she loved it. The other side of the rise was a wide sloping meadow, next to a tranquil pond that was nestled between tall willow trees. They were surrounded by swaying grasses and golden and purple wildflowers that gently waved in the wind.

"You're just one surprise after another, aren't you, Matt?" Lizzie said in a teasing way.

"I'm trying to keep you on your toes. Let's pick out a place to have our picnic before all the butterflies swoop in and take all the good spots," Matt said.

At the time, Lizzie had thought to herself, *Can this guy be for real? Maybe he's seen too many Disney movies.* Then she looked around and could hardly believe he was telling the truth. She saw a bunch of butterflies flittering here and there and heard the sweet music of songbirds singing in the branches above. They had found just the right spot under one of the weeping willows near the pond. A light breeze, the shade of the tree, the blanket spread out—she was in love with every bit of it.

Matt was not in any rush. He carefully spread out the black-watch plaid blanket and opened the latched picnic basket, revealing a nice bottle of white wine that had an insulated sleeve to keep it chilled. *This guy thinks of everything.* Next, he took a corkscrew and handed her two plastic stemmed wine glasses. As he started to open up the bottle, she shook her head in disbelief.

"I figured you to be more of a six-pack kind of a guy instead of a wine connoisseur, but I guess those are on your abs." Lizzie giggled and then complimented him on his selection of a fine white Burgundy.

"I'm full of surprises," he said as he expertly opened the wine and poured wine into the glasses. As he took one glass from her, he said, "I'd like to make a toast. Here's to spending a lazy, gorgeous Sunday with the most beautiful woman in the world." And they laughed at the dull tap the two plastic glasses made.

"Thank you," she said as she blushed and smiled over the rim of her glass taking her first sip. Lizzie actually still had fond memories of that time. He went through so much trouble to make everything special and romantic. Matt laid out some cheeses, fruit, and a fresh loaf of ciabatta bread. As they ate, he gazed at the pond.

She had liked him for that. He was funny, smart, and intuitive enough to know that a picnic by a picturesque pond in an unspoiled glen would score a twelve out of ten on her "just what I needed today" meter. He had such a larger-than-life presence. When he shifted his gaze from the pond to her, she knew he wanted her as much as she wanted him.

Matt was a persistent man who knew what he wanted and knew how to get it, and he wanted Lizzie making no bones about letting her know it. Excuses for his excessive and outrageous flirting were unnecessary; she loved every minute of it. But on that day, he had shown her a softer side, and she knew she was falling in love with Matt Bowlyn.

After another hour or so of jokes and laughter, and their appetites satiated, Lizzie was definitely feeling relaxed and happy.

"You can't see that? It's as clear as day, and it's definitely a horse racing. See the strong neck there?" she asked as she pointed to the sky, following the outline of the cloud with her finger. "And there, that's absolutely without a doubt a tail on the butt. Don't you Detroit boys have any sense of imagination?"

"Oh, I have a lot of imagination . . . just not when it comes to clouds," Matt said. "In fact, my imagination is working quite fine right now. In overdrive, if you must know," he said with a slow smile, his eyes dark with desire.

He definitely wants to kiss me, she thought to herself. It didn't take much of an imagination to figure that one out. Her heart started beating faster, her mouth moist with the prospect of his sensuous lips lowering to hers. He moved in toward her and gently met her lips, cradling her face in his hands and kissed her, barely at first with small nibbles, and then moved back, looked into her eyes, and smiled. Then Matt let out all the stops, lowering his head again, and his mouth and tongue consumed her. Lizzie was hot with desire; he was pressing every sexual button. *Holy Mother of God, did this man know how to kiss a girl!*

"Wow," she said when she finally came up for air. That was the only thing she could say.

Matt chuckled, "Lost for words again? I'll take that as a good sign," and he assumed she was ready for more. And she was. She lost herself in the sensation, and she ran her hands under his shirt while he did the same thing to her. Feeling his smooth skin against hers sent their making out into overdrive. She tugged frantically at his shirt, his erection pressing hard through his jeans against her belly. *Lizzie was ready to give herself to him that day. How badly she had wanted him.*

On a frustrated groan, Matt stopped what he was doing. "Babe, we can't go any further. We have to stop now. I don't have any protection because I know you're not the type to feel good about having sex on the first date. If we continue at this rate, you won't like yourself or me in the morning, and I want you to really like both of us."

Lizzie remembered how she had to catch her breath and slow down her racing heart and how could she forget about suddenly feeling really embarrassed. She had never lost control like that, and Matt knew it. She had never gone that far with someone she hardly knew and *never* on the first date. Matt was quick to change the subject and asked her if she could skim stones. So they meandered down to the pond, and Matt showed off yet another thing he was great at doing. He could have taken advantage of her but didn't.

"Hey, you ready to hit the road? Let me get you home, and I'll see you at the barracks tomorrow morning bright and early." When they got to Lizzie's house, he kissed her softly and sensuously, making her feel like there was more to come when the time was right.

How could he have changed so much? By the time she realized he was a player, her marriage was over, and that sweet man was long gone. The man she married had changed. Or had he? These were questions Lizzie constantly asked herself, never satisfied with the answers. Perhaps through jealousy or some other manifestation, she wasn't sure. Maybe it had been the job since they often saw the worst of humanity on a daily basis, and some of the men let the power of being a cop go to their heads. Maybe Matt just had too many women coming on to him, and his ego just got too big. Whatever the reason was, she never saw what was coming, what he was capable of, drunk or not.

Lizzie came back to the present, an empty bed, an empty home. *At least Mandy cares about me.*

Chapter 45

"Hellooooo! Anyone home?" came a friendly voice through the door, followed by three quick taps. Lizzie knew it was Scott, so she quickly finished her conversation with Remmi, hung up, and started panicking. She opened the door and was blown away by his big beautiful smile. He was good-looking to begin with, but with that smile, he was devastatingly handsome. Lizzie started perspiring, and her heart nearly skipped a beat. Scott stepped in and drew her into his arms with a toe-curling kiss that seemed to last forever.

"Lizzie, you drive me crazy. My insides are all twisted into knots. Just say no and tell me you don't want this, and I'll leave right now and never bother you again, but I want you so badly, I can't wait any longer—not another second. I need this, sweetheart. Please, tell me you're with me."

Lizzie felt dizzy. She pulled out of his arms, motioned that they move into her living room, and they sat down on her white big overstuffed sofa.

"We have to talk," Lizzie started to say.

"That's never a good way to start. Please don't," he put his finger up to her lips. She kissed it but continued anyway.

"No, it's not like that. You just have to listen. Then you'll understand why I'm like this." She couldn't look him in the eye, so she stared at the floor as she started to recount her history with her ex-husband. She went on to tell him of how two summers ago, they had rushed her to the hospital and thought she was going to die. She spent three weeks in intensive care, her life hanging by a thread, almost beaten to death by her husband.

She gave him all the details she had kept to herself for so long. "Matt and I were both on the Memphis Police Force, and one night, after a rather long and tiring evening, I entered the locker room and caught Matt with one of the new recruits. He, with his pants down and she was on her knees with her mouth full of him."

Scott remained quiet yet captivated by every word.

"It started a screaming match, and our boss overheard the commotion. Since Matt was apparently the recruit's superior officer, he was immediately fired, without benefits. If he were to stay, he faced a sexual harassment lawsuit. He was stripped of his gun and badge and thrown out the front door. Not a pretty sight."

As Lizzie continued, Scott gently took her hand. He had a sense that the next part was the hardest.

"Matt said that he went to a bar and got wasted. That was the last thing he remembered until he woke up the next morning, covered in blood with both hands bruised and swollen. He figured he must have been in one hell of a bar fight. The next thing he knew, the door was kicked in, and he was arrested. That's when he found out he had beaten me to a pulp, and I was fighting for my life. He felt horrible and didn't even try and fight the charges. He just pleaded guilty. You know, I never expected in a million years I would have to defend myself against my own husband. But the betrayal on top of his brutality was overwhelming. I just shut down in the 'relationship' department. I told a few of my closest friends about the cheating but not the rest."

All of a sudden, Scott put his arms around her and gently pulled her into his lap. He just held her like that, whispering comforting words and kissing her forehead. She didn't know how long they stayed that way. He finally turned took her face in his hands and started off with a gentle kiss, hardly touching her lips.

It was like a dam broke. Lizzie threw her arms around his neck, unabashedly thrusting her tongue into his mouth. She kissed him with unreserved passion. Not like before, not a kiss to say she was interested in him, but one to steal his breath away, the way he stole hers. She wanted that kiss to say, "This is what I need. I need you like I've never needed anyone before in my life."

When they finally pulled apart, Scott said with a smile, "Now that's a kiss!" The next thing she knew, he was all over her. He pushed her back onto the soft sofa, kissing and touching her while many fingers fumbled to get their clothes off. First, shirts were unbuttoned and pants unzipped; then her lavender panties went flying to the floor to join her lace bra. They were breathing loudly, their hands exploring each other, hungrily graveling for the next caress. She had forgotten how good it felt to be held . . . *and to be wanted.* Their mouths came together, softly almost hesitantly at first, then hard and demanding. He kissed a hot trail down her neck, intoxicated by a hint of lilac perfume. He took his time with each breast, moving his tongue at the tip of the nipple to swirling around the entire breast. He loved the way she was moaning and panting to his every move. Skin to skin, Scott lay on top, then rolled her over on top of him. He wanted to savor the moment and take his time loving her.

She had never experienced foreplay like this, kissing and stroking her gently in sensitive spots and more aggressively when the moment was right. As he moved lower down to her flat, smooth stomach, he started kissing her between her legs. She called out his name softly, then again more loudly as her passion escalated. His tongue and fingers quickly moved up her body in unison, and he entered her in one long stroke. Just then, Lizzie felt something change within her. She didn't just love being with him; *she was in love with him.* It warmed her down to her very soul and terrified her at the same time.

She felt an electrifying current run all over her skin, and every tiny hair was standing on end. His grip was tight, holding onto her so he could enjoy her orgasm as much as his own. He gave everything to her at that moment, and she gave it right back—not only with her body but also her heart. Their bodies moved rhythmically, slowly at first and then faster and faster as their passion was fully released. Finally, mindless with desire, Lizzie tightened around him as he surged deeper inside her. They shuddered together, and Lizzie climaxed, as did Scott. The two exploded, coming together, their bodies trembling as her fingers clutched at his shoulders. Lizzie felt bliss and exhaustion as never before. She hoped that this was the start of the most wonderful thing in the world. She thought that she could finally live again and not give up on love.

As they lay trying to catch their breath, they were returning to earth, staring into each other's eyes, comfortable in the silence. Finally, Scott pulled out of her, disposed of the condom, and brought her a warm cloth. He lay down next to her to cuddle with her, holding her tight against his large strong body. He found a blanket folded on the back of the sofa that he threw over them, pulling her closer to him.

Lizzie looked at him with tears in her eyes.

"What's wrong, sweetheart?"

"Nothing. I'm so happy I can't help it. I don't know what to do. Where do we go from here?"

With a big smile breaking out on his handsome face, "Let's sleep on it first. I think that a trip to the bedroom is in order. Then maybe we'll get a snack and try out the kitchen table—a hidden fantasy of mine, but now, I have the perfect partner to share it with."

Chapter 46

Paul and Diane had a fabulous time at the barbeque. Sue and her coworkers were so much fun. There were four lawyers there, including the stunning Alexa. She was an Indian woman with almond-shaped eyes, long black hair, and the most gorgeous face Diane had ever seen. *She should be an actress or a model of some kind. She is so exquisite and such a lovely personality,* Diane thought. Linda and Harriett were two associates, but they talked mostly to each other, so Diane never really got a chance to speak with them. The most senior attorney at the barbeque was Paula Guthner, an attractive brunette who had great personal style. Even at the barbeque, Paula was "designer" all the way. She looked stunning in a navy Dolce & Gabbana skirt, a navy-and-white-striped Gucci T-shirt, and red Jimmy Choo espadrilles. She was the one responsible for the civil litigation against a pharmaceutical product, and she proved the drug was linked to the deaths of twelve patients around the country. Nothing ever got by Paula. She was extremely dedicated, and the client was always number one in her mind. She could be a tough cookie, but she never gave up. Diane told her a little bit about herself, and Paula gave her more details about the case they had just won.

"We waded through boxes and boxes of research material and found the elusive memo dated shortly after the FDA had approved the drug, and it was already being used by many patients. It proved that the company had known about several patients who were developing life-threatening heart complications, which, in the extreme, could cause cardiac arrest. So many millions of dollars had been used in the research stage that if the company didn't release the drug on schedule, the stock would have been crushed and the company out of business. Well, guess what? It ended up costing them millions, and they're out of business anyway," said Paula emphatically.

The weather was mild, and the party lasted a long time. Diane loved watching Paul play with Rob's kids and a couple of the other children that showed up with their parents. The smaller kids were having a blast getting "horsey" rides on the "bronco." When they tired of that, Paul and Rob were throwing a football around and playing running bases with the older kids.

"It never ceases to amaze me. When I watch those two actually take a moment to relax, it seems like they never grew up, just big kids at heart," Sue said to Diane as she sat next to her at the picnic table in the sunroom.

"I don't really know Paul that well. I just met him a little over two weeks ago."

"He's really nice and a great friend to Rob. Me too for that matter. When we had the twins, we were clueless. Paul had his mom come visit us—or should I say rescue us—with a bunch of fabulous ideas to organize the nursery and answer all our questions about raising twins. Rob still calls Paul when the twins are being crafty. Peter and Paul wrote the book so our girls don't get away with too much. It's still pretty amazing how they trick people—even their own parents!" And the two ladies laughed at the thought.

"I've been privy to a few of those stories, Diane said.

"Wait 'til you meet his mama, Sharon. She's such a hoot! The woman is amazing to watch. She has all her kids wrapped around her little finger. Paul's older brother is about three inches taller and about fifty pounds heavier. She handles all the boys and she's barely five feet tall. Her daughter is just like her, really cute and petite. They're a great family."

"I hope I'm lucky enough to meet them someday."

"I think you will, based on the way Paul has been staring at you all night. I've never seen him this way around a girl before. You must be special."

Diane just blushed, not knowing how to answer that statement. She was special all right, just not the way Sue meant.

Chapter 47

They made love two more times that evening. Lizzie was too wired to sleep, so she curled up in her grandmother's overstuffed chair gazing at Scott sleeping soundly, his body gleaming in the soft moonlight. *Just look at that beautiful, muscular body.* The crisp linens were now a tangle just below the curve of his ass, and she could not believe how perfectly masculine he was. She also was smitten by how all that manliness was very sensitive and caring. She never wanted to let him go, just keep her in his arms forever.

There was a rustling of the sheets, and Scott got up and stretched, gloriously unashamed of his nakedness. "What are you doing over here? Not good enough company in the bed?"

"No, it's perfect, you're perfect. I was too wound up to sleep, and I didn't want to wake you up. I feel like New York at midnight with all the lights burning brightly and the city bustling with activity. It's going to be hard to go back to the way things were."

"Why would we want to do that?" Scott asked as he shuffled her along so she was now sitting on his lap. She wiggled to get comfortable and could feel his erection starting to rise.

"I mean like at work, like nothing is going on between us."

"We can still be professional and date at the same time." His fingers gently fondled her breasts. "You don't have to worry. We won't be those kind of partners anymore. This case will end, but we don't have to. I want you, and I want to make this work. I've wanted you ever since I first met you. Mark said you were married, so I never pursued you." He started kissing the back of her neck sending chills down her spine. "I told you we wouldn't be working together as partners forever."

"Where does that leave us?"

"Come home with me. Work as a cop in DC or join us, or I'll see if I can station myself here. Just please, let's see where this thing takes us."

His hands were all over her in a nanosecond, and once again, she felt a rush of desire. He picked her up, carried her over to the bed, and laid her flat, with her blond hair fanned out on the pillow. It could have been a great mattress advertisement, just too X-rated. He leaned in and started kissing her, gently nipping at her lips. One touch led to another, and they indulged themselves for the third time.

"This just keeps getting better and better, doesn't it?" Scott asked with a deep whisper in her ear.

"You can say that again . . ." she whispered back. And he did.

Chapter 48

Diane was tired of waking up shaking and sweating. She was connecting with the Servant again: this time, he was looking into a match, fantasizing about his latest victim burning in her bed. She could smell the sulfur, and she could see the match flickering before it burned his fingers. He had smoker's hands and large bulbous fingertips, yellowed from the cigarettes. She got flashes of sports memorabilia probably in a bar where he was located. She could make out the image of a moose head. Once the connection faded, Diane immediately called Paul.

"Hello," a very groggy Paul answered his cell phone.

"It's Diane. Did I wake you up? I'm sorry, I didn't realize that it was so early."

"No, that's fine. I was getting up in five minutes anyway. I like to take a run in the morning to get my blood flowing. What's up? Anything wrong?"

"Not wrong, but I've seen the Servant again. This time I think he was at a bar, smoking and staring at a match. He's identified his next victim and has been following her. There was a moose head . . . maybe. Do you know where there is a bar with a huge moose?"

"Holy shit, Diane, you saw all that? I'm not from here, but we'll ask Rob and the precinct guys if they ever heard of a place with a moose head. That's a great tip!"

Before they hung up the phone, Paul and Diane made arrangements to meet up with Rob.

The precinct was full of activity. Both criminals and police alike were walking around the main entrance, and of course, the crooks were easy to spot since they were the ones being led around in handcuffs. Diane Benson arrived early and made her way into the area where Rob and Paul would be waiting for her.

"Hi, guys," Diane said with unreserved excitement while her curls bounced around even more than her body.

"Morning, little Miss Sunshine," Paul said with a large grin on his face. He was slightly intoxicated by Diane's scent of verbena, which somehow permeated his brain and groin at the same time. All his blood seemed to leave his brain, making him three steps behind in the conversation. Why is it that a man's brain never wins that battle?

"Good morning, Diane," Rob said, a bit more reserved than Paul and giving Paul a noticeably annoyed glare.

"Okay, Diane, please describe the bar, etc. All the stuff you saw in your vision."

"Well, it is someplace that still allows smoking, like a bar, because the Servant was staring into a match as he was lighting his cigarette. That part was very clear. He has long fingers, and they're clubbed and yellow at the tips. The main thing about the bar is that there was sports memorabilia all around the walls. I couldn't quite distinguish each item, but there definitely was a huge moose head. The ceiling must be pretty high because the moose head was above a man's head. I'm assuming he was the bartender.

"A bar with a moose head inside does not ring an immediate bell, but let's ask around and do a check," Rob said.

None of officers in the squad room knew about a bar with the moose head. Rob and Paul went up a level to the White Collar Crimes division, and two older guys suggested it might be the Towne Tavern. Paul got the address, and the three of them left to check it out. They arrived at the bar situated in a rather nice area of South Philly and parked Rob's Dodge Durango close by.

"What can I get you folks?" John, the bartender, asked.

"Some information please. Did you see anyone who you thought was weird or acted a little odd in the past week or so?" Rob asked.

"You cops?" John asked cautiously.

Rob got out his badge, "Fire Marshall. We have reason to believe that an arsonist may have been here recently. We were hoping that maybe you or another worker had noticed him. Strange dude playing with matches, probably a heavy-smoker type."

"Did you notice someone who was staring into matches that he lit and then let burn down to his fingers?" Diane asked, giving a more precise description.

"Hmm, yeah, now that you mention it. I do remember this nothin' kind of guy—you know, brownish hair, not that tall, average height, wearing jeans and a shirt with the sleeves rolled up, like everyone else. But he kept lightin' matches and talking to himself. He gave me the creeps, but he didn't do nothin', so I didn't think to call the cops."

"Could you work with a sketch artist and come up with his face?" Paul asked.

"I don't know. I could try," John said. "He wore big glasses and was pretty much in the shadows most of the night. He sat over there at that table in the left corner. As you can see, it's pretty hard to make out any details of the people who are over there now. Sorry, wish I could help. He was just really average, nothing special about him."

Oh, there's something special about him, Diane thought. *He's murdered over twenty people, my mother included.*

Chapter 49

Scott walked into the squad room early that morning. He saw Lizzie standing in the corner over by Dubowski's desk reading a piece of paper. Her golden blond hair was pulled into a chignon at the back of her head, and the severity of the style only emphasized her beautiful skin and high cheekbones. The tailored blue slacks and cropped jacket she wore over a simple cream silk blouse would have made most women look too plain and unapproachable. Yet somehow the austere style only highlighted Lizzie's sexual femininity.

The whole room was buzzing with beeping faxes, phones ringing, and personal computers blinking. Energy was all around them, good and bad. Good energy emanated from the hustle and bustle of following up on leads. Unfortunately, it couldn't suppress an underlying feeling of negative energy depressing everyone. All this time and effort was not bringing them any closer to finding the unsub.

Lizzie was in heaven and could not contain herself. An enormous smile spread across her face when she finished reading a memo from the chief and saw Scott standing by her desk. She didn't care who saw her; of course, it was Dubowski.

"Well, it was about time," said Dave.

"What are you talking about, Dubowski?" Lizzie asked, unable to control her embarrassment.

"I thought the chemistry between you two was too hot to handle. I'm glad to see you finally let off some steam last night. You slept with him, right? It's about time. I was getting tired of all the puppy dog eyes he's been givin' you for the past week."

"Oh my god! I can't believe you just said that!"

"Please. How long have we known each other? When would I *not* say something like that? It's obvious that I don't know how to be appropriate."

"Okay, can we be serious now? What's the latest news?"

"What are your plans from here on out?"

She just gave him a huge grin and shrugged her shoulders. "News, Dubowski. Now, please."

Dubowski proceeded to tell her about the latest video, and as of early this morning, Susan was still alive although probably wishing she wasn't. They entered the conference room for the daily task force meeting.

There was a big fat file in front of every seat that contained all the past cases that might relate to the current one. Lizzie briefly went over what they discovered in Charlotte and then handed the floor over to Mark Lewis. Lewis started addressing the group, going over what he and Rafe discovered in Durham. "Basically, there were five girls murdered within a ten-month period two years ago. They all fit with the current series of killings. You'll see in the file that each victim was held for a number of days, sometimes up to a month. She was repeatedly raped, tortured, and finally killed either by a stab wound into the heart or a horizontal cut to the liver, slicing it in half."

Lewis went into more detail with the working profile of the unsub. "The unsub would definitely not have had any lasting relationships, probably had a dominant female figure in his life that made him feel helpless, absent father figure, may have been beaten or sexually abused as a child, and is a thirty-something white male." The more they watched the videos, the more they discovered about him: the words he used, the torture methods he inflicted, all leading Mark to a more refined profile.

"Strange and insane as it is, he obviously has an enormous ego, and he feels he's in a competition against us, which will work in our favor. He thinks he's smarter than we are and that he's unstoppable. We'll catch him when he's at his strongest. He'll be overconfident and make a careless mistake, giving himself away. There will be one simple detail that he overlooked and that's how we'll get him."

Chapter 50

She opened her swollen eyes. She wasn't dead yet. *God, when would he just end it?* She had passed out four times from the intense pain. He used a blowtorch on her feet; that was too much for her to bear. He kept reviving her by throwing cold water on her chest and face.

As he rammed into her, she tried to think of something else. At least, this wasn't intolerable pain. All of a sudden, he took the large knife that had been on the metal table next to him.

"This is it, Susan, the big ending. SCREAM FOR ME! Oh god, I'm coming, ohh," he shouted as he lifted the gleaming knife with both hands over his head, and he came down hard in the center of Susan's liver. The cold stainless blade cut into her like warm butter. In an instant, hot blood flowed out of her on both sides. She felt the sweet darkness overtake her. And it was enough to get him to climax. Susan stiffened, and a final jolt lifted her body like she had been electrocuted. Then, a slackening of death.

Chapter 51

Bart Jeffries was going over the videos frame by frame. There had to be something there that would help identify this guy. He knew these films so well, knew every moan and scream. Pretending it was a fake horror movie helped get him through the scenes. *He knew there was something he was missing.* He could feel it in his bones.

Sully walked into Jeffries's office with a grim expression on his face. "Not a damn thing! Absolutely nothing! He uses public places with no video surveillance, and he keeps creating new .live accounts. They're free, so literally untraceable. Is that the latest date?"

"Yeah, he hasn't killed her yet, but soon, she'll probably think of it as a blessing." Jeffries said. "I see this shit every night now in my sleep. We have to get this sick perv. Look closely, there has to be something besides the glimpse of a tattoo that sticks out underneath his wifebeater T-shirt. I can't tell what it is, just that it's large. Maybe a dragon or a snake. Check the background. Do you see *anything* that we can identify where he's filming the video?"

"Stop. Look at that picture," Sully said. Bart stopped on a split screen with the caption on the top of "I just wanted to see her TITS! Wat a sexual experiance!" It showed on the left a very attractive blond-haired blue-eyed girl in her late teens wearing a blue flowered bikini. It was modest as far as two pieces go; the shorts were boy shorts cut with large yellow daisies on the suit. On the right was the horrific image of the same girl with her top pulled up to her chin, multiple stab wounds to her torso, her breasts removed, and her face so swollen from a beating that it didn't look human, stained from blood and dirt.

"I remember that girl. She was Justice Martin's daughter. I think she was visiting her college roommate's family for Spring Break in Charlotte about four years back. She just disappeared, and they found her about a month later fifty miles from where she was abducted. I was working with Mark to create a profile of the abductor. After seeing what he did to her, I was totally wrong in my assessment. We initially thought that he was a collector, older white male, and never figured anything this violent. I knew she was found dead, but I never saw a photo of the body. That poor girl."

"It also fits one of the VICAP sheets. Mention this to Lewis as soon as we're done here."

They looked at the video together for another fifteen minutes when all of a sudden Sully said, "Wait! Go back, I think I saw something!"

Jeffries backed it up twenty seconds. "There. Enlarge that right there, in the background," he pointed to a door in the far left of the shot.

"I'm not sure how to zoom-in on that."

"Oh, move over. Let me at it. Jeez." Sully's hands moved like lightening over the mouse and keyboard. A few keystrokes and clicks later, he knew what he was looking at. "Hot dog, I thought so."

"Sully, what is it? What do you see that I don't?"

"*That . . . that doorknob thingy!* That's a lever used on all RV doors. He's in some kind of mobile home or trailer. I spent every summer in one of those things. They don't have round door knobs like a regular house, they have lever handles. Lewis and his cousin have determined the killer has got to be a living locally, otherwise he wouldn't be so invisible. There are less than a thousand people in Arcadia Lakes, so it shouldn't take us long to check DMV for trailer registrations. We've got a place to start, *finally!*"

"I'll call Lewis right away and let him know the good news. You start pawing through DMV records," Sully said.

Chapter 52

He went to the store to buy supplies to fix Mr. Hopewell's cellar stairs. He needed a lot of lumber, nails, and new blades for various saws and his table saw. He looked around Peters Hardware for anything else he might need. Satisfied, he paid Mr. Peters and left.

He figured that he would stop into the diner, grab breakfast, and listen to the local gossip. No one could figure out what was happening or why it was happening. He just loved that and the feeling of superiority it bred. *Look at them shoving their mouths full of pancakes and donuts every day. All such blithering idiots, meeting in the same diner, doing the same thing day in and day out. Nothing important.* Not like he was. He was striving for greatness. He took a particular satisfaction in everyone's fear, and they didn't even realize the very monster they were talking about was sitting in the booth next to them.

"If I had a gun, I'd shoot that bastard myself," said Mrs. Winston.

"Why can't the police find him? He's got to stand out like some strange maniac," chimed in Jerry Rhinehart.

"Well, I'm terrified. And I'm not goin' anywhere 'til they find that pervert," said Tilly Shaw.

Listen to them babble. The cops are on the lookout for a monster; they were all high and mighty talking about what they would do if they could find the animal. He just laughed to himself. They were looking right at him, and no one knew it was him. He paid for his breakfast and left a hefty tip for all the entertainment.

Chapter 53

L ewis got off the phone with Bart Jeffries and waved Lizzie over. "Good news, they've got a lead."

"THANK GOD! What is it?" Lizzie asked anxiously.

Lewis explained that apparently, Sully and his family were avid campers and always rented RVs. He recognized the doorknob as being unique to Coachmen RVs. He says it's either the standard mobile home or the large towable trailer. They're running DMV records now of everyone that lives in Arcadia Lakes and the surrounding area and generating a list to e-mail to them for follow-up. *They finally had a viable lead.*

The task force was buzzing with activity as Rogers opened up the e-mail containing the list of RVs. It was amazing, there were over a hundred registered vehicles. They each decided to take fourteen names and check out the list. Several of the names could be knocked off the list at the same time because the trailers were being stored at the trailer park on the outskirts of town. Everyone had their assignments and headed out to find a killer.

Chapter 54

Thunderclouds glazed the roof of the barn, and the lashing rain soaked the animals, but he could care less. Lightning flashed and lit up the blackened sky over thrashing trees. A storm unloading its violent furry as if protesting the lurking horror. *Boom!* The barn shook with the force of thunder following a brilliant explosive light. He herded the nervous animals into their stalls and started his chores. All the while, he was thinking about how he was going to edit his final video of Susan. He was highly motivated to finish quickly and get back to his room to finish his work. The need to see everything again was almost as strong as his desire to kill. He could handle himself for a while, act normal and be the shy, quiet guy he had been during school. No one ever knew what he was dreaming about when he would drift off in class. Most of the girls thought he was stupid. He didn't get good grades; school just wasn't that important. The teachers were boring, so he didn't bother studying. He had better things to do.

He finished in the barn and worked his way back to the rambling Victorian. It was well-maintained and creatively painted in multiple hues. It had pale-green detailing under the eaves that was all but hidden by the plethora of flowering vines cascading down around the extensive front porch. Small potted plants decorated the stairs. *Such love and attention was put into this house . . . but certainly NOT by him.* It was out of a fairy tale, the type Hansel and Gretel would surely want to stop to visit, never suspecting a witch was lurking inside. His grandma was that witch. She'd beat him regularly, so he wouldn't turn out like his pa. She never hit Pa when he was young. She wouldn't make the same mistake with him. *"A firm hand," she always said.*

He made his way up the large center-hall staircase that led to his bedroom on the second floor. He had his laptop set up on the small desk that he used as a child. It covered the deep scratches he dug in with a key that spelled out, "I hate skool and everywon." His grandma beat him pretty bad when she found what he had done. His room hadn't changed much since eighth grade, and neither had he. Except now, he didn't just dream of torturing girls; he actually experienced it over and over again. He sat down on the wooden ladder-back chair and started editing his video. After an hour of hard work, he got into his truck. Time to head over to Columbia and post his latest and last film of Susan Starks. He would dump her body tomorrow, first thing in the morning.

As he was driving into Columbia, he recalled, with intense pleasure and satisfaction, his last "playtime" with Susan. He would never tire of the scenario, especially the bloodcurdling screams meant just for him. The cleverness, artistry, and symbolism of all his work instilled such confidence in him. *So much smarter than the police, than those dopes in the diner.* All this time, and they never saw him as a person of interest. He smiled with the rightness of it all.

Chapter 55

The alarm clock startled Lizzie, and she awoke hugging her pillow. Her wonderful dream had been rudely interrupted, and she swatted at the clock, desperately trying to shut it off and go back to her dream.

Lizzie was in bed with Scott, his strong, soft hands stroking her back down to the tip of her ass, not going inside but tempting her with playful fingers. He stroked the edges of her breasts—so enticing. She sighed with arousal, and her breathing was picking up tempo—

Just then, she felt a wet kiss. Mandy's. Lizzie scratched the puppy's neck and kissed her between her little ears. She wanted back in that dream, not the reality waiting for her at the office. *Progress, yes, but barely.* They still didn't have a name for the killer, and he still had two young women, still torturing Sarah and placing films on the Internet. *That fucking bastard . . . I will nail his ass!*

That thought motivated her to forego the dream and start the shower. Lizzie had to give the water a chance to warm up, so she let Mandy out and went back upstairs. She examined her naked body in the mirror while brushing her teeth. She didn't look bad for thirty-eight; in fact, she looked damn good! She still had great legs, large firm breasts, and a svelte waist. Scott had commented on her body, and obviously, he liked it. She moved her own hands around her breasts, down her stomach, and between her legs. *Here we go again . . . Snap out of it!* She blow-dried her hair and dressed herself in her usual personalized uniform; today, she would wear a cream linen blazer, a pink and orange striped Faconnable button-down, a pair of tapered navy slacks, and low-wedge Cole Haans. Her badge and gun were her only accessories. Mandy trotted behind her the entire time until she walked out the door to her Altima.

It was raining again; streaks of water pelted the car's windshield and roof. It was like the town was weeping because the nightmare was uncontrollable and seemed to be accelerating. Carver wasn't keeping the women as long, and he was kidnapping them more quickly. The escalation was scary and unpredictable, making it the most difficult and frustrating case Lizzie had ever worked on. Whenever she let her mind wander, she would constantly see the poor victims in vivid, terrible detail. She zipped into the parking garage and took the stairs to her floor. She entered the squad room and was immediately bombarded with questions on next steps.

"Listen up, everyone! First things first: Dubowski, Griff, Peer, Finnegan, and Santos, conference room, *now!*"

Her morning meeting with the task force was under way. Scott and Mark were absent because they were concentrating on another follow-up. Lizzie began with a review of the perp's profile and what was being done to locate the RV with the telltale sign of a lever on the door. So far, every RV was clean, so they had to get this into a more efficient search.

The day progressed, checking out RVs, and the list was being refined and many eliminated. Scott Rogers had returned to the squad room and approached Lizzie's desk with a megawatt grin.

"What?"

"Have dinner with me tonight."

"Dinner? Not a date? Or a dinner date?" Lizzie said with a smirk.

"Dinner date, a real date. Not a 'let's pretend it's not a date' . . . date," Scott was quick to retort.

"Sounds good to me. Where do you want to go?"

"I'll pick you up early evening, say around seven o'clock. I'll take care of the reservations."

"Where are we going so I know how to dress. Casual? Fancy? In between?"

"Fancy all the way," Scott said raising both eyebrows quickly up and down a couple of times. She burst out laughing, knowing what the gesture suggested.

Chapter 56

L izzie couldn't concentrate because all she could think about was another fantastic evening in Scott's arms. She left the office way earlier than usual, trying not to feel guilty. She felt nervous, anxious, and wired as hell. She decided to stop at Sweet Nothing's Lingerie Boutique and treated herself to a sexy garter belt, with black lace, little pink roses, and bows on it. *Naughty but nice!* Once she made it back to her apartment, she canvassed her closet. She was hoping that something would scream "wear me tonight" and be exactly what she wanted to wear. But every piece of clothing fell flat. *Too much work wear, not enough date wear.* She must have taken out ten outfits, throwing them in the reject pile which now nearly covered her queen-sized bed.

She finally decided on a black skirt that stopped midthigh. It seemed longer than it was because it had a wide band of lace on the bottom so her slim legs could still be seen through the lace. She paired it with a two-toned grey-striped jacket and a black camisole. She would wear black stockings with her Gucci patent leather four-inch heels. She had no idea what possessed her to spend a week's salary on those shoes, but soon after she got out of the hospital, she wanted to buy something really outrageous. A pair of four-inch Gucci stilettos on a girl "five feet, thirteen inches" fit the bill.

She piled her light blond hair on her head, taking a quick shower using her favorite jasmine rose shower gel. She wanted to smell extra nice for Scott. She dried off while checking the time. Seven o'clock. Right on schedule. She started putting on the black lacy bra and matching thong, her garter, and stockings when she heard the buzzing of her doorbell. She quickly threw on a robe and went to answer the door. It was Scott, thirty minutes early.

"I'm not ready yet! You're half an hour early! No fair."

"I couldn't wait any longer. I've been standing outside for about twenty minutes." He looked at her in the short robe, black stockings, and high heels. He swallowed hard and got a glint in his eye and a smile that meant trouble. He came closer to her and said, "I was always the kid at Christmas that couldn't wait to unwrap gifts. So what da ya say? Can I unwrap you now, before dinner?" He took the belt from her robe and started untying it.

She pulled him inside the room and shut the door, turning around and putting her back to the door. Mandy was doing her happy dance greeting Scott with a tail that wagged so hard it might have fallen off.

"I don't want to advertise to the neighbors. Let me finish getting dressed," she said glowing.

"Please, let me take a tiny peek. I'll be good, promise. How 'bout if I say I won't touch?" He opened up the robe and was speechless. She looked like a Victoria's Secret model; her athletic body was wrapped in black lace, thigh-high stockings, and the most provocative garter belt he'd ever seen. He swallowed loudly and gasped for air.

"You are a goddess," he whispered. He moved closer and reached out to cup both her breasts.

"No touching, remember?"

"Saying and doing are two different things. You can't expect me to go out and behave myself at dinner knowing what you're wearing under those clothes! Impossible and very cruel." He pulled her into his arms for a lengthy, passionate kiss.

Scott dropped his blazer to the floor, and Lizzie wrestled his cashmere turtle neck over his head. He pressed her up against the door and slipped off her bra, his big hands sensuously handling her full breasts, his lips kissing where his fingers had been.

He picked her up and carried her to the bedroom and closed the door, keeping Mandy outside the room. The not-good-enough-for-a-date clothing pile on the bed was quickly kicked to the floor. Scott placed her down, and it was his muscled body now hovering over hers. He expertly peeled off her stockings, kissing her long smooth legs along the way. He took off the thong with his teeth and again kissed up her body, taking his time teasing her, kissing her everywhere.

"Scott, please . . . Now . . . I want you so badly," Lizzie said, barely managing to exhale audibly.

He spread her legs apart and entered her part of the way. Lizzie was so wet, and Scott groaned at how turned on she was. With ease, he pushed in the rest of the way, both of them moaning with pleasure. Her long legs were fabulously athletic, grabbing around him around the waist with ease. The sex became faster and more rhythmic, and as he moved in and out of her, he looked over her beautiful body, noticing nipples as erect as nail heads. They were loving each other, and both never wanted it to end. The only thing keeping Lizzie in one piece was Scott's massive arms around her body, arching her back. Lizzie was breathing hard and let out a small series howls and then climaxed. Scott came shortly after. Entwined in each other's arms, the lovers let their breathing return to normal, looked into each other's eyes, and laughed.

"I think we both could use a shower before dinner. What do you say?" asked Scott, winking while he spoke.

"I'm too exhausted to make it the ten feet into the bathroom," Lizzie answered.

With that, Scott leapt out of bed and disposed of the used condom. *When did he have time for that?* He started the shower and then dashed back, swooped Lizzie into his arms, and carried her into the steaming bathroom. He put her hair up into a high ponytail and then started lathering her body under the spray. He lingered on certain areas, enjoying her pleasure as she came again. She started bathing him and got down on her knees, lingering in a few areas of her own. As the water started running cold, they took it as a sign to finish up.

She got two bath towels out of the closet, handing one to Scott. He put it around his waist, took the other towel, and started tenderly drying her with it. There was an unspoken comfort level, and neither was bashful about being naked in front of the other. Lizzie put on her barely worn bra and thong and snapped the garter belt in place.

"I heard that. I'm going in the other room because we'll never get to dinner if I see you in that outfit again. You're making me so crazy," Scott joked as he gave Lizzie a quick kiss, left the bedroom, and faced a very put-out doggie.

"Did we miss our dinner reservations?" Lizzie called out.

"No. I planned ahead. Our reservations are for 8:30 p.m., so we still have twenty-minutes. Want to? Just once more?" Scott said with a sly grin.

"After dinner. It will be the best dessert you have ever tasted," she said flashing open her robe to give him a glimpse of her sexy lingerie one more time.

Chapter 57

Mark Lewis and Dave Dubowski were in early that morning, another grey day, the rain letting up and only misting now. The list of RV owners was not as promising as they thought. "This sucks. None of these RV owners fit the profile. Let's start putting together the owners that we still need to check out," said Dubowski. "Good. I'll start on a schedule to efficiently locate them," offered Mark.

"So what's with the limp? You move all right with it, but I know it must hurt like a son of a bitch. Would have thought you'd have been DLed with that sucker a while ago. How come you're still on active duty?"

"You're not shy are you?"

"Nope, not a shy bone in my body. Ask Bowlyn. I'm always saying the wrong thing. Must be some kind of wiring problem, don't know when to shut the mouth. So what's with the leg?"

Mark proceeded to tell Dave the details of his undercover assignment dealing with a Russian mob child slavery operation. "We were really close to nailing them, but somehow our cover was blown and we got kinda *blown up with it*. I still carry around a lot of baggage. The limp is the least of it. So what's your story? How long have you been partnered with Lizzie?"

"Lizzie was assigned to partner with me two years ago when she came. Took a long while before she opened up. Never talked about Memphis, but I can tell somethin' bad went down. I'm just working to get my pension. Full retirement in two years. I just have one kid left in college, and then I'll be able to settle back and enjoy some fishing."

"How's your wife with a life of fishing?"

"She died from injuries from a car accident. She had a subdural hematoma. They didn't find out right away, and she slipped into a coma and never regained consciousness," Dave said as he bowed his head slightly.

"Sorry, man, I didn't know. I figured she was okay when I saw all the pictures on your desk . . . and you still wear a ring."

"Yeah. Keeps all the young hotties away," Dave said with a sad smile.

"It's been six years now. I still feel like she's with me, complaining about the way I leave my socks on the bathroom floor. My daughter just started her own business, a paint-your-own-pottery place. She has fun with kids' parties, a great way to use her art major. She enjoys every day, and she can make a decent living at it. I have my buddy at home, Buster. He keeps me company, gives me love without the nagging. The perfect roommate except when it's cold outside and I have to walk him in the middle of the night. He's a real brute, part basset hound and who knows what else. His legs are so short that he doesn't walk anymore, he waddles." At that, they had a quiet chuckle and went back to revising the RV list.

Chapter 58

Bart Jeffries and Christian Eriksen were sitting with Sully in the disorganized office, papers strewn over every surface, piles on the floor, three coffee mugs sitting on the side file cabinet. Bart's coffee was steaming, and for the moment, he enjoyed the wonderful aroma. Christian had an open bottle of Fiji water in his hand.

"There are some really good blueberry muffins out there. You should get some before Peter gets to them and they're all gone. What are you working on now?" Christian asked.

"Don't get too excited, but I'm trying to get a list of names from the past ten years that have registered vehicles in Durham, Charlotte, and Arcadia Lakes. I figure that our guy had to have a heavy-duty vehicle to pull this off, so he had to have it registered in both states, probably changed his address with DMV. On top of that, he's thought to be a local, knows too much about the area and blends in too well. I've gotten through to the Gs and found four people so far. It's taking a while to compare all the DMV records for same DOB and name against addresses. I thought that there would be one name and that would be our unsub, and I would have saved the day with my incredible computer genius yet again. But no, there are multiple people that have lived in both states. In Charlotte or Durham, North Carolina. I should have the entire list by this afternoon. What's up with you guys?" Sully asked.

Bart Jeffries thought carefully before he answered. "Something that Feldman said to keep a lid on. Need-to-know basis, it has to do with what went down with Rogers and Lewis, the Russians. Christian and I have determined that there are some viable leads on that kiddie slave ring, and Feldman doesn't want Rogers and Lewis to know about it until we have something solid. He has me, Christian, and Rafe working on a possible lead with an Internet site that auctions kids worldwide to the highest bidder while he is negotiating with some pedophile politician for information. I'll need your expertise with the computer later; right now, Feldman wants all resources on Carver unless something breaks on this child trafficking ring."

"When you get a list together, we'll fax it to Lewis, and then we'll hop on the jet and go to them. We're closing in on that creep, and I want to be there for the takedown. We'll need to get a plan of action together. I'll talk with Feldman, let him know where you're at and what resources we'll need when we land. Great work, Sully Boy." Christian said, taking a long drink from his bottled water.

Sully continued watching name after name flip up onto the computer screen, flashing by at lightening speeds, comparing one to another. While this information was running through his program, he decided that he would go out into the main area and see what there was to eat.

"Hey, Sammy. What's doing?" Sully asked.

"Working."

"Wow, we have that in common. What da' ya know? What do we have today to munch on?" Sully asked

"There are cranberry orange, blueberry, bran, and corn muffins. I'm sure that you can find something to tickle your fancy."

"Of course, I'm Mr. Easygoing when it comes to food. You know I'll eat anything—well, anything except liver. No liver," he made a funny face and gave a mock shudder of his shoulders in disgust.

"Sully, Mark is on line 3, pick up please," Sammy said.

"Hey, Mark. Sully here."

"How's the search going? I was hoping for an update. Any progress naming someone who was in Charlotte and/or Durham from Arcadia Lakes during the murders? Wondering if you might do a cross check," said Mark.

"Way ahead of ya, boss. I've got at least four names that are crossovers, and I'm less than half way through the alphabet. I should have the complete list in about an hour. That should narrow down the suspect pool to about ten or so names," Sully said.

"Only in America. We have the most serial killers of anywhere else in the world . . . , hidden monsters living next door. It's like a freakin' epidemic. What happens in this great country that breeds this shit? Someone should figure out how to stop it," commented Mike Freeman who came up behind Sully and could overhear part of the phone conversation.

After about an hour, Sully came into the main room. "Are you guys sitting down? The list is finished and one name is registered in all three places! *We've got him!*" Sully yelled triumphantly.

Chapter 59

"I need the cross," said Diane Benson. "I've connected with him before, and I need to connect again. He's close to finding another victim, and I want him caught. I don't want another family to lose everything and mourn the way I did. He needs to be stopped. I need to stop him. Please, let me help!" she pleaded.

Rob and Paul looked at each other. Then Rob spoke. "All right, it can't hurt."

"Gee . . . Thanks. Your vote of confidence is underwhelming," Diane said with a combination of hurt and sarcasm.

"What do you want me to say? This isn't routine police work. I'm not the only one having problems with this. It's like hocus-pocus. I'm doing my best here to believe. Show me something to make me shut up and stop giving you a hard time," Rob said.

Paul just looked at her and saw the tears she was holding back. He just wanted to put his arms around her and tell her it would be all right. Not what he should be doing, so he didn't. He would try to comfort her at dinner tonight. Maybe that would lead to something more.

"Hey, Paul, over here," Rob said waving his hand over Rob's face to get his attention.

"Yep. Let's get started already. Keep things moving, or you'll lose me again. ADD isn't just for kids."

"Okay. Just give me a few minutes of your undivided attention, and I know you'll be convinced." With that, Diane took a deep breath.

"I've been in his head before. He sees what he is doing as fighting the worst kind of sin. He's got a thing for adultery, and he's the one who has to stop it. He thinks that God has spoken to him. Not the forgiving New Testament God. This is the Old Testament God of fire and damnation, the vengeful god. He sees this as a way for them to atone for their sins, by facing the fires of hell. If God chooses, they will be able to walk through the fires of hell into the halls of heaven. If they burn, they've earned their way into heaven through the Servant's intervention. He is constantly talking to God while he is setting the fire. I believe the Servant blesses the victims as he sets the fire, hence the cross. He must first identify the 'sinners' and then watch them for several days until it is time for their salvation. Plus, he gets off on watching the fire, how it dances and calls to him."

Rob and Paul just looked at each other in amazement. She was citing facts that had not been released. Diane continued.

"The day before, the Servant usually checks out the house posing as some type of service man, utility, cable, plumber . . . someone who won't arouse suspicion. But he's way smarter than any of those guys. In my visions, I see him breaking into the basement to enter the house, disabling the alarm system, and carefully setting the scene. He soaks a pillowcase and the pillow with chloroform that will put them into a deep sleep. He uses whatever is in the person's home—newspapers, magazines, old rags caked in a gel accelerant—and hides them under the bed, behind the drapes, in the back of the closet."

Again, no one knew about the pillowcases or the rags. They didn't know about the hand-carved cross, nor did they know about entering in through the basement. *This girl is for real . . . A psychic.*

"Since he is an ordained minister—although through the Internet—the Servant feels he has God's official approval," Diane said.

"Unfortunately, anyone can get ordained over the Internet. That won't narrow down the suspect field," Paul interjected.

"He needs to leave his calling card, something to show that he was there so that you will know that it was him, that he was there to do his good deed, that he has saved more souls. If you give me the latest cross, I'll try to connect with him again. I'm not sure what will happen. I may connect with him or I may connect with the victim. It's a crap shoot. I'll do my best to help."

Rob opened up the evidence bag and handed the cross to Diane. Paul noticed a slight tremble to her hand as she was about to receive it.

"Whatever you see, whatever I say, whatever you think is happening, you can't touch me, or I'll lose the connection. It may look like I'm in pain, I'm not really. I think I'm feeling what the victim is . . . and I'll be fine. Remember, don't touch me." Diane looked into their eyes and saw their heads bobbing up and down in agreement.

Diane took another deep breath and cleared her mind and shook her head, movements in preparation for the connection. She gently rubbed her fingers over the charred cross, blackening her fingers while noting its rough groves and outline. Paul and Rob were mesmerized. Diane looked like she was having a conversation with herself. Finally, she closed her eyes, but instantly, they opened again. *Creepy.*

Chapter 60

The squad room was buzzing with activity, and everyone was working at top speed: looking over VICAP sheets, checking computer data, talking on the phone. Lizzie entered the room walking with newfound confidence and purpose.

"Morning, people! Ready to nail that SOB CARVER today?" she called out for all ears to hear.

A chorus of cheers rang out. "Yes! You bet Detective Bowlyn! Today's the day!"

"I want to get the RV lists taken care of today. The names are clustered alphabetically into four groups of fourteen each. Since those listed in the first group are mostly located on the outskirts of town, Dubowski and I will handle those. Everyone else should be able to breeze through the rest. But be cautious: this psycho is really smart and really dangerous and has eluded the police for a while. Santos, you and Griff take the next group of names, and Peer, you and Mike Freeman take the next fourteen. I'll get Peter Frank and Chris Medina from VICE to take the last set. I want Mark Lewis and Scott Rogers to stay here and work point, coordinating information coming in from the field and to keep the FBI lines open in case Sully and his magic computer come up with anything else. People, I'm instituting a mandatory report-in every forty-five minutes with an update. This way, command will have the most current information. LET'S MOVE!"

Over the cacophony of voices, Lizzie gave a yell and hand motion to Dubowski. She was anxious to leave and start on their portion of the list. Lizzie didn't like going out into the field except to examine a crime scene. This was an exception. It seemed best to keep Mark at the home office so he could act on an update from Sully.

Throughout the morning, the officers in the field checked-in as commanded by Detective Bowlyn. So far, they did not have one suspect. As the afternoon approached, Santos, Griff, Freeman, and Peer returned to the squad room having completed checking the names on their lists. Frank, Medina, Bowlyn, and Dubowski were still out interviewing RV owners.

Mark's cell rang, and he answered, "Lewis."

"Sully here, boss. Got some good news for a change. Bart is faxing you a list of names with only one registered in all three places. We're gassing up the plane, and we'll see you within two hours."

"Guys, we've got a name of somebody who owns an RV registered in Arcadia, Charlotte, and Durham!" Lewis yelled into the air. "Wait 'til Lizzie hears this!"

The cheers got louder as the fax machine beeped and slowly churned out the list. There it was, on the last page, the name Travis Johnson. Arcadia Lakes address. RV owner, who had lived in Charlotte and Durham within the past five years. Twenty-nine years old, unmarried, currently living with his mom. *Bingo*.

"Let's see if we can't set up a meeting at the Arcadia Lakes Sheriff's Office with Mr. Travis Johnson. Rogers, call Lizzie and Dubowski right away so we can get them over to the office to question this guy. They're still out following up RV leads," Lewis said.

As ordered, Scott Rogers called Lizzie's cell phone, but it went straight to voice mail. He tries Dubowski's next with the same result. He leaves a message to meet at the sheriff's office. The rest of the task force is already in Arcadia Lakes.

The drive over was filled with anxiety and stress. The crew was tense, like strings on a violin. They waited a long time for this moment, wanted this guy badly, and they wanted to get the girls to safety. Once they arrived, Lewis took control and was very professional. He briefed the sheriff and a couple of his deputies about the information and matching profile of Travis Johnson. The sheriff wanted to be part of the questioning process, but Lewis made it clear that this was an FBI interrogation and not his show. The sheriff understood, and they all headed to the Johnson house.

As they pulled up to the house, the first thing they saw was a Ford flatbed F150, a perfect truck for hauling an RV. Travis Johnson was outside, cutting his lawn, wearing a black Rolling Stones T-shirt soaked with sweat. Grass-stained painter's paints hung loosely on his tall thin frame. He had the right build to be Carver, but facially, it was hard to tell. In every video scene, Carver's head was covered with a mask. When Johnson noticed the police cars, he spooked and took off toward the house.

"Travis Johnson, freeze! FBI!" Rogers yelled as he was leaping from his car, sprinting after the fleeing suspect. Johnson ran up the large front porch stairs, knocking over a flowerpot on his way up. He got to the front door, stopped, and put his hands in the air.

"I didn't do nothin' wrong! Don't shoot!" Johnson shouted with surrender.

"Why did you run, Johnson, if you didn't do nothin' wrong?"

"You wigged me out with all these cars flashin' and comin' up on to my lawn like that. What da ya want?"

"You need to come with us and answer some questions. Let's go!" Then he read Johnson his Miranda rights, keeping with protocol. Johnson did not resist when he was frisked and cuffed but complained that they were rough when Rogers shoved his head down and practically threw the rest of his body into the back of the sheriff's vehicle. Griff and Santos went around back looking for the RV. It was nowhere to be seen.

Mark Lewis and his men went back to the sheriff's office where the sheriff had Johnson detained in an interrogation room. Lewis was pleased that the room was well-equipped with a large two-way mirror. Rogers was looking through the glass at Johnson, sitting, looking around the room, nervously twitching. Taking his cell phone out of his pocket, he tried Lizzie again. Still, no answer. He was getting a queasy feeling in his stomach but pushed it aside so he could get into interrogation mode.

Scott Rogers began the questioning, and poor Travis Johnson was scared out of his mind, confused, and sweating profusely.

"Are you arresting me?"

"Do we need to arrest you?" Rogers prompted.

"No! I didn't do nothin' . . . like I already told you!"

"You keep saying that. We'll let you know if you did something. Where were you at six o'clock last Wednesday morning?" Rogers asked.

"Home. Sleepin' in bed. I don't git up 'til around seven o'clock. I gotta be at work by eight. Ask my boss. I was at work by eight on Wednesday mornin'. Why do you want to know that? Wait a minute . . . That's when that girl, Sadie Mae was kidnapped! Yeah, last Wednesday. Me? You think I'm the one raping and killing those girls? You got the wrong guy, mister!"

Rogers and Lewis heard a knock on the glass and left the room for a moment.

"Travis's mother gave us permission to search his room. He's got a lot of porn magazines and videos with bondage and submission. We also checked his computer, and he has all the Carver videos saved to his desktop. We haven't found the raw feeds, but he's got the edited versions. I think he's our guy."

Chapter 61

Lizzie rolled down the window and let the breeze blow back her long yellow hair as they drove east on Route 12 toward Arcadia Lakes. They were passing two- and three-story Victorian houses that were spread out along the road, just as they had been for the past hundred years. So much had changed around them, yet so much had stayed the same. Dubowski asked her if she had any plans for the evening, with a double raise of his eyebrows and a wink. Lizzie turned pink, shrugged her shoulders, and mentioned something about sexual harassment. He quickly started whistling.

"We've got fourteen names on this list that we've got to check out. Where do you want to start?" said Dubowski, quickly changing the subject.

"Let's go alphabetically and then whoever lives closest. Who's up first?"

"Larry Alcott."

Larry Alcott worked as a plumber in the area, grew up in Arcadia Lakes, and went to college for a year in Charlotte before dropping out. He trained to be a plumber with his cousin in Atlanta before returning to Arcadia Lakes to open his own business. He was a bit of a loner and didn't really date any women. They pulled up to his modest two-story colonial, noticing the RV was parked around the side of the garage. They pulled up in front of the house by the pale blue mailbox with a big number 46 stenciled on it. Dubowski got out of the car and went directly over to the RV, looking in the windows, glancing around. He knew instantly that this was not the right trailer.

After he heard the doorbell, a slight man of about thirty came to the door, dressed in a faded plaid short-sleeved shirt and stained blue jeans. Alcott's tousled hair suggested that they woke him up from a nap, or else he had a late night.

"Howdy. May I help you folks with sumthin'?" he said in his very heavy Southern accent.

"Mr. Alcott, I'm Detective Bowlyn, and this is Detective Dubowski from the SLED, and we were wondering if we could have a few words with you."

"I know who you are, Ms. Lizzie. Detective, please come in. It's a bit of a mess. I'm not a real good housekeeper," Alcott said with a drawl.

They stepped into the sparsely decorated living room filled with take-out containers, newspapers, and few empty fifths of Jack Daniel's. Alcott tried to move the mess around so his company could sit on the sofa.

Lizzie and Dubowski questioned Larry Alcott about where he was on the days they had discovered the bodies. He had been working on plumbing jobs around Arcadia and willingly offered the names of those whose houses he had serviced.

"Listen, Mr. Alcott. We're sorry to have bothered you. We'll check out your information and let you know if we need anything else," said Dubowski.

"No problem, detective sir. If you and Ms. Lizzie want to come back, just give me a little warnin' so's I can tidy up a bit."

That pattern repeated itself for the next four names on the list. Each proved a dead end due to credible alibis and RVs set in plain view. This was taking longer than Lizzie had thought, and she was wondering how Peer, Santos, and the others were making out. She had checked in twice, the last time about an hour and a half or so ago, but cell coverage was spotty, and it made her nervous when she didn't communicate with the team. After interviewing the next name on the list, Lizzie would find a way to update Mark and learn what information he had as well. The detectives came to the sixth name on the list, Timothy Ray Dutton. He lived with his grandmother, Sylvia Dutton on Dutton Dairy Farm. It used to be a thriving dairy farm, but when the grandfather died about four years back, she was not able to keep up with the work, so the business died out. Grandma Dutton now had just a couple of cows, a pig, and some chickens.

Dubowski drove up the long driveway and spotted the barn first and then the large farm house behind it. Victorian in nature, the house had gingerbread trim with many contrasting pretty colors, making the house seem cheerful and welcoming. This was the opposite feeling they got when they approached the house.

"What do you want?" said a stern older woman sitting on the front porch in a creaky rattan and wood rocker.

"Looks like she might pull out a .22 rifle any second," Dubowski uttered under his breath.

Grandma Dutton was a plump old lady with a tight scowl on her face that seemed to say, "You look like you're trespassin', so git to gittin'! A bright yellow house coat draped her larger frame, and what a surprise, her hair was up in pink curlers. Maybe getting ready for a wild night of bingo. Wire-rimmed glasses completed the stereotype and were perched at the end of her nose in front of cold blue eyes filled with malice. The old woman spoke first.

"My grandson is a good boy, so whatever you're looking for, you're not gonna find it here."

"Mrs. Dutton, this is Detective Dubowski, and I am Senior Detective Bowlyn, and we just have a few questions regarding an RV that is registered to this address. Is there a Timothy Dutton living here? We'd like to speak with him about his RV, that's all."

"Timmy Ray is out somewhere on the property. He stays in that trailer sometimes 'cause he's grown and needs time alone. The boy ain't too thrilled about livin' at home with granny, but he's a good boy, helpin' me keep up with the animals. What do you want him for anyways?"

"Just some routine questions we've been asking people who have trailers in this area," Dubowski said.

"Well, good luck findin' Timmy Ray. He's here somewhere, maybe over the ridge." Mrs. Dutton pointed a crooked finger in the direction, wishing they would just leave and never come back.

"Much obliged, Mrs. Dutton. We appreciate your time," Dubowski said.

Chapter 62

Lewis and Rogers walked back into the interrogation room and started in on Johnson again.

"So, Mr. Slicer . . . Chopper . . . Or was it *Mr. Carver?* Want to talk about the Sally Anne, Sarah, Susan Starks, and—oh, let's see—how about the pretty Sadie Mae? You got a thing for blonds with names that start with an *s*?" said Rogers flippantly.

"Are you shittin' me? You think I'm that Carver psycho? You really think I could do that eff'd up shit to another human being?"

"Well . . . hmmm . . . You just happen to have all his videos on your computer desktop. You also have quite an extensive collection of bondage pornography in your room and bookmarked on your Internet browser, and you have numerous books on forensics, serial killers, and all the seasons of CSI on DVD. Sounds a little eff'd up to me," said Lewis.

"You guys are wasting your time! A bunch of dumbasses with a badge . . . I can prove you're wrong, and you don't even have to check a single alibi!" With that, Travis Johnson whipped off his shirt, turned around, and said, "See my back. Take a good look!. No tats!" he spit as he screamed. "Your killer's back is loaded with tattoos. I may be sick, twisted, perverted, depraved, and whatever else you want to put in front of 'sexual fantasies,' but that's all they are: sexual *fantasies*. I would never actually do that shit! That's the job of a sick bastard."

"The guy has a point, boss. Plato said it best: 'the virtuous man is content to dream what the wicked man really does.' In this case, the virtuous man is a creep. Nevertheless, I say we let him go," said Rogers.

Chapter 63

Carver had been so excited about finishing his latest video that he had left Susan Starks's mutilated body on the performance table in one room of the trailer, and the lovely Sadie Mae ready and waiting in the smaller room. He was anxious to go and edit the footage. Once he was satisfied with the final version, he grabbed his laptop and tried to determine the best place to get an Internet connection. *His next masterpiece was ready for distribution.* He ended up at Sweet Treats, a tiny bakery on the outskirts of Columbia with just a couple of small tables and no one in the shop. Carver loaded the video and sent off an e-mail to his boy, Seth Roberts, over at *The State* newspaper so that this video would start getting hits. He was amazed and proud at how popular his work had become and how many people were enjoying it. *Clearly, better than anything on YouTube!*

With all that done hours ago, Carver needed to clean up and dump what was left of Susan Starks's body. He would place it somewhere special that would confuse the stupid cops even more. This time, he planned on leaving her at Arcadia High School's Giambrone Baseball Field. *Right at home plate. Like another home run. Get it?* He was parking his Silverado by the farm's ridge area, the opposite side of where the trailer was stationed. Finally, he arranged the wood in the back of his truck, laid out the tarps, and was ready to transfer Susan's body to the flatbed. He was behind his trailer when he heard a voice cursing in the woods.

"Jesus Christ! Who wants to live out here in the boonies? Shoulda worn sneakers. Aahhh! Hope I don't have a freak'n heart attack," Dubowski grunted.

Who the hell would be out here in the woods on his property? He crouched down and peeked around the back of the trailer. He recognized the detective from the TV and newspapers. "Shit! It's that old cop, the partner of the blond detective. *He's going to ruin everything! How could he have possibly found me?*"

Dubowski saw the trailer by itself out in the middle of nowhere and no truck to haul it around. *Suspicious*. He stumbled and cursed a few more times, clearly expressing how much he hates the woods and worried that, at the very least, he'll get poison ivy. For the first time, Dubowski gets an uneasy feeling, unsnaps his gun holster, and pounds on the trailer door. He thought he heard something, but he wasn't sure, so he tried the handle. Locked. He went around to one of the windows by the door and looked in but wasn't able to see anything through the dark curtains. He banged again, put his hear to the metal siding, and swore he heard a muffled cry for help.

"Hold on! I'll get you out! Just hold on!" Dubowski yells.

Afraid that using his gun will cause a bullet to ricochet unsafely, Dubowski spots a rock to break open the door. As he bends over, he feels a hand slap his forehead and pull it back. Warm liquid started flowing down his chest. Dubowski fell to the ground, clutching his neck, unable to say a word. He lay there for about a minute, convulsing as he was bleeding profusely next to the trailer.

Timothy Dutton had gotten rid of that idiot although it was a very anticlimatic and just a bit too easy. He would have thought the cop would have more fight in him. *Very disappointing*. He knew the blond must be close by and was getting excited for a good fight with her. *Hmmm . . . What to do now?* Dutton had two bodies to dispose of, so he quickly cleaned up any evidence that he might have left on Dubowski. *Such a pro!* He looked around for the blond, who couldn't be far behind. She had to be missing that fat bastard by now. Clearly, the cops were onto him. He must escape and start over somewhere else. He had the trailer ready to leave at a moment's notice. *He just has to get rid of the bodies*. He hastily covered Dubowski with debris from his truck and then started to dig out an area to hide the bodies, just long enough for him to get away.

Chapter 64

Lizzie leaves Mrs. Dutton rocking contentedly on the front porch. She speed-dials Dubowski. No signal. *Shit!* She tries Rogers next. No signal. *Damn it!* Lizzie walks toward the ridge where Dubowski headed about twenty minutes earlier. This blond detective's instincts were kicking in. She thought something felt off, so she started reaching for her Glock.

Timothy Ray Dutton just finished digging a shallow grave to conceal the gruesome remains of Susan Starks and Detective Dubowski. He hears the lady cop yelling for her partner. Dutton hides around the back of the trailer to wait for her to investigate it, the way her dumb dead partner did. He finds a dirty rag and bungee cord by the trailer and stuffs them into his pocket. He picks up a gnarly piece of wood, a decent size so he can swing it like a baseball bat, a homerun, out of the park.

He sees Lizzie and delights in her striking good looks. He couldn't resist. Another leading lady has just walked into his life, and he couldn't pass up the opportunity. *She will be the perfect end to my Arcadia Lakes productions. I've got a nice performance table all ready for you, cop lady!* Dutton is in position to strike; his breathing increases, his heart pounding . . . and a growing erection.

Lizzie had her Glock out and carefully approached the RV. *Too quiet*, she thinks, then notices what looks like a loafer sticking out from under a pile of wood to the right of the trailer. *A present from his daughter. Too expensive for him to buy. He wore them every day.* She hurried over to the wood pile and started clearing away the debris. She quickly and shockingly uncovered Dave Dubowski. She saw so much blood on his shirt, she started shaking and saying softly, "No, no, no! Not you, Dubowski."

Something struck Lizzie, hitting her hard in the shoulder and knocking her down, her gun flying somewhere to the left. She tried to turn around and block the next assault with her right arm, but Dutton hit her hand, breaking bones. Someone was trying to kill her, beat her to death. *Not again, not another son of a bitch. Not this time. Especially not from you, you psycho bastard!* Lizzie wasn't going to let this asshole kill her. Her adrenaline surged just as Timothy Ray dropped the stick and grabbed her from behind. She kicked back, missing his groin but slamming his knee. He yelled in pain like a little girl and let her go. He started kicking her in the ribs with his left leg, his right one throbbing. Lizzie rolled over with the wind knocked out of her, trying to claw at anything that could be used as a weapon since her gun was out of sight. She was too slow, so Dutton was able to land a solid punch to the back of the head, knocking her out. Dutton quickly shoved the rag into her mouth and tied it and then wrapped the bungee cord around her wrists, securing them. "Let's go, miss detective. We've got a movie to make!" Dutton spewed victoriously.

Now, there was more work to do. Timothy Ray took Susan Starks's body from the trailer and dragged it over to the spot where he left Dubowski and arranged the two bodies accordingly for the best camouflage. He then picked up and carried Lizzie to the trailer and strapped her to the table. "I just know you'll enjoy this as much as I will, blondie," he said in a low growl. Dutton went into the other room and regagged Sadie Mae. *Got to tie up a few loose ends before the fun can start.* He crossed over to the other side of the ridge to get his truck and hooked up the trailer so it was ready to roll. Timothy Ray came up the gravel driveway and saw granny sitting in her rocking chair and sipping sweet tea.

"Two police come by. Went lookin' fer ya. One was a lady cop. I said you was probably stayin' in your trailer. Did you see them?"

"No, Grams. Must have just missed them. What'd they want anyway?"

"Just checkin' all RV owners. Said they was lookin' for one that might be involved with a crime, so they was just checkin' all registered ones so they could go crossin' them off the list. I hate them damn cops."

"Well, they can cross me off the list. I'm gonna go campin' this weekend, Grams. I'll just get my stuff together and head out for a couple of days. Don't worry, I'll be back real soon."

"Have fun! Gist feed the animals before ya go," she said.

"Yep, will do," he said as he went into the house to gather his belongings. He grabbed his computer from his bedroom, along with his clothing and his keepsakes from the other girls. He had quite a collection of small trinkets in a lockbox that was hidden in the floorboards of his closet. He loaded everything into his truck and drove out as fast as possible without raising suspicion. *He did not take the time to feed the animals. He wondered how long it would take dear old granny to figure out that he was never coming back. He smiled at the thought.*

Chapter 65

M ark Lewis and Scott Rogers were back in Columbia, sitting in their makeshift office, looking out the windowed wall. They really thought they had found their serial killer. But no, he was still on the loose. They meticulously scrutinized all the lists again. Oftentimes, police work wasn't like the *Law & Order* type you would see on TV, where the police have fantastic leads that they follow up with and get the bad guy in some exciting takedown. More often than not, it's the boring administrative work that uncovers the missing piece. It's the little details that catch the criminals.

Scott's concern was mounting as he checked his Blackberry for the tenth time, now getting ready to throw it against the wall. "Why haven't we heard squat from Lizzie or Dubowski? She's the one who made it very clear to check in every forty-five minutes, and it's been over three hours now since they checked in," he said, clearly upset and worried.

Mark went over to the desk sergeant, "Sergeant, can you tell me the location of Detective Bowlyn and Dubowski and when they last checked in?"

"That would be at the Dutton Dairy Farm, sir, at around 11:30 a.m. Nothing since then."

"Okay, thanks. Please notify me immediately should they call in," Lewis ordered.

"Look at this, Mark," said Scott as he held out Sully's list and Lizzie's. Scott ran his finger down each name until he stopped at the fifth one, Timothy Ray Dutton, which appeared both on Lizzie's list of interviews and on the one Sully had faxed to them.

"Notify the desk sergeant! We're out'a here now!" Mark said, making sure his gun was in its holster. "Griff, Peer, we've got to get to the Dutton Farm, five minutes ago. Bowlyn isn't answering her phone, and neither is Dubowski. And we've got another possible suspect. Let's go!" Griff had a worried look on his rugged face, his brown eyes turning serious, "Shit, Dave's cell is going to voice mail too. Not a good sign."

"Call the local police and tell them to proceed with caution!" Lewis yelled to the desk sergeant.

They made their way to their SUVs as quickly as possible, Lewis's limp barely noticeable. Rogers was driving like a maniac. *If that SOB has done anything my Lizzie*, he thought, and pressed the gas pedal nearly to the floor, reaching over a hundred in the Tahoe.

They descended onto the Dutton Farm like a black cloud. At first, they couldn't believe the Victorian was the right house. So pretty, so welcoming. What deception. Three local police cars were parked with lights flashing. The two black SUVs pulled up, adding to the serious mix of police vehicles filling up the front yard. Mrs. Dutton was not helpful, continuing to claim she had a "good boy" and said that the two other officers were out in the woods searching for who knew what.

"Where's your grandson, Mrs. Dutton?" Lewis asked.

"What do you want with him? He's a good boy, never did nothin' to no one," she answered back.

"We need to ask him some questions." Rogers said.

"I don't want you on my property anymore! Git lost, you're not welcome here!"

"Sorry, ma'am, but that's not possible until we find the other officers who seem to be unaccounted for right now. We'll find them, and then we'll talk about what kind of questions we have for your grandson."

With that, she made a disgusted kind of a snort, a rather phlegm sound, and got up out of the rocking chair and walked into her house. They thought she may have given them the finger but weren't sure. In any case, she refused to answer any more questions. She didn't want to see Timothy end up in trouble like his father.

The eight of them started to spread out and look for Bowlyn and Dubowski. Lewis stayed with the vehicles to watchdog the house and surrounding area. The others divided up the four walkie-talkies; Rogers was paired up with one of the Arcadia Lakes sheriff's deputies, Charlie Daly. Scott was in charge, motioning for them to spread out in different directions: Griff and Peer headed north; two state troopers, Chris Medina and Rodney Watson, headed east; the sheriff and his deputy, Ryan Peters, went south; and Rogers and Daly went west. They fanned out with guns drawn, highly alert and carefully searching for anything that would tell them what went down at the farm. They continued called for the missing officers and got no response.

Scott Rogers and Charlie Daly continued west for about an hour, moving slowly and fanning out to make sure that they covered the entire area until they came to an area that had indents and tire marks made by one or more large vehicles. They also noticed a pile of new lumber that seemed out of place in the woods. Rogers and Daly started moving some of the debris around and found the shallow grave. Both bent down and started digging, knowing what they would find, Scott Rogers with tears forming in his eyes as he dug. *Please, God, no, he prayed.* They unearthed a male's shoe and beneath it a cold naked female's foot, no pedal pulse. Scott fell to his knees, not wanting to believe that it was Lizzie. He knew he could not touch the bodies because he might disrupt forensic evidence, yet he was desperate to know for sure if it was Lizzie. As hard as it was, Scott wiped his eyes and told Daly to call it in to the others and Lewis.

Deputy Daly relayed the details of what they had found. Lewis called CSU and the ME to come out immediately. The troopers, the sheriff, and the rest started toward the area where Rogers and Daly found the dead bodies, making it to the scene in about twenty-five minutes. The sheriff sent Ryan Peters back to where Lewis was stationed so that he could lead investigators and medical personnel to the scene quickly.

Mark called back to his offices, "Sammy, who's there right now?"

"Peter, Bart, Sully, Mikey, Christian, and Bryan. Why, what's going on, you sound upset."

"We found the unsub. His name is Timothy Ray Dutton. Get Sully to put out an APB on his vehicles and try to figure out a way we can track him. He still has at least one hostage, maybe two that we know of. Let me speak to Bryan."

"Feldman."

"It's me, Mark. The shit has hit the fan here big time. We've finally got a name, Timothy Dutton, looks like he might have killed the two detectives that came out to question him. One might be my cousin. I want this guy so bad I can taste it. What can you do on your end?"

"I'll get the team together, brief them, then we'll fly right down. I'll put Sully to work on possible locations the unsub might try to flee to, and we can send a search helicopter. How much lead time does the unsub have?"

"About two hours," said Mark.

"How's Rogers taking this? You mentioned earlier today that he and your cousin were getting involved."

"Don't know. He's at the scene waiting on forensics, and I'm staying at the house with one of the sheriff's deputies, waiting for the troops to arrive. From what Ryan Peters said, he's not doing well."

"We'll be there in about five hours. Call me back if anything changes, or you get new intel; otherwise, I'll call you when we land on Columbia. When you can, check on Rogers. And hey, Lewis, real sorry about your cousin."

"Thanks, sir."

Mark let it sink in that Lizzie might be dead. He hung his head and let out a long breath. Sirens were in the distance. The circus was about to start. Emergency vehicles started appearing on the farm like locusts, and Mrs. Dutton refused to cooperate. No surprise. Mark already had Santos working on search warrants for the farmhouse and the rest of the property.

Emergency personnel made their way out to the crime scene, and they started the dirty chore of digging up the shallow grave. As the earth was moved, the body of Dubowski was visible through the shifting leaves and debris. Below him was the destroyed body of a tall naked blond, visible through his legs and lying facedown in the grave. After numerous photographs, they managed to lift Dubowski off the girl, placing him in a body bag. Next, the female body was finally turned over, and Scott saw her bruised and distorted face. He was nearly ecstatic, producing a huge sigh of relief. A few CSU techs looked at him like he was losing it.

"It's not her! It isn't Lizzie! She's still alive! She has to be alive . . . where the fuck has that bastard taken my Lizzie?" Scott said to himself in an inaudible whisper. They had found Susan Starks, the third victim. As they moved her body, Scott felt like the crushing weight of a Mac truck was slowly lifting off his chest. They exposed the rest of her body, preserving what evidence they could, and placed her in a large black body bag. Everyone was quiet and respectful. They lost one of their own, and poor Susan Starks had finally found peace.

Mark made his way over to Rogers to update him on what he told Bryan Feldman. The two men bear-hugged, relieved that there was still hope that Lizzie was alive. They left the forensic team to continue collecting evidence and securing the murder scene. The SLED officers along with Rogers and Lewis headed back to Columbia to figure out what the next step could possibly be to catch Dutton before he did anything to Lizzie.

Chapter 66

Diane was now deeply entranced. The first thing she noticed was the thick cigarette smoke twisting and curling, rising into the air, and engulfing the bar and the people inside. She spoke softly, uttering descriptions about what was around her. Diane could not hear if Paul or Rob were speaking to her; she was totally absorbed in her vision now. Paul started the digital recorder. They wanted this all on tape.

"He's in a bar, dark, dingy, no young people. Older people. Thirties. Forties. Has a strong sense of purpose. Watching over his flock. Keeping them from being led astray by evil," Diane revealed.

She could feel his emotions, see what he saw, hear what he heard, think what he was thinking as if it were her own thoughts. It was scary how deep the connection could go.

"He's waiting. He knows his victim. That slut will be here. She'll lure a man with her low-cut blouse, perfume, short skirt, makeup. They'll sin together. Disgusting. He's scanning the room, the door, the bar, the bathroom entrance . . . Not here yet, but soon. Patience," Diane said and then remained silent for a couple of minutes with her eyes tightly shut.

Rob and Paul listened to the stream of consciousness that was coming out of Diane's mouth, amazed and wary at the same time. She was talking softly, not really in a conversation, just telling what she was seeing or what he was thinking.

Diane took another deep breath, as if meditating, and her eyes were still closed. Then she started speaking again. "Only through death can they be cleansed. Only he can help them enter the kingdom of heaven. A humble servant of the lord . . . Those two, on the dance floor, rubbing, rubbing their genitals together, almost having sex, in public . . . Shameful . . . All the drinking, the flirting, the sex . . . Evil everywhere . . ." And Diane put one hand to her face to shield her eyes from the horrible sights the Servant saw, the other hand gripping the burnt cross so tightly her knuckles turned white.

"Two weeks of watching . . . She will be here tonight. A woman approaches . . . short skirt. Not her. The waitress . . . bends over . . . Get your breasts out of my face . . . No, thank you . . . No more to drink. Take this . . . a wink . . . twenty-dollar tip . . . She likes him, wants him . . . After midnight when she's free . . . A smile and wink . . . Walks away . . . The Devil is tempting him. No, won't give in to that jezebel, that tormentor . . . Better than these people. Eyes to the bar's entrance—*she's here*," Diane said and then stopped talking and seemed to gasp for air.

Diane continued streaming his thoughts. Paul glanced at his watch; it was eleven o'clock before she finally said, "They're leaving . . . Following them . . . White Honda Civic . . ." The connection was about to break, but Diane held on a few more moments, desperate to get the license plate number and know where he was going. It was too dark, so she could only see the last three numbers: one, six, three.

Diane's face was flushed, and both Rob and Paul were worried that she might pass out. "Don't touch her, Paul!" said Rob. "We need this information and remember what she said."

"She just looks like she might faint, and I don't want her to get hurt," said Paul.

Diane continued her diatribe, describing how the Servant drove off toward the woman's house, and he didn't have to trail too closely since he knew where "they" were going. Diane needed an address and tried to pull one from his mind but couldn't. She was looking for street signs but couldn't see any. Rob and Paul could tell Diane was struggling, but they just had to watch in silence.

"Statues of Hindu gods and goddesses . . . An elephant, many jewels, many arms not representing the lord. Just decorations . . . Look at the Shiva and Kali statues . . . *and another showing fornication! Such blasphemy!* But the lord wants her to be saved anyway." Diane's tone suddenly shifted. She was now describing what she noticed. "I see homes spread apart, far back from the street. The Servant is slowing down, parked in front of a house . . . Lights are on and two cars in driveway. I see numbers—two, four, three . . . Two hundred forty-three . . . Need to see name of street. What is the name of the street? He's still outside . . . Show me the name of the street. Show me the name please!" she begged, trying to look through his eyes for a signpost.

"Can't see where he is now . . . By the basement window. Same pattern. Go inside through basement, listen until no noise," Diane uttered.

She gave so many details. He actually stops to sniff the daffodils. *Freak. It's dark, and daffodils haven't got any scent.* As he goes around the back, he opens up the gate to enter the large backyard. He walks by the deck and sees the table and chairs, a built-in grill, and a pool. He enters the basement through the window that he broke earlier today.

"More waiting . . . hate this. Those two going at it, touching, naked, noises of sex, groaning, moaning, laughing. His blue thin rubber gloves go on. Lights are off . . . More sinning sounds upstairs. Sits on the stairs. Patience . . . waiting do the lord's work." Diane is desperately searching for an image that will give a location. She must find a location now, or these two innocent people will be set on fire and murdered. She can't let that happen. Walking through the kitchen . . . to front hall . . . pass the piano . . . pictures on the back of the piano . . . Diane tries to focus on the pictures. She sees the same face in picture after picture, a beautiful Indian woman, the most stunning face she has ever seen. She's seen that face before, but where? It was at the barbeque . . . YES! "It's Alexa! It's Alexa's house! You have to save her!" Diane said and started shaking, almost convulsing. Paul thought that she might be having a seizure and was ready to catch her in case she fell over.

"No," she screamed, feeling like she was free-falling, and nausea hit her when she realized that she was back in her own head, not in his. "I told you not to touch me! Go to Alexa!" she said, then shook violently, intense pain behind her eyes, and then blissfully passed out.

Holy shit! They were definitely believers now! Knowing that Alexa was his next victim, Rob called his wife and got Alexa's address, then contacted the fire dispatcher to roll out the trucks. The next call was to the detectives handling the case. He gave them quick details that the arsonist was about to start another fire, and two more people were at risk. Finally, Rob made a call to the EMTs to make sure that they came to examine Diane. Before Rob left for Alexa's house, he asked Paul if he was coming with him.

"I'm staying with Diane. Go ahead and catch this asshole." It was the first time Paul felt that it was more important to stay back and not be part of the action. "I must be out of my mind! I've never even been out on a date with this woman, but I feel drawn to her. What's wrong with me? This is so strange, but I have to stay with her," he admitted to himself.

Chapter 67

F eldman got off the phone with Rogers. "I want to know everything there is to know about Timothy Ray Dutton, and I want it yesterday!" Feldman yelled to the room. "He has two hostages, one being Lewis's cousin, Detective Elizabeth Bowlyn."

Everyone filed into the luxurious conference room, Bryan, Bart, Christian, Peter, Mike, Sully, and Sammy. An entire glass wall offered a magnificent view of the beautiful sunny spring day with apple blossoms out in force lining the edge of the lake and adding to the picture-like quality that no one really noticed. The group anxiously took their seats in the fine leather chairs, making each feel like they were a guest in an expensive home rather than a business conference room.

"We need to do a complete background check. Friends or family, school mates, coworkers, anyone that Dutton might go to. Any land registered to him or family members. List of all of the vehicles registered to him, anything that will help us get a handle on what he is thinking and where he's headed," said Feldman, very much in control.

Laptops and notepads were clicking and scratching away while everyone was brainstorming different ways to figure out how to track this monster down. The murmurs were back and forth as everyone had an idea to talk over with the person sitting next to them. Any idea that had merit was projected to the whole group. The mini-brainstorming session was going full tilt, with Feldman writing the "to dos" on the smart board at the one end of the conference room. That way, they would be able to save the writings as a document and e-mail it to Lewis for his briefing with the SLED officers. With SLED working while they were flying, no time would be lost in trying to apprehend Dutton before he was able to do anything other than escape.

"Too bad we didn't have time to plant a tracking device in his truck. Then we'd be able to locate him in a second," Jeffries plainly stated.

"Whoa, that might be it, might be his one big fuckup. Let me check on something, and I'll be right back," Sully said excitedly, his eyes excited looking toward his office. He took off like a bat out of hell and sat down at his bank of computers.

"Tell me what you're thinking, Sully," Feldman yelled across the hall.

"Telematics. More commonly referred to as OnStar," Sully said as he walked back in with a different laptop and sat back down, typing furiously on one computer and then the other. "It comes standard on over twenty-eight different GM models. The service originally started in May 2005, offering the first year free. Dutton has a 2010 Silverado which might still have the feature, or he may have let the service lapse, but it won't matter. We'll need a subpoena to get his truck's tracking locater beacon code. The code is unique to each vehicle that has OnStar. It works kind of like a dedicated phone line, providing service between that specific vehicle and OnStar call centers. Best part: it's definitely traceable. If not, I can see if he has Lojak on the RV. Either way, I'm sure that we can get him as long as he didn't disconnect the tracking locator. We need to figure out if he still has OnStar and whether we can activate it from the OnStar Service Center," Sully said.

"Pure genius, man," Christian said in awe.

"In the meantime, let's look for any other property that is registered to the Dutton family and see if any of his relatives are living within the five-state area where he could go and hide," said Mike. "He could theoretically be in any number of states, depending on which direction he headed in. If he went north, he could be as far as Tennessee or Virginia or as far south in Georgia or Florida. Not much east, North Carolina, but if he headed west, he could be in Alabama by now. He's been traveling for almost five hours."

"I'll check into previous areas where Dutton might have lived and for how long. Since he has Lizzie and Sadie Mae still alive, he'll need to go where he's comfortable. I'll check where his parents are from, see if maybe he has ideas of heading to their home towns," Bart added.

"Peter, coordinate with Scott and Mark and find out what they are doing on their end as soon as we land and let's coordinate information. Rafe is still at the precinct with Bowlyn's man, Santos. I want to know what they're doing, and in turn, we'll update them on our end. I want you to keep up-to-the-minute with them!" Feldman ordered.

"Sammy, call over to the hangar. We need to have the jet fuelled and ready for a flight to Columbia, South Carolina. I want full operation equipment to be loaded on. This will be a major operation. Also, I need vehicles ready for us when we land. Contact the local FBI offices and have them meet us at the airport with at least four vehicles. I want you to stay here and call me if any news comes in here from other field offices."

"This creep is toast. We've got him now. How I love this part!" Sammy said, secretly cheering inside.

"Listen, people! We are very close to catching this killer. I have great confidence that you will all work together, communicating every step of the way, keeping Chief Walter Montgomery in the loop. Timothy Ray Dutton won't be able to hide for long. Let's make sure we get to him before he gets the chance to kill again," Feldman stated firmly.

Chapter 68

Bryan Feldman, Bart, and Sully grabbed their prepped overnight satchels, which every member of the Pit was required to keep at hand for any emergency. Peter started gathering communications equipment, making sure that there were enough sets for everyone. Christian was making sure that the jet was loaded and ready. Sammy contacted the local FBI office in Columbia to secure vehicles.

Sully was in his office packing up his laptop. Trying to go through proper channels, he had alerted the people at OnStar first to connect with Dutton's vehicle. The OnStar people were very helpful, but as suspected, they would not move forward without a subpoena. There was no way for them to verify that Sully was FBI, and their rules were very strict about administering any information over the phone. Sully was able to get the local Detroit FBI office started on the subpoena since the command center was located at the Renaissance Center in Detroit. There was a call center in North Carolina, but it didn't have the resources to do what the Pit needed to get done. Sully wanted the exact location of the vehicle which would enable them to determine Dutton's course and where he might end up.

Feldman hurriedly ushered everyone and everything into the large black Suburbans, and they made it to the airport in record time. The Pit's private jet took off for South Carolina. Through the satellite link on his laptop, Sully would know the minute the subpoena was being served on the OnStar corporate offices, and then he would immediately start tracing Dutton. They tried to find Lizzie through the tracking component of her cell phone, but Dutton must have thrown the phone out the window because it was found on Dutton's property, not far from the bodies, and Dutton had no registered cell phone in his name. The grandmother said that he changes his phone number a lot, so they figured that he used disposable cell phones.

The flight from DC went by quickly, and as planned, they were met by local field office agents who had rented vehicles at the main terminal of the airport. The cars were parked at the terminal where private jets land. They got their equipment secured within their vehicles and started to the SLED offices to meet up with Scott Rogers, Lewis, and Dominguez. They were all on pins and needles, waiting for the subpoena for OnStar to come through. If they didn't get that subpoena, they would be losing valuable time. So far, nothing came from the APB or BOLO. The only good news was that there were no new postings on the Internet, which hopefully meant Sadie and Lizzie were still alive. Lizzie had been missing now for seven hours.

Chapter 69

Walter Montgomery hung up the phone in his third-floor office, staring out the window in shock. Dave Dubowski, a friend and one of his more senior detectives, was just found murdered by the sick bastard known as Carver, and Detective Lizzie Bowlyn has been abducted by him. The chief liked Lizzie, and he knew she was a damn fine detective even if he didn't always show it. Now, that psycho has got her, and the images of her being cut apart by that asshole were more than upsetting. Although self-described as a tough son of a bitch, Montgomery was having a hard time trying to control his emotions. *I'm the goddamn chief of South Carolina Law Enforcement Division, for Christ sake! I can't be falling apart like a pansy-assed Nancy boy!* he thought, trying hard to convince himself. But tears welled up in his eyes anyway. "Got to suck it up and get going," he said quietly to himself. He adjusted his bolero and blew his nose and headed downstairs into the SLED detective offices to find out what the fuck was going on and what the FBI could do to find Bowlyn.

As he walked into the room, the heaviness hanging over everyone's heads was palpable. Sad defeated eyes looked up, waiting for something, some kind of direction. Montgomery put on his game face and addressed the group.

"Listen up, people!" he bellowed. "We're pros, and we are the best goddamn team in the state. Yes, Dave Dubowski has died, and Detective Bowlyn has been captured. But we will not let that fuck head get away with it! So get your heads together, use your brains, go over the details for the hundredth time, and let's nail this piece of shit!"

That seemed to do the trick. Everyone rustled uncomfortably and began to compose themselves. A hum of activity grew louder. Officers, agents, clerks, desk sergeants, and the like were all busy doing something, anything they thought could help. Montgomery was yelling out instructions to analyze information, get alerts out, and make sure they had the most up-to-date information about happenings at the crime scene. Tapping sounds on computer keys were nearly deafening as everyone searched for information on the Dutton family, specifically Timothy Ray.

Santos and Watson were coordinating information for AMBER alerts; Finnegan and Peer were taking care of the APBs and BOLOs that needed to be placed on Dutton's vehicles; Griff was checking with the forensics techs to see if there was anything new at the crime scene. He was also coordinating with the local sheriff's office, talking to Officer Daly about how the questioning of Dutton's grandmother was going. The sheriff was trying to question her, they went back a long ways, but she refused to say anything, mostly because she really didn't know anything, and of course, she hated cops. They were also waiting for the FBI agents to finish their conference call with their offices.

Scott and Mark were in the conference room on the speaker phone with Feldman and the others at the Pit, having connected just before leaving for the airport. Mark was updating Feldman and the others about Dubowski and the blond whose body was buried with him, as well as the prospects of finding Lizzie before she was raped or worse. Scott was beside himself not just because they were talking about Lizzie but also because all he could focus on was the table and his beautiful Lizzie being cut and tortured, needing him, and he was helpless to save her. *Fuck! God, help me help her, I'm begging You, help me please!*

Mark reviewed Timothy Ray Dutton's current state of mind. "He's obviously devolving and decompensating, a bad state for a serial killer. He knows that we know who he is, but he still thinks that he can get away with what he's doing. He feels superior to us to the point of being delusional and has no fear of the law. We need to approach him with extreme caution because he has a superiority complex and is convinced he will not be caught even if he encounters any police. He will not be taken alive; it will be suicide by cop. We just have to make sure that he doesn't take anyone with him."

"Bryan, can you think of any way to get to him? Sully, we need your tech expertise to find a lead, and you are usually the one who always comes up with them. Don't let that go to your head, but it happens to be true. We have to pull out all the stops. Please, we have to find Lizzie!" Scott pleaded with a loud voice, then noticed everyone was staring at him.

"Rogers, pull yourself together. You can't help her if your head's not in the game. Take a walk around the block, get some air, and come back ready to work. Stop thinking of her as Lizzie and start thinking of her as 'the vic.' Depersonalize it now, or you are out of the op. Do you understand me?" Feldman threatened over the phone.

"Loud and clear, sir! Pulling myself together now, sir!" Scott said while taking in a deep breath.

"Don't be a wise ass!"

"Seriously, sir, I'm not. Agent Scott Rogers, reporting for duty, sir!"

"Rogers, anything less than professional from you and I'm pulling you. This is not a threat, it's a reality! Understand?"

"Yes, sir!" Rogers said. He blocked his thoughts about Lizzie and concentrated on finding Dutton. He actually felt a little relief.

"Scottie, don't worry, I've got something up my sleeve. I've got a good idea on how to get the bastard, but just checking my idea out now. Got the Detroit field office on the line, and I think our lead will pan out. Has to do with using OnStar. I don't want to say anything more. Don't want to get your hopes up," Sully answered.

Montgomery walked into the conference room and started his rapid-fire questions to the two FBI agents, not realizing that they were on a conference call with others from the Pit, and the wireless polycom unit was activated. With veins popping out of his neck, the chief was in rare form, dropping the "f-bomb" with practically every other word.

"What the fuck happened out there? How did we not know what the fuck was going on for so fucking long? How did he get over a two-hour lead on us, now pressing to nearly five hours? Christ, he could be fucking anywhere by now, in any direction! Georgia, North Carolina, Tennessee, even Alabama . . . He could be fucking anywhere! Do we know for a fact that he still has the girls? We can't cover two-hundred fucking miles in all directions. What the fuck are you doing? You're the fucking experts, now coordinate and get my Lizzie back and fry Dutton's ass!"

Mark stood up and calmly addressed the chief's questions. "Sir, we are coordinating that right now, and when we have a game plan, we will tell you first and then everyone else." Mark turned his eyes from Montgomery to the polycom unit set in the middle of the conference room table and said, "Feldman, get over to the airport now, we've covered all that's current, and we'll reconvene when you land." Looking back to Montgomery, he continued. "Right now, we are checking into a couple of tracking options to find the unsub. My boss and several other members of our team are on their way here as we speak. We'll get her back, Chief. She's my cousin, and believe me, I'm as concerned as you are. I want her back as badly as you do, but we have to remain objective and not make this personal. We'll lose her if we don't keep our focus."

"You think I don't know that? We're doing our best. I'll be out in the room with my detectives awaiting your briefing, and if you have something, I'll listen, but if you've got nothing, I'm not sure we can work together, which would be unfortunate. I'll get my men working leads," Montgomery said with a matter-of-fact tone. "We're not backwater idiots, you know. We're SLED, elite detectives who know what the fuck we're doing! Enough talking! Let's do something."

"Chief, just hold on a second, please," Mark said. "Your men are excellent. There is no doubt in my mind that they are highly skilled people, and we are relying on them heavily. Our computer expert is trying to work out if there is any way to track Dutton's vehicles using LoJack or OnStar. Right now, we think this is our best shot at locating Dutton—the proverbial needle in a haystack. We should have answers in a few minutes. Why don't you join us in the conference room? I should have suggested it at the onset of the conference call. Bring in your team and let's nail this bastard!"

"I'm all for that," Montgomery said and blotted the beads of sweat from his brow with a starched handkerchief.

Chapter 70

How the hell could they have found me? It was a thought that temporarily consumed Dutton. He was more than careful. It must have been some kind of fluke. They wouldn't find him again. He had chucked both detectives' cell phones after he gagged the lady cop, so they couldn't track either of them. He only used disposable cell phones. Dutton cruised down the back roads, purposely avoiding Route 106, humming the tune to "Midnight Train to Georgia." He liked Georgia, been there a while back with his cousin. He remembered some old abandoned apartment buildings in Allenhurst, really old tenement projects that were just thrown away, like the people who were living in them. About ten years ago, the state moved the tenants into more modern condos. It was actually a cool idea that allowed the people who were going to live in the condos the opportunity to help build them. It was a project that received a lot of funding and notoriety during the Clinton Administration. The tenement ruins were perfect for his needs. Dutton had liked playing hide-and-seek with his cousin in those buildings. Of course, that was before his pa killed his ma, and he had to live with the sadistic old witch.

He tried to relax by thinking about what he would do to the blond cop. Hopefully, she was still unconscious with the chloroform to knock her out, but he knew she would be too weak to escape. He got a few good hits to her head when she stopped fighting. When Dutton finally thought it safe to stop for the night, he might just give a little preview to his playtime with Detective Bowlyn. She was a bit older than he liked, but she would still look good on film, and she would scream for him the way the others always did.

Timothy Dutton and his two captives had been on the road for about eight hours. He had a really good sense of direction and headed north first, on 95, then doubled back. He picked up Route 20 west toward Augusta and then headed down to Pelion. He went through a bunch of small towns, Sylvania, Newington, Springfield, Register, and Clayton. Currently, he was in Glennville and only had Hinesville to go through before he would be in Allenhurst. He knew that the police would be looking for his truck and RV, but they didn't know which direction he was headed, so he would be good for a while until he finished with miss detective and was able to trash the body. He might just bury it, and then no one would be able to find her. They'd know she was dead because he would immortalize the moment on film. He couldn't wait.

Chapter 71

Mark addressed the group with a profile update on Dutton. "Okay, people, at this point, Timothy Ray Dutton is rapidly decompensating, which means he is falling apart. His identity has been revealed. He's got two women, and one is a cop. He has two more movies to make but wants to escape. Yet escaping is getting more difficult. This smooth operator is worried . . . and for good reason. Everything that rises must converge. He will begin to make rash decisions, and I want us to be ready for the explosion, so to speak."

Sully made an announcement.

"We've got the subpoena! Now, we're gonna get our killer!" The squad room roared with happy screams and wolf whistles. Sully was then able to tap into the OnStar system and watch the progression of Dutton's truck and trailer. OnStar was working like a charm. *He was on US 25 heading out of Glennville.*

"I'm out of here! Lewis, you coming with me?" Rogers asked while checking his guns, one in his shoulder holster and one attached to his ankle.

"Hey! Hold up there! What do you think you're doing, Rogers?" Feldman demanded.

"I can't sit here any longer. I have to get down there, even if I just work surveillance. I won't do anything stupid, I promise."

"Okay, but, Lewis, watch him like a hawk. Are you sure you're not too emotional to handle this? You can stay with Sully, and I'll send Peter and Rafe." Feldman looked deep into Rogers's eyes to try and determine his state of mind.

"I swear, I can handle this, boss. I feel like I have to be the one to help bring the bastard down. I'm a pro, remember."

"Okay, but don't make me sorry I did this!"

"No, sir," Scott said and saluted Feldman.

Scott Rogers and Mark Lewis took a selection of sophisticated technology equipment, such as night-vision scopes, video- and audio-recording tools, and tracking devices, along with a selection of lethal weaponry. They started on the three-and-a-half-hour trip to Glenville. Feldman and the others would prepare for an intercept while Rogers and Lewis handled surveillance. Well, that's what everyone thought except Rogers. He had to save Lizzie, and it had to happen now. "I'll drive!" he said to Lewis and took off with the gas pedal to the floor, making it to Glennville in a little over three hours. He was talking to Sully most of the time for specific locations and was told that Dutton stopped at a destination and hadn't moved for over thirty minutes. Rogers was crawling out of his skin, worrying about Lizzie and what that prick could be doing to his girl.

Chapter 72

Just as he remembered them, the abandoned buildings in Allenhurst brought back such fond memories for Timothy Ray Dutton. But that was then, and this was now. *Let's get some action!* He parked in a hidden spot behind the complex and began the routine. With his mask already on, he set up the cameras in under fifteen minutes.

At this point, he wasn't as interested in Sadie Mae . . . let her rot in the other room for all he cared . . . she would have to wait her turn. Or maybe, he'd just shoot her and dump her along with miss detective.

"Detective Bowlyn, nice to spend some quality time together. I know we'll have a ton of fun. You are just way overdressed for the occasion, so let's just start cutting away some of those nasty clothes," a masked Dutton said to Lizzie as she squirmed and struggled fruitlessly against leather restraints, her eyes glaring with contempt and hatred.

Unlike Dutton's other victim, Susan Starks, Lizzie knew all too well where she was: in the torture chamber that Dutton used to post his nightmarish killings on the Internet. She saw various blades and tools, even a gun. If only she could get that gun. He came at her with a large knife, running it up her shirt, pulling the shredded white blouse away from her body, exposing a light blue demi-bra. "Nice bra, miss detective. Did you wear that just for li'l ole me? Do you also have on matching panties, Liz? Let's see. I love a matching set. You can always tell a lot about a woman by the underwear she has on." As he cut away her black slacks to reveal light blue thong panties, he reveled in being correct.

Dutton took off her shoes and ran the knife up the soles of her feet with a kind of a tickling manner, not yet cutting into them.

"I learned something with Susan: she was so much more responsive after I shot her up with some junk. I think that I need to see what it's like with you too. Would you like that, Liz, huh?" He put the knife down and started with the drug paraphernalia. He tied a rubber tourniquet around her right arm while she struggled desperately to move her arms as much as possible. Dutton put his knee up on the table to hold her arm in place. She was screaming, but the gag in her mouth muffled most of the sound. He found a vein and pricked the needle into it. Lizzie felt the pinch as it poked into her skin and then the burn of the drug permeating her body.

Timothy Ray watched Lizzie for about five minutes, loving how her eyes, like Susan Starks's, rolled around when they first got that rush from a high. He took off the gag, picked up the knife, and started with her feet.

Chapter 73

The smoke was becoming denser, so he was sure that the bedroom was totally engulfed. The Servant's work here was done. He calmly went out the back door and then ran around to the front door to leave his calling card. As the Servant cornered the house, he heard the far away sounds of sirens, so he really had to move quickly to get back to his car, parked a couple of blocks away. He nailed the cross to the front door, put his hammer back into his tool box, picked it up as he straightened up, smiled, and turned around, only to be met with a fist to the face. It knocked him flat on his back. He was immediately flipped over onto his stomach, and his hands were cuffed behind him. Fire trucks screamed up the street, followed by police cars and ambulances. Interestingly, the Servant was sort of pleased to see all the vehicles since he was never around for this part. He had a big twisted grin on his face. Rob was holding onto the Servant's arm tightly, awaiting his arrest.

As several police detectives approached Rob, six firefighters surrounded the house. Three of them busted down the front door and started reeling the hoses directly up the stairs. The firemen could see the thick black smoke pouring out from under the door directly in front of them. They got to the bed, but sadly, the bodies were charred beyond recognition.

"Yeah, Donnie, this is the scumbag that has been setting the fires and killing all the couples," Rob said.

"I haven't killed anyone. They were all cleansed by the fire. But you ruined it for that harlot and her boyfriend. They will never walk through the halls of heaven with the lord. Vengeance is mine sayeth the lord." Didn't they understand that it wasn't him? It was God's decision. He was simply the lord's servant.

"And the flames will set them free! The fire of salvation will wash away their sins, and they will be reborn in the lord. I am God's servant saving their souls, and you know, God's will must be done." The Servant stopped talking. He wasn't smiling anymore. *He felt he had failed the Lord and must be punished.*

Chapter 74

S cott Rogers and Mark Lewis, turned onto a nondescript road, dirt, not tar. The shoulder was badly potholed and overgrown, with thick weeds and wild shrubs growing densely on both sides. Although the road was less than fifty yards from the highway, they couldn't see anything but the packed dirt in front of them and several overhanging bushes. They were the first police vehicle to arrive in Allenhurst, Georgia. Scott Rogers's heart was nearly beating out of his chest. *No way was he going to just survey the area and wait for backup. No telling what horrors Lizzie has already had to endure.*

Rogers clicked off the safety on his gun and opened the door of the SUV. "Hey, man, we've got to sit tight. This dude is a psycho killer. The guys are right behind us," Lewis said.

"There's no fuckin' way I am sitting in this car waiting for that bastard to torture and kill Lizzie. Now, you can sit there and be a good boy, or you can follow me in and cover my ass. Which is it?" Rogers said dashing outside without giving Lewis an opportunity to answer. Leading with his gun, Scott Rogers started moving through the deserted apartment complex like a maze. The old apartment buildings looked like a hollowed-out prison, cold grey cinder block walls surrounding the bunker style units. It was an extremely depressing place, not unlike other housing areas in the rural south that were left like rotting corpses. There, off to the right of the bunker-like buildings, was a large open-aired rusty-roofed shed, constructed from the same grey cinder blocks as the rest of the buildings. There were half-dead fluorescent lights flickering and throwing faint shadows over the ground, adding to the already oppressive visual. *Was that supposed to provide some sort of security?* Even in the late afternoon daylight, this was a creepy place, and Rogers felt the hair on the back of his neck stand on end. He motioned to Lewis about the next direction he was headed, and Lewis got out of the SUV, knowing that backup was less than fifteen minutes out.

Rogers spotted the Silverado and Coachmen they had been frantically searching for under the open-sided shed. He struggled to remain calm, knowing that Lizzie was being held captive and possibly being hurt in some horrible way. As Rogers stealthily moved closer, he could see how this provided the perfect camouflage for the truck and RV, especially from the helicopters searching. It would be invisible from the air, and it was impossible to see from the road since the old apartment buildings hid the shed from direct view.

With the tiny audio device Scott had in his ear, he heard Sully say, "Where are you guys? Have you got a visual on the target?"

He also heard Feldman's order, "Stay put, maintain visual surveillance until we arrive. We're less than ten minutes out."

"Can't do that, sir. I'm goin' in," Rogers interrupted.

"Damn it, Rogers, you fucking promised. You were trained better than that. Hold position," Feldman ordered again.

"I'll go closer to get some type of audio from the trailer."

"Hold position."

"Yes, sir." But he had no intention of waiting another second, let alone ten minutes, while Lizzie was in there. He crept closer to the trailer, his heart pounding faster and adrenaline pumping. He could hear Dutton talking and say Lizzie's name. Every step seemed laborious, and although Scott felt like blasting through the increasing darkness to announce his arrival, he took every precaution to be even quieter. He heard Lizzie's muffled scream, and it took every ounce of strength and all his training to restrain himself from kicking in the trailer door. He looked across the lot and saw Lewis, he motioned for him to stay put, giving the hand signal that he was just doing recon.

The windows were covered with heavy fabric, and he couldn't see a thing. He silently got out his tools to pick the lock. He was very careful to gently turn the knob, moving it the slightest bit so he could peek through the narrow slit. He saw Dutton standing over a naked Lizzie with a large knife, making long, thin cuts along her legs. He burst down the door, gun first. Scott Rogers went through the opened door, and all hell broke loose.

"FBI. Freeze!"

Dutton immediately got behind Lizzie using her as a shield and placed the knife against her carotid artery. "No! You freeze! Drop your fuckin' gun, or I'll slit her throat. Don't think I won't do it!"

Rogers quickly cocked his gun upward to show he was backing off and said as calmly as possible, "Just step away from her. I'll move aside to let you by. I just want the girls." He slowly began moving away from the door. The space was very cramped with the cameras and torture table taking up most of the room.

"Drop the gun or she's dead. A few more slices and dices, and she would have been ready for this anyway. At least, she's got some fight in her, more than I can say for her partner, tubby the detective," Dutton jeered.

Rogers crouched down carefully, looking like he was going to drop his gun while trying to see if there was any shot he could take that wouldn't hurt Lizzie. Dutton, while still holding the knife, grabbed a gun from the utility table next to him. *Boom!* Everything began to play out in slow motion, with every second seeming longer than the next, each movement distinct from the one before. Rogers flinched, rolling to the left as he felt the bullet rip through his right shoulder. Another shot hit him above his right hip. Rogers couldn't chance a shot because of Lizzie between him and Dutton. Voices in his two-way earpiece were yelling for an update, and he tried to call for Lewis. He still had his gun in his hand but had to be careful not to hit Lizzie. Then he was starting to see black and went down, losing consciousness. Dutton was now screaming at Lizzie through his mask, wildly flinging the gun, and pressing the knife harder to her throat; a trail of blood was trailing down her throat. It only pierced the skin, not the artery. *Lizzie was still mostly out of it. Thank God.*

As Dutton realized that the FBI agent was unconscious, he came around the table with the gun in his hand and put the knife down on the small steel utility table that held his "carving" tools. He was lining up his shot to shoot Rogers in the head, execution style.

Boom! Boom! Mark Lewis double-tapped the center of Dutton's chest. Backup arrived seconds later and found Dutton leaning over Lizzie's bloodied legs. There was an eerie silence after the gunfire, and the small room smelled of gunpowder and sweat. Through the haze of her half-shut eyelids, Lizzie saw two men rush over to Scott.

Peter knelt next to his brother, fighting the need to throw up, and hot tears started streaming down his cheeks. "Scottie, stay with me, man. Scottie, look at me, damn it!" Rafe knew Peter was about to have a meltdown and pushed him aside to administer medical attention since he was the field medic for their unit. Peter slumped heavily against the wall.

"Peter, get Sadie Mae. In the other room, through that door. See if she's still alive. I'll get Lizzie out, and you can check their injuries. Rafe has your brother," Feldman said with respectful urgency.

Peter looked down at Scott and knew he was too emotional to help him. Rafe and Bryan could handle him better than he could right now.

He kicked open the small door and saw Sadie Mae still bound and gagged, nearly unconscious; the room stunk of urine and feces.

Feldman came around to Lizzie, cut off her restraints, and draped a jacket over her naked body. She started to speak.

"Scott . . . Scott Rogers, answer me. *Scott!*" she pleaded in a rough whisper.

"Shh. Lizzie, shh. Quiet. The boys are with him now, and I can hear the sirens. The ambulance will be here any second." Scott was in and out of consciousness, and he could feel the wetness of warm blood pooling underneath his back from the bullet wounds. He tried to speak but couldn't. He looked up into Rafe's eyes, then opened his eyes wide trying to communicate, but passed out before a word was spoken. Rafe and Bryan were putting pressure on his wounds. *So much blood.* The first medics on the scene entered the room and immediately started working on Scott to get him out of the cramped area to work on him. They secured him to a backboard with bright orange straps and placed a stiff collar on his neck in case one of the bullets traveled to his spine and moved him out of the trailer to the awaiting stretcher. Bryan motioned for one of the medics to move Lizzie out of the trailer, telling them agent Peter Rogers would be waiting to help her and Sadie Mae.

They quickly moved Scott into the ambulance. One medic started an IV while another cut off Rogers's clothes to look at the wounds and apply dressings to help stop the bleeding. There was air coming out of the bullet wound near his shoulder, which was not a good sign. The medic was swearing as he tried to put on an occlusive dressing, a special nonabsorbent bandage used for trauma victims which provides a seal to the wound site so the air stays in the lungs. The other medic, listening to chest sounds, said that they needed to intubate him to help his breathing.

"Shit! Punctured lung. Move him out of here. Go to Winn Army now!" ordered the first, referring to a hospital at Fort Stewart which was the closest trauma unit available. They had excellent trauma surgeons, and Rogers would get the best care.

Lizzie couldn't focus on what had happened, the heroin still clouding her perception. "Help me . . . No, help Scott first. Don't let him die, he can't die. Please, help him." She looked up into Peter's eyes. "Those are Scott's eyes . . . How do you have his eyes? Please, help him." She just lay there and started to cry. Peter thought her behavior was odd and then saw that she had very dilated pupils. He also noticed the tourniquet on her arm and figured that she had been drugged. "Lizzie, do you know what he shot you with? Do you know what he gave you?"

"Junk."

"Shit."

Three ambulances were called to the scene, the first having already left with Scott. The other two were working on Lizzie and Sadie Mae, who sat huddled underneath blankets. Lizzie had cuts up and down her legs and on her feet and was still high from the heroin injection. Sadie had severe rope burns from her bindings where she tried to break free. She was also quite dehydrated. A female medic brought a sweatshirt and track shorts for Lizzie to put on, and the women were guided to the waiting ambulances. Peter rode with Lizzie, calling his mama from the ambulance.

"Mama," Peter said.

"Petie, how are you doin', honey? It's kina late to be callin', isn't it? What's wrong, sweetie?"

"It's Scottie. He's been shot. It's real bad, Mama. We need you and Sammy to go to the hangar. The plane will be there for you in two hours. You need to get there as soon as possible, Sammy will pick you up. I don't want you drivin'."

"What happened?" his mama asked.

"Shoot out with that Carver guy who was mutilating and murdering all those young women on the Internet. Scott's been working on that case. Lizzie, Mark's cousin, was held hostage. He likes her, a real lot, Mama. He wasn't thinkin' right and was supposed to wait for backup but went in before he shoulda. I'm on my way to the hospital now. Wait for Sammy, and you'll be here in a coupla hours. I'll see you then. Call me as you're taking off and when you land. I'll give you whatever update I can," Peter said, clearly choked-up but in control.

"Was anyone else hurt?" she asked in a brave but slightly cracked tone.

"The girls had minor injuries. Lizzie will need a lot of stitches, but she should be fine. That bastard hadn't started yet on Sadie Mae, so she'll be fine physically. Mentally is another story. The killer is dead. We shot him before he killed Scottie. Gotta go. Love you, Mama."

"Love you too, sweetie. He'll be all right, you know, I feel it in my bones. He'll make it through this," she said, praying to herself it was the truth and thinking how much he was like his damn daddy.

Chapter 75

"They never had a chance. It was a death trap, all right. The room quickly became a seething inferno. They most likely died within three minutes of the fire being set," Rob said.

"I'm so sorry . . . I thought that I might be able to save them before he set the fire," Diane said with tears in her eyes.

"It's not your fault. It was that asshole who thought that he was the divine servant of the lord. Why are there so many freaks in this world?" With that comment, Diane's tears dried up quickly, and Paul realized his goof. "What I mean is . . . what causes a person to lose it so bad that they think God wants them to burn people alive? I just don't understand it at all."

Then Rob commented. "Who knows why. But at least we got this one, and God knows how many lives were saved today. Your mother would be so proud of you, Diane."

"So true. I'm sure Mark Lewis could shed some light on the reasons. He's an amazing profiler, but of course, we have our own amazing *ultra* profiler right here. Thank you, Diane. I really can't express how much we appreciate everything you . . . ah . . . saw," Paul said with gratitude mixed with a little confusion.

Luckily, they were interrupted by a ringing cell phone.

"Rogers here," Paul answered. They watched as his face instantly changed from relieved to distraught. "Shit, Peter, what happened?" He listened some more, his face becoming graver as he listened. "I'll be there as fast as I can."

Rob and Diane looked at him waiting for an explanation.

"My brother was shot. It's bad. I have to go. Diane, this will seem weird, and I kind of expect you to say no, but will you come with me?" Without hesitating, her eyes lit up, and she said, "Yes!"

Chapter 76

S cott Rogers was rushed into surgery. The bullet in his right shoulder entered on a downward angle and punctured one of the lobes of his lung. The other bullet tunneled into his hip and burrowed into his kidney. Once Peter was sure Lizzie was being treated, he talked with Sadie Mae Reynolds, making sure she was okay. They were keeping her overnight for observation, and she was given IV fluids to treat her dehydration.

Lizzie's cuts were stitched up by a resident plastic surgeon, and she had been given a dose of Narcan, a drug that counters the effects of opiate overdoses. She looked around the sterile light green waiting room and didn't know what to do. She sat alone, feeling as empty as the Styrofoam cup she was holding on to, like it was her lifeline. She really missed her dog, Mandy. *Boy, I could go for a nice lick on my face and a wagging tail right now.*

She just stared out into the waiting room cluttered with magazines and a TV tuned to a cooking show and not really focusing on anything. Lewis, Feldman, and Dominguez were providing details to the local police, and CSU personnel had arrived to collect evidence from the old apartment complex. For someone who never left a trace of evidence, Timothy Ray Dutton had left more than enough this time.

There was a flash of movement by the door and a flurry of activity in the waiting room, startling Lizzie out of her half sleep. The room was no longer quiet as it started filling with people. The entire Rogers family had come to see her; *they cared about her*. She had met some of them four years ago when Remmie had a surprise birthday party for Mark. There were also a few others that she didn't know. Remmie, of course, showed up and came right over to give her a big, but gentle hug. Sammy had called her, and she flew in with her and Sharon. As introductions were being made, Lizzie couldn't help getting emotional when she looked into the eyes of Scott's brothers. They all had the same eyes. She couldn't move, she just sat there, her knees trembling, hands shaking and lots of tears

A small woman, who looked like an older Sammy, came over to Lizzie and put her arms lovingly around her. "Don't worry, honey child, he's put us through a lot more than this. You'll see. He'll be just fine in a couple of days. I can feel it. I know these things. I raised strong boys. I'm Sharon, Scott's mama."

Lizzie looked up at her with her light-blue eyes full of tears and whispered, "I'm so sorry, I couldn't stop him. It's my fault."

"Now why on earth would you go thinkin' it was your fault? There's nothing for you to be sorry about."

"I broke protocol. I should have waited for backup, not gone looking for Dubowski myself. I should have waited . . . I should have . . . ohhhh . . . Poor Dubowski." And more tears streaked down her cheeks.

"Here, honey, take this tissue. That's better," said Sharon Rogers as she wiped away the streaks and placed the box of tissue on Lizzie's lap. "I was told he disobeyed a direct order from his boss not to move his butt until backup showed up. But that doesn't matter now. We just have to keep prayin' to God so he'll let us keep Scott. He's not ready for Scott to die. I swear, he'll be fine."

They sat around the waiting room for what seemed like days but actually was about ten hours. A surgeon came out wearing green scrubs, his name embroidered in white over his left breast. Marvin G. Platt, M.D. F.A.C.S. Dr. Platt proceeded to explain that the repair to the lung was successfully done, but the bullet to the kidney was still worrisome. In order to remove the bullet, they had to remove part of the kidney too. "We'll have to wait and see if what remains can still function or if we may have to go back in and remove the rest of the kidney. Hopefully, he will be able to recover without more surgery. He was extremely lucky to survive this shooting. We'll know more soon. The next forty-eight hours are critical to determining whether he'll be able to keep the kidney. Barring any complications, he should pull through. Hang in there," the doctor said before going back into the OR. *Should pull through?* That comment made everyone even more concerned. The nurse said he would only be allowed one visitor an hour and only for five minutes while in intensive care. Sharon Rogers went first.

Chapter 77

Detective Lizzie Bowlyn was determined to stay in the small plain waiting room plastered with bad art and "Please Don't Use Your Cell Phone" signs everywhere until she could talk with Scott. She felt weary but also zombie-like, as dull as the neutral grey walls. As she looked out of the drab hospital room window, it was an absolutely beautiful day, almost too perfect, like a little kid's drawing with a big round yellow sun, squirrels running around, birds tweeting, and a blue cloudless sky. But in her mind, the scene was far from idyllic, and she didn't enjoy the view. She felt helpless and sad while waiting for some kind of news about Scott's condition. Even Remmi and the others were almost invisible to her right now. She couldn't believe this had happened. She hugged herself tightly, only aware of a searing pain around her heart, far worse than what she had suffered under the demented hands of Timothy Ray Dutton.

It had been more than forty-eight hours since Scott Rogers's surgery, and he was still hanging on. He hadn't woken up for more than a few minutes at a time, but the fact that he was opening his eyes at all was good news. The nurses were being very restrictive, and when it was Lizzie's turn to visit, Scott was never awake. She would hold his hand, talk to him, but he wouldn't wake up for her. They had taken the intubation tube out the night before, and he was just on oxygen. She was more than grateful that he could breathe on his own. *Sharon Rogers did raise strong boys*, she thought and smiled.

Scott opened his deep-blue eyes, hoping to see Lizzie, but instead, it was the damn hospital room, no one with him this time. He wanted to see Lizzie and make sure she was okay. His mama could tell him that all day long, but until he saw her, held her, he couldn't rest easy. He pressed the button to call the nurse, and she came right away.

"Is there something I can get you?"

"I need to see Detective Bowlyn, and I need to see her now," he said in a horse whisper, like a smoker. It seems his throat wasn't working too well and his mouth was as dry as the Afghan desert.

"You're not allowed to have visitors for another forty minutes. Try to get some rest and I'll send her in then. Dr. Platt was very insistent," she said.

"Listen, I'll roll myself out of this damn bed and crawl down the hall to find her. Please, I need to see her now!" He tried to sit up, and the nurse could tell he was getting agitated because the Beep! Beep! Beep! of his heart monitor was speeding up.

"Sir, please, no, okay. I'll get her but don't move. You'll rip your stitches out. Please stay still, calm, I'll be right back with her."

For the first time in many hours, Rogers felt relief and lay back onto his bed. That little demonstration really hurt. He must have been hurt worse than he thought. A few minutes later, Lizzie walked into the room. She saw that he was awake and ran the rest of the way to the bed. She gently held him and gave him a tender kiss on his forehead.

"God, Lizzie, if anything had happened to you, I don't know what I would have done. I love you with all my heart. I was so worried about you," Rogers said softly into her ear.

"Worried about me? I've been frantic worrying over you! At first, they didn't think you'd make it. Your mama was the only one who knew all along that you'd be okay."

"Do you like my mama?" he asked with a smile on his face.

"What's not to like? She's the sweetest lady in the world." That gave Scott a nice, warm feeling in his chest. Lizzie didn't say anything about his declaration of love, but he continued on with what he planned. The nurse walked back in and said that the five minutes were up and that he needed his rest. Scott was having problems staying awake anyway with the pain medication, so he said okay.

This pattern continued for a day or so, and everything was in a holding pattern. Lizzie only left the hospital to go to the hotel and take a shower. She even slept in the waiting room, visiting Scott when she was allowed. They were finally moving him to a regular room, a week after incurring his injuries.

Lizzie found Scott sitting up in a chair, next to the bed. He motioned for Lizzie to move onto the bed; he took both her hands in his. "I've thought about this, a lot, and I don't want to scare you, but I don't want to lose you. I think I fell for you when I met you at Mark's surprise party years ago. There's something I want you to have, Lizzie." He reached under the pillow next to her and pulled out a small black velvet jewelry box and placed it into her hands. "Open it."

"I don't know if I can," she whispered.

"It's really easy. There's a small gold latch on the front and two tiny hinges on the back that will spring it open. Just lift the lid, Lizzie."

She opened up the box and the sunlight coming in the window caught the diamond in such a way that the prism spread sparkling rainbows all around the room. It was the most perfect cushion-cut diamond with pretty filigree around the band. It was not so big as to be ostentatious but big enough to be beautiful on her hand.

Lizzie hesitated, perhaps overwhelmed or maybe not ready to be engaged. Either way, Scott felt compelled to fill in the silence.

"This isn't exactly going the way I pictured it. I know this may be too soon for you. I can tell by the look in your gorgeous eyes. If you're not going to put the ring on right away, just hold onto it, and when you're ready, just know that you'll make me the happiest man in the world."

Lizzie stared down at the ring and said, "When did you have time . . . How did you manage to—"

"Mama. I told her what I wanted, what would be perfect for you. She came back with a jeweler when you went to the hotel. He brought several options, but I knew what I wanted, and he set it for me, and here it is. I kinda guessed the size." Scott rambled on a little more. "I know that we will be perfect together, and I understand your reservations with another whirlwind romance, but I'm not Matt, nor will I ever be. I'll take care of you, the way you deserve to be treated and loved."

The disappointment was written all over Scott's face. Lizzie's heart was breaking to see that expression. He seemed lost for a moment but then smiled at her, saying, "I'm not going to change my mind, and I'll do everything to change yours. I can see the hesitation in your eyes. How about this? When you're ready, I'll put this ring on your finger, and I'll do it right at some fancy restaurant with a flaming dessert and a bottle of champagne. How does that sound?"

"That will be perfect. I want to say yes so badly, but I need a time to do some things with you. I can't rush into a marriage like I did the last time. I know you're not like Matt, but I need to do couple things with you like waking up with you, arguing about toothpaste caps and drinking out of the milk carton and leaving your underwear on the bathroom floor. I want to wake up with you, bed head and all. I don't have anything keeping me here. You have your whole family back in DC. I want to come with you but let me find a small apartment first and then maybe try moving in with you. I want you to know, I do love you too, and I plan on having you in my life." With that, the two kissed, which was in Scott's book was almost as good as yes.

Chapter 78

"I'm still trying to get into the site. They change the passwords frequently, but at least, I found a way to get to the log-on area of the website," Sully said.

"This is unbelievable. This *www.kidsworldwide.com* site is a pedophile's dream come true! It's the equivalent of a kid in a candy store," a disgusted Rafe commented.

"Whoever set this site up was 'my caliber' brilliant, and that's saying a lot coming from me. Except that I work for the law not against it. Big difference. The homepage is fairly generic and if you visit it by accident, there is a banner that says 'full site coming soon, site under construction.' In the foreground, there's a harmless photograph of a very pretty woman, midtwenties, who is totally Miss American Apple Pie. She's smiling, wearing a professional navy blazer and starched white blouse, a few buttons opened at the top, holding a kid's plaid binder. That's the only give-away. There is an image of an older gentleman in the background that is blurry. The focus is off, but I'd say he's in his forties. It looks like your very professional office and what little copy that appears on the homepage makes it out to be an organization affiliated to providing safety and protection of children. What a lie!" Sully exclaimed with vehemence.

"Is it what Feldman said? An online auction house for child trafficking?" Christian asked.

"Totally. I haven't been on the site for a while now. The password that Senator Stevens gave us expired, but I'll figure a way back in. I always do eventually. What I saw is deplorable. They actually had a menu under the heading 'hot favorites.' The subhead said 'worldwide flights' that arranged for the transportation of the child, and 'momentum worldwide' offered the places to buy different types of porn, books, magazines, films—disgusting stuff. 'Data entry' is what you entered to find what you specially wanted, and they either found 'it,' or they had that kind of child in inventory. They referred to the children as 'units' or 'it.' Can you believe the low form of human that does this shit?'" Sully said.

"I wonder how they got so big. How does one go about finding this? It's astounding, really," Christian asked, now moving to strategic analysis.

"Unfortunately, child trafficking has become a lucrative business that is directly linked with highly organized criminal activity. The ugly truth is that human trafficking is a horrid reality for millions of children. After selling drugs and gun running, it is the third largest illicit activity, earning about five billion dollars annually. About four hundred thousand children are sold each year. These guys are the biggest organization that we've seen," Rafe said to him while looking over some old printouts that Sully had made while they still had access to the site.

"Good homework, man. Do Lewis or Rogers know what we've found yet?" Christian asked.

"Don't think so, or one of them would have jumped on me right away for any information. When Feldman's ready to start an op, we'll give them the details. And there are a lot of ugly ones," Sully said shaking his head.

Chapter 79

I t was a sweltering September summer day in DC, and autumn was definitely not in the air. The streets had that blurred effect when the tar is almost melting and the heat rises. Lizzie was heading home from her grueling day of training at Quantico. It had been four months since that horrible moment in the trailer and Scott nearly dying from bullet wounds. She couldn't wait to be home and take a shower to get off the sweat and grime. It was a particularly strenuous workout at the Academy that day, and every muscle hurt. Lizzie couldn't wait until graduation and start working full time. There were only four more training modules that she had to complete before she was officially an FBI agent.

Lizzie was in a good mood. Approaching her apartment complex, she parked her trusty Altima underneath a large oak where she always liked to park. She loved the majesty of the tree: it was large, healthy, and happy, and it covered the whole side of the Academy Arms apartment building. Although steamy hot outside, the sky was a spectacular china-blue with only a smattering of fluffy white clouds. She started up the slate stairs and pulled open one of the heavy steel and etched glass doors, entering the lobby of the building. She waved to the doorman standing to the side of the nicely decorated lobby with marble floors. "Hi, Bruce! Hope you're keepin' cool!" she said. The doorman smiled and waved back, and Lizzie went to the elevator bank, and when the door opened, she hit the button for the fourteenth floor. This apartment didn't have the same feeling that her little house had in Arcadia Lakes, but it was home for now.

Mandy met her at the door, ready once she heard the key turn in the lock. That sweet pup gave Lizzie the usual high jumping "hello" greeting that she just loved so much. Lizzie adored that little dog. She was only five pounds, but what she lacked in size was made up in personality. She landed in Lizzie's arms and started licking her face voraciously.

"Mandy, okay, girl, want to go for a walk? Let me get changed, and we'll go out for a little jog around the complex."

"Can I come too?"

"Damn, you scared the pants off of me! And this isn't the first time. You're lucky I don't have my Glock handy! How long were you standing there? I can't believe that I didn't notice you. You're kinda hard to miss."

Scott walked over to her and gathered her in his arms for a soul-searing kiss. He always took her breath away. His wounds had healed beautifully, but Lizzie still handled him gently, ignoring the scars where the bullets had entered.

"When did you get back? I thought you wouldn't be here for another week."

Scott held her tighter and whispered in her ear, "We finished early, so I came home as soon as I could. Want to go out to eat tonight? Go to my place or just stay here, dealer's choice."

"I bought a few things at the market that I was going to make for me and Pander, so I'll just make a little more. You'll stay, please?"

"Wouldn't want to be any place else," he said and started kissing her again. He missed her on his last assignment. He couldn't wait until they were working together, and he wouldn't have to be separated from her for so long. He gently started pulling her shirt from her pants.

"I need a shower. I've been training all day, and I was going to run the Pup n' Chow for a while before I took my shower."

"Don't care. Can't wait. Quick, put the pups in her crate. I haven't seen you in three weeks, and Mandy has been with you every day."

"You have a point. Mander, in ya go," Lizzie said ushering Mandy into her crate.

With Mandy safely at bay, Scott backed Lizzie up against the door and continued to kiss her. She put her arms around his neck and kissed back, dizzy with passion.

He quickly rid her of clothing, kissing her body every time a button was undone. Scott touched her body, her skin soft as silk. The scars on her legs looked like faint scratches. Scott was naked before Lizzie could blink, and he lifted her up and entered her in one long stroke, pushing her into the wall. They moved in a fast mesmerizing rhythm, clutching onto each other, coming apart in each other's arms. They gasped for breath, feeling each other's heart thumping wildly.

"God, you're amazing. I missed you so much," he said as he let her down gently.

"Missed you more."

"Impossible," he whispered in her ear.

"Not impossible. Let's head into the bathroom for a shower. I know I certainly need one after those *two* workouts!" She kissed his cheek tenderly.

Lizzie released Mandy from her crate, knowing how much the tiny dog wanted to be with them. They walked arm in arm into the bathroom, started the shower, and got in, closing the door on Mandy. She wanted a play in the water too!

After a passionate shower, where they started by washing one another and ended up joined together in passion, Lizzie and Scott finally made their way into the kitchen and started preparing dinner together. Scott had just finished cleaning the shrimp and looked over at Lizzie chopping the scallions and almost dropped the box of rice. There, glistening on her left hand was the engagement ring, the one he had given her months ago.

"What is this?" he asked as he picked up her hand to give it a soft kiss by the ring.

"Well, your birthday is next week, and I wanted it to be a kinda present for you. The best birthday present ever—*me*. I was just tried it on, and what do you know? A perfect fit! I tried to take it off, but it wouldn't budge. No, really, I want to grow old with you. I missed you so much these past three weeks that I know for certain I can't spend my life without you. Will you marry me, Scott Rogers?" she said as she got down on one knee.

He joined her, in the same position, pulling her onto his knee, cuddling her close to his body. "Hey, you stole my line, but to answer your question, yes. Now, I have a question for you: will you marry me, Elizabeth Bowlyn?"

"Yes," she said as she kissed him and Mandy . . . well, she kissed them too.

Chapter 80

Seth Roberts was working on his next assignment. Although that whole story he wrote exposing Carver was nasty, he was still the one who gave the cops a lead when they had nothing. His popularity had grown, and now, he was a feature writer. Sadly, it was a demented killer who got him this far. But this next story was going to blow the old one out of the water: a retired senator who was involved with child pornography.